Praise fo

'[Walter Bain is] a classic crea
tenements, and his affection for   lly
animates *Close Quarters*. There w   1ise
some of their own lives here'
The Herald

'The author re-imagines the Glasgow tenement lifestyle, fuelled by his own
experiences of living in flats. There's a touch of humour but there's also an
element of crime, the combination of which makes excellent reading'
The Scots Magazine

'*Close Quarters* isn't, oddly, really a crime novel, it's far more a gentle satire
about Glasgow and some of its denizens. The murder of Walter Bain is
certainly central to the plot, but finding out who committed the crime
turns out to be almost incidental to what follows, and to the considerable
enjoyment this book gives the reader'
Undiscovered Scotland

'A refreshing and well-written read'
That's Books and Entertainment

'*Close Quarters* has a cosy, farcical, stage-like quality that I really enjoyed . . .
funny and poignant'
Mystery People

'Some laugh-out-loud moments . . . a comedy wrapped around a whodunnit
. . . will be enjoyed especially by anyone familiar with the West End'
The Westender Magazine

'Tenement life gains a whole new perspective in Angus McAllister's recently
published murder mystery, and it's a local novel that has particularly
appealed to Glasgow's bibliophiles . . . Full of witty observations about
tenement life, this is a whodunnit with a decidedly Glaswegian twist'
Rachel Walker, Scottish Writers' Centre, *Books Set in Glasgow*

A note on the author

Angus McAllister worked as a solicitor and university professor, and is now retired. For many years he wrote academic books and articles, as well as fiction. He is the author of *The Krugg Syndrome*, *The Canongate Strangler*, *The Cyber Puppets* and the bestselling *Close Quarters*, and he lives in Glasgow. See www.angusmcallister.co.uk for more information.

Murder
in the
Merchant City

Angus McAllister

Polygon

First published in Great Britain in 2019 by Polygon,
an imprint of Birlinn Ltd,

West Newington House,
10 Newington Road,
Edinburgh
EH9 1QS

www.polygonbooks.co.uk

1

A short story entitled 'The List', which included material from this book,
was published in the online version of *The Strand Magazine* in 2017.

ISBN 978 1 84697 471 7
eBook ISBN 978 1 78885 174 9

British Library Cataloguing-in-Publication Data
A catalogue record for this book is available on request
from the British Library.

Typeset by 3btype.com, Rosyth

Contents

'For the wages of sin is death'
—*Romans 6: 23*

Author's note

The events in this book take place in and near Glasgow sometime in the 1990s.

1

A Night Vigil

It's eight o'clock and I've been waiting over an hour. As I stand in the doorway, holding up my coat collar against the wind and spitting rain, I think how easy it would be to give up and go home. But justice demands otherwise, as do weeks of patience and careful preparation.

And the night is perfect. It's dark and there's no one around.

I check my tools again. One large claw hammer and one kitchen knife, freshly sharpened. Common household items, and innocent enough, as long as they remain in the house. Carried inside your coat on a dark winter evening, they acquire a more sinister significance.

A man walks past, the first for several minutes. He glances briefly across at me, but pays me little attention. I don't recognise him, but note as much about him as I can, in case he is a new candidate for my list. Tall, mid-thirties maybe, wearing glasses. Colour of hair? Difficult to tell under this street lighting.

Then it becomes irrelevant as he carries on up the street, without slowing for a second.

I relax again, but only for a moment. The street is empty when *he* appears at last.

I ease back slightly within my doorway, then walk boldly forward, as if I'm coming out of the building. From the corner of my eye I can see him walking towards me and that the street behind him is still clear. Then I turn my back on him and walk quickly along the pavement, about fifteen yards ahead of him. The street in front of me is also empty. I know where he's going because I know where his car is parked. I take a right turning and carry on walking, then slow down and stop, appearing uncertain, as if I'm suddenly unsure of my way. As planned, I'm opposite an empty piece of ground, a derelict site between two buildings. It's separated from the pavement by a high wooden fence, part of which has been knocked flat.

He has almost caught up with me as I turn. 'Excuse me.'

'Yes?' He looks slightly startled, but not at all alarmed. I don't present a very threatening figure after all, hardly the stereotype of a mugger. I get a good look at him as he faces me. He's not particularly tall, about the same height as me. About fifty, overweight and not too fit. All to the good. He has coarse, ill-proportioned features unappealingly arranged around a wide, flat nose; his receding grey hair is hidden by a hat and his poor complexion is less obvious in the bad light, but even under cover of night he is a very ugly man.

I ask him for directions to a nearby street and he gives me the information.

'That's great. Thanks very much.'

'No problem.'

As soon as his back is turned, I bring out my hammer. Moving quickly, I simultaneously flick off his hat with my left hand and, with all my strength, bring down the hammer on the back of his head. As he stumbles and falls, I leap forward and batter him twice more. He hits the ground and lies still. He's unconscious, maybe already dead, but I've got to make sure. I look quickly around. No one's there. He hardly made a sound.

I grab him by the ankles and haul him, by stages, into the empty site. He's very heavy, but in my triumph I seem to have extra strength. He doesn't stir as his head bumps over the slats of the flattened fence, across the rubble and weeds. As soon as we're well hidden from the road, I completely let go and unleash my fury. I stab him in the back, again and again, haul him round on his face and renew my attack. *Bastard, bastard, bastard, bastard, bastard, bastard, bastard, bastard, bastard, bastard, bastard . . .*

I hear footsteps in the street. I stop and hold my breath. A figure passes the gap in the fence and walks on.

When the footsteps have receded into the distance, I check that the street is empty and return to my car, parked only a few yards away. My planning has paid off. It's just as well: though I knew there would be blood, it was much messier than I'd anticipated. The worst of it is on my coat, so I bring out a black bin bag from the boot and put my coat in it, as well as the hammer and knife. No knowing when I might need them for some household task. I put the bag back in the boot, lock it, and clean myself as best I can. Can't leave stains in the car. I'll have to check it carefully when I get home.

The street is still empty as I drive away.

It's a long time since I've felt so pleased with myself, so content and full of peace. I know it won't last, but it's good just the same. With my new-found calmness, I realise that this business of street killing, though exhilarating, is far too dangerous. In time, my luck may run out.

Next time I'll need to think of something more original.

2

Another Day

When her radio alarm switched on at seven a.m., Annette had the usual impulse to turn it off again and go back to sleep. But there would be little point. The alarm had been designed for people like her and the radio would switch on again after ten minutes. Instead she compromised by leaving it on and turning on her other side.

She eased herself gradually from the desire to sleep on, while half listening to a news bulletin, a pop song, the inane patter of the DJ. There was no need to get up for another twenty minutes. She had deliberately set the alarm early in order to give herself this space.

When she finally got out of bed, she checked on the children. Lisa was still asleep but Andrew was awake, fortunately showing no desire to get out of bed just yet. With any luck she would have time to get showered and dressed before they were under her feet.

An hour later, they were definitely under her feet, but she had almost completed the process of getting them washed, dressed, breakfasted and ready for school. By the time she was driving off, with the children safely locked in at the back, she felt as if she'd already done a day's work. This was one respect in which she some-times missed her former husband David. While they'd been together she hadn't had to do all of the work in the morning, only most of it. This was probably the only thing about him that she ever missed.

Just before nine, she dropped the children outside the school. It wasn't too far from her house and, with enough time, she could easily have walked them there. But they never seemed to have enough time. She kissed them both and pointed them in the right direction.

'Are you coming for us today, Mummy?' Lisa asked.

'No,' said Annette. 'Linda's picking you up.'

'Why can't you come for us?'

'I told you before. I'm working.'

'Looking after the sick people?'

'That's right. I'll be home at six o'clock.'

'She told you before,' said Andrew. He took his young sister by the hand and pulled her towards the school gate. At least, Annette thought, he was beginning to assume some protective responsibility without having to be told. She sat watching until they had entered the school building together.

She drove back home and parked her car outside the house. On the way in, she stopped to have a look at the garden. The house was at the end of a terrace, giving her more ground than any of her neighbours. This had been David's idea. From the limited choice the council had offered them, he had gone for the house with the biggest garden. He had been full of ideas about developing it: it was simultaneously to be a floral showpiece, a market garden supplying half of their food needs and a leisure area for them and the children. In the end, after his neglect had brought complaints from the neighbours and a warning from the council, it was Annette who had got to work with the lawnmower and shears. She had concentrated on preserving the more modest achievements of the former tenants; usually she just kept the grass cut and the hedge trimmed, and dabbled with the rest when she had time.

6

In some parts of the council estate it wouldn't have mattered. But this was one of the better areas. Annette had good neighbours, ones who tended their gardens, didn't make too much noise and kept their children under reasonable control. Drug taking and violence were mainly confined to other parts of the estate, those furthest away from the town centre. Several of her neighbours, like Annette, had even bought their house from the council.

She was still examining the front garden when she paid the penalty for lingering. Norah appeared from the house next door. Norah had more time on her hands than Annette: her children had grown up and left home, and her job as a shop assistant was only part-time.

'Forget about it,' said Norah. 'It'll be OK till the spring.'

'No, it won't. There's so much of it, there's always something needing done. I'm thinking about getting a garage. It would fill up half the side garden. I could even put my car in it.'

'A garage? You're really givin' that man of yours a showin' up.'

'He can do that well enough on his own.'

Norah didn't respond. She came from a generation that thought you should make more effort to preserve a marriage. When her husband went off to the pub on his own, she simply dropped in on Annette for company.

'Are the weans safely delivered then?'

'No, I just left them on the main road to play with the motors.'

Norah laughed. 'Have you time for a cup of tea?'

'I'd better not. I'm working today.'

'Oh aye, you cannae keep your patients waitin'. No' when you're doin' so well out of them. Buyin' your own house, and now a garage as well.'

'One of these days I'll go back to the health service,' said Annette, not having time for an argument. She brought the conversation to an end and got safely into the house.

❖

She left again at ten fifteen. One advantage of shift work was being able to avoid the rush hour. Without too much delay, she made her way across Paisley and on to the motorway for Glasgow. The road was still busy, but at least the Kingston Bridge queue had dispersed. Soon she was parking her car in a side street only a short walk from her work.

She was sharing her shift with Miranda and Sylvia. By ten past eleven they had all assembled, dressed in their white medical coats, waiting for the day's work to begin. Typically, Miranda was saying very little and Sylvia was making up for it.

'I was lucky to get here in time. Charlie wouldnae let me go. Get me this, get me that. He'd had a hard night.'

'Poor guy,' said Annette in a sarcastic tone.

'I'm no' kiddin'. He was in a bad way. I didnae like to leave him.'

'I'm sure he'll be fine. As long as you left him enough money for opening time. Or was he in withdrawal from something different?'

'I've nae idea what you're talkin' about. We were in the pub last night and he brought home a carry-out. I didnae want any, so he drank it all himself.'

'That was good of him.'

'He's like a wee kid sometimes. I never know what to say to him.'

'You only need two words,' said Annette. 'I'll give you a clue. The second one's "off".'

'Is that what you told your man?'

'Something like that.'

'Did it work?'

'Eventually. With a couple of boots up the bum to help him on his way. If he'd left right away it might have seemed like decisive action.'

'I'm no' sure,' said Sylvia. 'What do you think, Miranda?'

Miranda had remained silent during the exchange, a faint smile on her face. A smile of superiority? Mockery? Annette found it difficult to tell. It might even be her way of trying to be friendly. You could never be sure what Miranda was thinking. 'I don't really know,' she told Sylvia. 'It's up to you.'

Annette found it hard to like Miranda, and she knew the other girls felt the same. It was difficult not to be a little jealous of her supermodel looks, but there was more to it than that. She was always perfectly pleasant and friendly, but somehow remote. She never poured out the details of her private life like Sylvia and some of the others, though Annette didn't do that either, preferring to keep her home life separate. But in Miranda's case, Annette sensed that the barrier she put up wasn't just for the benefit of her colleagues; she suspected that it stood between Miranda and the whole world.

As they waited for the first arrival, they drank coffee and Sylvia chain-smoked. She never seemed to relax; not at work anyway and, Annette guessed, not at home either.

The first two customers arrived and the day's work began for Miranda and Annette.

Annette didn't recognise the man, and was fairly sure that she hadn't seen him before. He was young, quiet, and seemed a little nervous. He wasn't particularly good-looking, but not all that repulsive either. She took him to the cabin, relieved him of his robe and got him to lie face down on the table. She massaged the back of his body with oil for some time, then asked him to turn over. She looked down on his naked front. 'Was there something else you were wanting?'

The man hesitated for a moment. 'Yes, I think so.'

Annette took off her white coat. Beneath it, she was wearing only her underwear: black stockings, held up by a pair of frilly garters, a low-cut bra and a flimsy pair of knickers. 'Would you like to know what's on the menu?'

The man made no immediate reply, but there was definite evidence of interest.

Annette's day of attending to the sick people had begun.

3

The Merchant City
Health Centre

'. . . has been identified as fifty-one-year-old Richard McAlpine, a Glasgow solicitor. It is not known why he was in . . .'

The background noise in the pub temporarily swelled to a level that drowned out the sound of the TV.

Jack Morrison, who until then had been paying it little attention, glanced up at the face filling the screen. Not a very handsome man. A coarse, round face scarred by acne, a broad, flat nose, a few scraps of grey hair framing a bald pate. Hardly the usual image of a solicitor, more like a mugshot of one of his clients. Jack almost expected a side view to follow, revealing new dimensions of ugliness in the profile. Instead he saw a piece of waste ground, an empty site between two buildings, bordered by a high wooden fence, partially flattened.

The announcer's voice became audible again: '. . . to have attacked his victim with extraordinary fury. The police believe that he was struck down in the street, with a hammer or some other blunt instrument, and then dragged into the waste ground, where he was repeatedly stabbed with a knife. Police doctors have identified more than forty stab wounds, most administered after death.'

A senior police officer appeared on the screen. 'The killer must

11

have been drenched in blood and it seems unlikely that he could have escaped notice. We are therefore appealing…'

Losing interest, Jack turned away. It was just another murder. If the victim had been a child or young woman, it might have attracted public interest for a day or two, exploited by the tabloid press to whip up some spurious moral debate. But the murder of a solicitor was liable to cause the public more satisfaction than outrage. Or so it seemed to Jack, who had recently paid the legal bill for his divorce.

Jack was not by nature a callous man, but at that moment he had something else on his mind.

He finished his whisky in a single gulp. Should he have another? That might be counter-productive. He looked at his watch. Quarter past two. Now that the working population had mostly finished their lunch break, the streets would be quieter; there would be less chance of him being recognised. The crowd in the pub had already thinned considerably.

If he hadn't been working that evening, he could have gone after dark. That would have been much better.

Before entering the pub, he had wandered about the area for some time, looking in shop windows, examining all the leaflets in the ticket centre at the City Hall, generally going round in circles. It was time to make a move. He went to the toilet, then walked out of the pub. Then he turned into the next entrance, a few yards from the pub door. Luckily there wasn't a security door and he didn't have to hang about in the street waiting to be admitted.

The close was dark and smelled as if it had recently been used as a public toilet. Jack climbed winding stairs, past a dirty window overlooking an overgrown back court, to the floor above the pub. There was only one entrance on the landing. A broad storm door had been swung back and the sign on the glass-panelled inner door read: BLACKFRIARS PAWNBROKING COMPANY. Jack continued up the stairs to the top floor and another single entrance. This time the storm door was shut. It was clean and newly painted, in contrast to the seedy appearance of its surroundings. The attached sign read: MERCHANT CITY HEALTH CENTRE.

Before ringing the doorbell, he had another attack of doubt. What if it was a genuine health centre, an up-market private clinic? How would he explain himself? Then common sense returned. An up-market clinic in this building? Using an advert, packed with innuendo, like the one that had led him here? He pressed the bell.

There was a buzzing sound and the storm door unlocked. He pushed it open and found himself in a brightly decorated entrance hall, where a plump, middle-aged woman smiled at him from behind a desk. 'Hi there.'

'Hello,' said Jack, taking a step forward.

'Shut the door behind you, love.'

'Oh, sorry.' He pushed the door closed and went up to the desk, trying to think of something to say.

'Sauna and massage?'

'Yes, please.'

'Have you been here before?'

'No.'

'What's your first name?'

'Ah . . .' He tried to think of an alias, then gave up. 'Jack.'

'Right, Jack,' said the woman. 'Let's get you sorted out.'

❖

Through the open door of the lounge, the girls saw him coming, hesitantly making his way down the corridor towards the changing

13

room, giving off waves of nervousness. He clutched his towel and wallet as if they were soft toys from which he could take some childish comfort.

'I think we've got a virgin,' said Annette. 'Whose turn is it?'

'Not mine,' said Candy.

'I should bloody well hope not. Otherwise the rest of us'll never get a look in.'

Candy laughed. 'I cannae help it if I'm irresistible.'

'How about you, Claudia?'

Throughout the exchange, Claudia's usual expression of boredom and contempt had never faltered. She shrugged. 'Be my guest.'

'On you go, Annette,' said Candy. 'Give him your nice-girl-next-door act. He'll think he's wi' his childhood sweetheart.'

'Fuck off!'

Annette kept her voice low. All the customer would see as she approached was her welcoming smile. As she left the lounge, she saw him open the door of a closet in his search for the changing room. She quickened her step. If he caught sight of Claudia's gear, he might run away. 'Hi,' she said.

'Hello.'

'This your first visit?'

'Yes.'

Annette suppressed her annoyance. That stupid cow at the door was supposed to show the new customers round, or call on one of the girls to do it. Not leave him floundering about, having to find his own way like a regular.

'The changing room's over here,' she said, indicating the door. 'I'm Annette, by the way. What's your name?'

'Jack.'

'Right, Jack. You'll find a robe in your locker. While we're here,

14

let me show you where you can find the sauna, steam room and showers. Take as long as you want there.' She took him on a brief tour. 'When you've had your shower, come through to the lounge and choose the girl you want.'

'Thanks.'

'No problem. See you later.'

She returned to the lounge. He wasn't too bad, she thought. Early thirties, not going to fat, still had most of his hair. Quite good-looking, in a shy sort of way. Like most of the girls, she preferred to deal with regulars: you knew where you were with them and there were no nasty surprises. But this one seemed all right.

The customers were free to select any girl they wanted. However, a new one would often choose the girl who looked after him on his arrival, so they took it in turns to play hostess.

Back in the lounge, Claudia had lit another cigarette and Candy was playing the fruit machine.

'You'll spend all your money before you've earned it,' said Annette.

Candy pressed a button and the wheels spun. 'It's due tae pay oot. I can feel it.'

'Aye, and Christmas is coming.' It was the beginning of February. 'Mind you, Sylvia put enough into it yesterday.'

The mechanism stopped, followed by silence. Candy gave the machine a thump with her fist and returned to her seat. 'Next time, definitely.'

'Only one person makes money fae that thing,' said Claudia.

'Watch it,' said Annette. 'She's probably got the place bugged.'

'Probably,' said Claudia. 'But who gives a fuck?'

'Is that no' what we're here for?' said Candy.

'No' necessarily. I'm a specialist.'

15

Annette and Candy sat down, at opposite ends of the long leather sofa. The TV, turned down low, was showing an old film, and in the silence the dialogue became audible. It had been a slow day so far. Two customers for Candy, one for Annette, and none for Claudia. The hoped-for lunchtime rush hadn't materialised. Maybe it would pick up later and there would be an influx of business men who had sneaked off work early.

They sat and waited. 'I think your new guy's got lost,' said Candy. 'We'd better send out a search party.'

'I'm sure he's OK.'

'Maybe he only came to use the steam room.'

'Not another one.'

There was one regular customer who showed up every week, spent a couple of hours in the steam room, and then went away. If he had figured out the real nature of the place, he gave no sign of it. When he first appeared, Candy had tried to broaden his horizons in her usual subtle way, wandering into the changing room half naked, showering in the next stall, sitting beside him in the steam room, her towel falling away in all the right places. But none of it had any effect. Either he wasn't interested, or was especially slow on the uptake. Or maybe he was just too mean to go to a legitimate health club, where the entrance fee was probably higher.

The new customer reappeared, dressed in a towelling robe. Annette got up to meet him. 'Have a seat, Jack. Would you like a drink? We've got coffee or orange juice.'

'I don't know if I'll bother, thanks.'

Candy looked at him provocatively, licking her lips. 'You want to try our orange juice. You don't know what you're missing.' She patted the sofa beside her, inviting him to sit down.

'All right then.'

16

Annette went over to the drinks table and poured a couple of inches of diluting orange into a plastic cup, topping it up with water. She gave it to the customer and resumed her seat. He sat between Candy and Annette, staring in front of him, sipping his drink, his legs pressed tightly together. Claudia was watching the TV and gave no sign of having noticed his arrival.

'Let me introduce you,' said Annette. 'This is Candy and this is Claudia. And I'm Annette, as I said.' Candy gave him a big smile; Claudia looked round briefly and nodded, before turning back to the TV screen. The customer nervously nodded back to each of them.

There was a silence. Candy lounged back on the sofa. The top buttons of her coat were undone, and the bottom flap had fallen back to reveal a length of thigh. Annette knew that Candy wasn't deliberately muscling in. Coming on to customers was so instinctive that she probably didn't realise she was doing it.

'When you're ready,' Annette said, 'just choose the girl you want.'

The man nodded stiffly, still staring in front of him. Then he finished his drink in a single gulp and turned to Candy. 'Are you free?'

'No, but my prices are reasonable. This way.'

Candy got up and left the room, and he followed her, avoiding the eye of the other girls. A man with a conscience, thought Annette, who feels sensitive about rejecting us. He would learn. The only thing she was sensitive about was going home with enough money to feed the kids, pay the mortgage, put petrol in the car.

'Never mind,' said Claudia. 'Bob the Gobbler might show up.'

Annette laughed. 'He'll take Candy too.'

'Probably. But I'll no' greet in my beer over it.'

This was about as talkative as Claudia ever got, and they settled down to wait for the elusive rush.

Annette couldn't be annoyed at Candy. She hadn't done it deliberately. She was too good-natured to dislike, and you always got a laugh when you were on with her. Now Miranda, on the other hand . . .

It was just her bad luck to share her shift with two favourites in a row, Miranda the previous day and now Candy. Candy had worked in the place for several years, and for most of that time had been the unchallenged top girl. She had worked three shifts a week – if she hadn't overslept after a heavy night – and gone home with more money than the other girls had earned in twice that time. Now she was slightly older, had put on just a *little* weight, and was having to put in an extra shift to keep up her earnings. Then Miranda had arrived and pushed her into second place. Candy, in fact, had as much reason to resent Miranda as any of the others. But there wasn't a resentful cell in Candy's body. She just made sure that she was always on a different shift from Miranda.

Another customer appeared at the end of the corridor. He looked familiar and seemed to know his way around. Annette was fairly sure that he didn't belong to Claudia's select band of regulars. With any luck, she'd be able to collar him before Candy returned.

4

The Centre of the Universe

After all the time he'd spent working up his nerve, it had all been over very quickly. It was the first time he'd had sex since splitting up with Margaret, and he hadn't been receiving much prior to that. Mainly, he discovered eventually, because he'd been sharing her with someone else. Since then he'd had a few dates, but nothing that had developed into a sufficiently close relationship. It had been too long.

And it was so easy. That girl Candy was the best-looking woman Jack had ever been with, and there she was on offer, just for the asking. As long as you had the money. A woman who normally wouldn't have given you a second look was yours, just because you handed her a few pieces of printed paper.

That other girl – Annette – had been very nice too. Much less obvious than Candy, not at all the sort you'd expect to find in a place like that. He'd been about to choose her, and then had hesitated. She'd looked so prim and respectable in her white uniform that he'd wondered for a moment whether she might have worked there in some other capacity. He'd quickly realised that this couldn't be true; however, after his period of abstinence, Candy's blatant appeal had been difficult to resist.

He would certainly have chosen Annette in preference to that other one – Claudia. She really looked like a hard case. Quite sexy with it, but not to his taste. Also a little on the mature side.

All of this was still going through his mind when he arrived at his work just before six. The bar was still busy with the remains of the five o'clock rush, and he was kept occupied for a while. Then they hit the mid-evening dead spot, when most of the teatime drinkers had gone and the closing-time fixtures had mostly still to arrive. It was a Tuesday night and only two bar staff were on, Jack and young Les Wilson.

Jack gathered in glasses and wiped the tables while Les cleaned up behind the bar. When they had finished, the place was still quiet. Taking advantage of the owner's absence, Les smoked a cigarette, then went on his break. Half an hour later, Jack succeeded him.

The Centurion, Jack's place of work, was on Byres Road, at the heart of the city's West End. Byres Road linked two residential areas: middle-class Kelvinside on the north-west, and working-class Partick on the south. It was also close to, or passed near, BBC Scotland, Glasgow University and the Western Infirmary. These elements alone created an interesting variety of people, which in turn drew in outsiders attracted by this cosmopolitan mix. In the West End, if you were only mildly eccentric you faded into the background.

Tennent's Bar, where Jack went for his break, was at the area's epicentre, exactly halfway down Byres Road. If you sat in Tennent's long enough, so it was rumoured, you would eventually meet everyone in the world, plus the occasional extraterrestrial.

In the past, Jack had never quite believed this. He was shortly to change his mind.

Tennent's was also quiet, even emptier than the Centurion. The few customers were spread thinly around its wide spaces; as well as being the most central bar in the area, it was also the largest. Jack stood at the counter, chatting to Morag the barmaid, making his single drink last as long as possible.

Five minutes before his break was due to end, three women came into the pub. At first Jack paid them little attention; they sat down somewhere behind him, and the one who came up to the bar to buy a round – an attractive girl in her twenties – was a stranger to him. It was only on leaving the pub that he happened to glance over at the group and recognised one of them. Someone who had been constantly in his thoughts for half the day.

It was Candy, from the Merchant City Health Centre.

Even in the West End, this was a ridiculous coincidence. She didn't appear to have seen him, so he quickly went out the door and returned to work.

He hadn't escaped so easily. Half an hour later the girls arrived in the Centurion. It seemed they were on a pub crawl. Candy came up to the bar to buy a round.

Both Jack and Les were serving. Jack carried on, hoping Les would be finished first. Candy was too impatient to wait for either of them. She seemed a little tipsy.

'Hi, handsome!'

Jack was on his way to the till. As he was passing Les, the other barman said in his ear, 'Don't you bother. I think it's me she wants.'

But Jack was now free and Les was still serving. He went over to Candy. How should he react? He didn't want to snub her, but mutual recognition could be embarrassing for both of them. And he didn't know her real name. Better to play safe, with something equally appropriate as a greeting to a friend or a barman's welcome to a stranger. 'Hi,' he said, smiling.

He could have saved himself the worry. If anything was bothering Candy, it wasn't the protocol. 'Come on, darlin', we're dyin' of thirst here.' She spoke good-humouredly, treating him to a smile he remembered well.

'I'm all yours. What can I get you?'

Candy was leaning across the bar towards him; above the low-cut top, her cleavage seemed aimed at his nose. Even with the image of the hidden part still fresh in his memory, it still grabbed his attention. 'You tell me, honey,' she said. 'But right now, make it two Black Labels and a Jack Daniels.'

'Two Black Labels and a Jack Daniels,' he repeated. She blew him a kiss as he went for the order.

As he and Les stood together, facing the gantry, Les released a shuddering exhalation; it was intended to indicate, Jack supposed, the extremes of lust.

'You sound like an elephant havin' a shit.'

'It shouldnae be allowed!'

'Elephants need to shit, just like anyone else.'

Jack liked Les well enough; he would probably be a sound enough citizen when he grew up. He turned to serve Candy the drinks.

'Thanks, darlin'. What's your name?'

'Jack.'

'No, that's the drink. A Jack Daniels. What's *your* name?'

'My name's Jack.'

'Is your second name Daniels?'

'No.'

She gave a drunken giggle. 'I'm gettin' really confused.' She opened her purse and offered him a twenty-pound note. It was possibly one of those he'd got from the cash machine and given her only a few hours before. Now it was going into the Centurion's till on its way back to the bank. If banknotes could give an account of their circulation, some interesting journeys might be revealed. 'Get a drink for yourself, Daniel.'

'Thanks a lot.'

She continued the flirtation when he returned with her change. The bar was now getting busier, but Les found the time to tell Jack what he'd like to do to Candy. It made up in fervour what it lacked in originality.

From time to time, Jack glanced over at the table where the women were sitting. If Candy hadn't been among them, he wouldn't have paid them much attention. Three good-looking girls having a night out. Were they all on the game? Under normal circumstances, it would never have crossed his mind.

He still couldn't figure out Candy's behaviour. She had treated him with total ease, flirting with him, buying him a drink, but without a single sign of recognition. Was she playing an elaborate game?

Then he realised that the explanation was much simpler. She *hadn't* recognised him. To her, he had been just another customer, one of many faces that had briefly passed her way that day. If he seemed at all familiar, she probably thought he was just a barman who had served her before.

Maybe he had. If he'd met her the day before, or the previous week, would she have been just another customer to him?

That wasn't how Les saw it. 'I think you're ontae a good thing there,' he said to Jack, as Candy waved goodbye on her way to the next pub. 'Let us know if she's too much for you. I might be able to give you a hand.'

If only you knew, thought Jack. But you won't be able to afford it unless you give up the fags.

5

The Most Beautiful Girl in the World

On the following Monday, less than a week later, Jack went back to the Merchant City Health Centre. He hadn't meant to return quite so soon. When withdrawing money at the cash machine he checked his balance, and the virtues of self control became even more apparent.

This time he was much less nervous; the premises, after all, were discreetly located in an area where he was unlikely to be recognised. The same woman was at the front desk, but didn't appear to remember him. Jack managed not to feel slighted. He preferred to be anonymous.

He made his way to the changing room. The property had once been a large flat, built in the last century, and occupied the entire top floor of the building. At the far end of the hall the door to the lounge, once the house's main living room, lay open; through it, he could see a girl, one he didn't recognise, sitting upright, her legs crossed, taking short, frequent draws at a cigarette. Also at the far end, the kitchen had been amalgamated with another public room and a bathroom to accommodate a sauna, steam room, showers and toilet; an adjoining utilities room, filled with metal lockers, served as the changing room. In the area nearer the front door two bedrooms had been subdivided into massage cabins.

He was alone in the changing room as he undressed, donned his robe and transferred his money into the little plastic wallet. As he was securing his locker, his back to the door, he heard another man come into the room.

He turned slowly, then relaxed on seeing a stranger. It was very unlikely to be otherwise, but running into Candy at his place of work had made him sensitive to the possibility of coincidence. The feeling of relief was quickly followed by one of slight embarrassment. The other man was similarly diffident. He was older than Jack – in his mid-forties at least – and a little plump. His receding hairline showed touches of grey and he wore glasses. An unlikely consort for the sort of women on display here; an impossible one, in fact, without the formidable matchmaking properties of hard cash. The man stepped aside to let Jack out of the door, nodding briefly, his eyes fixed on the floor.

Jack took a shower and was making his way to the lounge when one of the cabin doors opened. A client came out and headed for the shower area. He was followed by a woman who walked towards Jack on her way to the lounge. She greeted him with a warm smile. 'Hi there.'

Jack stopped dead and stared after her as she went through the doorway before him. He thought she must be the most beautiful woman that he had ever seen. Tall, elegant, with a perfect face topped by blonde wavy hair. In a completely different class from Candy, who seemed cheap and obvious by comparison. If you saw her in the street, she would also attract attention, but as an impossible fantasy.

He followed her into the lounge. Annette was there along with the girl he had earlier seen from the corridor. He had been hoping to see Annette again, but now he hardly noticed her, unable to take his eyes off the blonde girl. She sat down on one of the two armchairs and he sat on the other one, continuing to stare.

'Hello there,' said Annette. 'How are you?'

Realising that he was being rude, Jack turned to face her. 'Fine,' he said. It looked as if *she* remembered him at least. Or maybe she said that to every man who looked as if he knew his way around. The nervous girl put down her cigarette and got up from the sofa. 'Would you like somethin' to drink?'

'A glass of orange juice, please.'

She poured the drink and returned with it. 'I'm Sylvia,' she said. 'This is Annette and this is Miranda.'

He sat and sipped his drink. Annette and Sylvia made small talk with him, but Miranda remained silent. She just sat and smiled. From the moment he had first seen her, Jack knew that she had to be his choice, but found that he was lacking the courage. A girl like that couldn't be there just for the asking. There had to be a mistake.

He was impelled into action by the arrival of the man he had met in the changing room. For Miranda to go with him would be unthinkable, an obscenity. He looked across at her, trying to avoid the eye of the other girls. 'Are you free for a massage?' He found that his voice had gone hoarse.

'Of course,' said Miranda. 'This way.' She got up and walked to the door as if she were treading a catwalk.

Though she tried to hide it, he could see Sylvia's disappointment. He managed to avoid looking at Annette at all.

As Miranda was leading him to the cabin, a newcomer approached them on his way to the changing room, a slightly-built man of about thirty-five. When he saw Miranda with Jack in tow, he stopped short.

'Hi there,' she said, giving him an identical greeting to the one she had originally given Jack. This somehow made it seem a little less special.

The man stared at her with an intensity that should have been disconcerting, though she took it calmly enough. 'Hello, Miranda,' he said. 'Are you busy?'

'Afraid so,' she said, continuing on her way. 'See you later.'

As they passed each other, the man fixed on Jack a look of absolute hatred. For a moment it quite unsettled him, then his attention returned to Miranda and the man was quickly forgotten.

❖

When Miranda came back, the customer didn't give her a chance to return to the lounge, but ran out to the corridor to meet her. There was no need, there being no other customers who could have jumped in before him, but Annette was glad to see him go. He created tension in the room.

'Bloody bitch,' said Sylvia. 'Is naebody else gonnae get a look in? Charlie'll murder me if I don't take mair hame than last time.'

'You don't want that guy. There's something funny about him.'

'I know what you mean. You ever had him?'

'Fat chance. It's always Miranda. I think he's in love.'

'He's no' the only one. Fuckin' cow.'

'Aye, but there's more to it with him,' said Annette. 'He gives me the creeps.'

'I know what you mean. I couldnae talk tae him. I just played the machine till you came back. What like was that other guy?'

'Hard work. Did you smell his breath? You'd think he'd swallowed a dead rat.'

Sylvia laughed. 'I take it you didnae have a long neckin' session?'

Annette shuddered. 'Don't even talk about it!'

❖

The man Jack had met in the changing room was back there before him. This time he seemed disposed to be talkative.

'That Annette's a really nice girl,' he said.

For some reason Jack had been hoping that he'd taken Sylvia. 'Yes, she seems so.'

'You were with Miranda, weren't you? I've been with her as well. She's very nice too. All the girls here are really nice.'

Jack passed close by him on the way to his locker, and almost gagged at the stench from the man's breath. He felt sorry for Annette, having been confined in an enclosed space with him. No wonder the other man had made it back before him. She'd probably hurried things along a bit.

'I don't think I've seen you here before,' the man said.

'No. This is only my second time.'

'I suppose I'm becoming a bit of a regular. You see, my wife . . .'

Don't tell me, thought Jack, she doesn't understand you. Or does it just put you off when she lies in bed wearing a gas mask?

'She doesn't keep well. It wouldn't be fair to . . . you know . . .'

'I'm sorry.'

'Are you married?'

'Divorced.'

The man nodded. He had finished dressing, but seemed inclined to stay and talk. Jack said nothing more, but turned back to the open locker and concentrated on putting his clothes back on. The other man seemed to take the hint and made for the door. 'See you again.'

'Bye,' said Jack.

As Jack was on his way out, the woman at the front desk was on the phone. 'Yes,' she was saying. 'Today it's Miranda, Annette and Sylvia . . . No problem . . . Bye.'

It hadn't occurred to Jack that he could phone to find out which girls were working on any particular day. There had been no need to take pot luck. He handed the woman his locker key and wallet.

'Thanks, Jack,' she said. 'See you again.'

My second visit and I'm already a regular, he thought. But of course she'd written his name in her book when he arrived. By the time he came back, she would probably have forgotten it again.

6

Special Delivery

On the last day of his life, Arnold Bell arose at seven a.m., washed and dressed himself, helped his wife to the bathroom and back, and made breakfast for them both. Then they ate together in her bedroom. They enjoyed having this time to themselves, before the nurse arrived at nine. Especially if Ellen had had a good night and was feeling less tired than she would later.

Rosemary, his wife's nurse, arrived at nine o'clock and took over the care of Ellen while Arnold started work. Arnold was a partner in a city firm of chartered accountants but, since his wife's illness, worked at home as much as possible. He had been busy for over an hour when Rosemary arrived at his study to say that they were off for their morning walk.

Arnold followed the nurse to the hall, where Ellen was already waiting, seated in her wheelchair.

'Where are you off to?'

'It's quite nice outside,' said Rosemary. 'I thought we'd go to the park.'

'It's still cold. I hope you're well wrapped up.'

'Stop fussing, Arnold,' said Ellen. 'I'm not dead yet.'

Arnold bent down to kiss her. Years of training enabled Ellen to show no reaction. She held her breath until his face had withdrawn, then exhaled slowly. 'You're a good man, Arnold,' she said. 'I don't know what I'd do without you.'

Feeling slightly embarrassed, Arnold made no reply.

The Bells lived in a luxury penthouse flat on the top floor of a converted warehouse, having moved there from their Southside villa when Ellen became confined to a wheelchair. It was within easy reach of both the West End and the city centre, and gave a spectacular view across the north of the city – on a good day you could see Ben Lomond – as well as being on a single level.

Arnold saw them out to the lift, then returned to his work. About ten minutes later, the buzzer for the security door sounded.

Who could this be? Ellen and Rosemary could have forgotten something, but they had a key. He went through to the hall and lifted the handset. 'Hello?'

'Special delivery.'

'OK.' He let the visitor into the building and replaced the handset.

His curiosity was aroused. He wasn't expecting anything. The office occasionally forwarded urgent items of mail, but his secretary would generally phone him first.

A few minutes later the doorbell rang. Still curious, but not in the least alarmed – it was ten thirty in the morning after all – he went to answer the door to his killer.

7

Life Goes On

'My God,' said Annette, 'I don't believe it.'

'What's the matter?'

'That man. I knew him.'

'What man?'

'The one on the telly. The one who was murdered.'

'Good grief,' said Norah. 'How did you know him?'

They were in Annette's living room, watching the local news on television. They often kept each other company after Annette's children had gone to bed and Norah's husband had gone to the pub.

Now that the initial shock was over, Annette realised that she would have to be careful what she said. 'He was a patient. An outpatient.'

'Not his wife?'

'What do you mean?'

'She's got MS,' said Norah. 'They just mentioned it.'

'No, he was the patient,' said Annette, wishing that she hadn't let the news take her by surprise. 'It was just some minor complaint.'

'Another of your rich private patients,' said Norah. 'I see his wife had a private nurse. Was she one of yours?'

'No.' Definitely not! 'Poor man, he didn't deserve that. Attacked by a madman in his own home. Who'd think twice about answering the door at ten in the morning?'

'Are you gonnae phone the police?'

'The police? Why?'

'You said you knew him.'

'I don't see the point,' said Annette quickly. Too quickly, she realised. 'I mean, everybody at the clinic knew him, not just me. I'll mention it to the boss, see what she . . . see what he says.' She tried to imagine Edna's reaction if she suggested going to the police. It wasn't going to be an issue.

'It's up to you,' said Norah. 'Look, we've got company.'

Annette looked round. Andrew had come into the room. 'What's the matter, pet?'

'I can't sleep.'

'Well, you won't manage it here. You'll have to go back to bed.'

'Can you read to me?'

'You can read yourself now. You don't need me. I've got a visitor to look after.'

'I'm just goin',' said Norah.

'I was about to put the kettle on.' Annette grabbed Andrew by the arm and led him from the room. 'Come on. I'll tuck you back in and help you choose a book.'

'I'll get the tea,' said Norah.

Ten minutes later, they were back in front of the television. 'You're too hard on him,' said Norah.

'He's got to learn. He wants everything done for him.'

'He's only eight, for God's sake.'

Annette sighed. 'I know. I'm just scared in case he's developing some of his father's habits. I feel I've got to stamp them out early.'

'It cannae be easy, bringin' them up on your own.'

❖

34

At work, Annette found that the murder caused less of a stir than she had expected. As they were changing for their shift, she mentioned it to Candy, who as usual had been out drinking and hadn't seen any news bulletins.

'What murder?' Candy asked absently, as she struggled into her working clothes. 'See thae crotchless panties? You never know where tae put yer leg in.'

'It was on the news last night. He was one of our regulars.'

'Bloody hell!' said Candy. 'I hope it wasnae Bob the Gobbler.'

'No. You'd know the guy. Middle-aged, baldy, wore glasses. Terrible bad breath.'

'Sounds like a real honey. Cannae say I can place him.'

'He was in the other week.'

'Well, he'll no' be in again.'

Annette knew that Candy wasn't really a callous person. She was just indifferent to anything that didn't affect her directly. Claudia was a different matter. As the three of them waited in the lounge for their first customer, Annette mentioned the murder again. Candy's reaction hadn't surprised her, but Claudia's did. The news of the killing – she hadn't heard of it either – seemed to afford her considerable satisfaction.

'One less of thae bastards in the world. Cannae be bad.'

'Come on,' said Annette. 'You're talking about your own livelihood.'

'There's plenty mair where he came from. For every one that gets the chop, another two'll crawl oot the woodwork to take his place. I wouldnae piss on one of thae swine if he was on fire.'

'I thought your customers paid you to do that,' said Candy.

'What do you mean, for every one that gets the chop?' asked Annette. 'Do you expect this to be a trend?'

Claudia shrugged. 'Wi' any luck.'

'Still, you can't help feeling sorry for the poor guy. They say he was battered to death with a hammer and stabbed more than forty times. In his own house.'

'I'm devastated.'

'Apparently he was devoted to his wife. She's got MS.'

'They're all devoted tae their wives,' said Claudia. 'It doesnae stop them comin' here.'

Annette wondered if Claudia's customers knew just how genuine was her contempt for them. It might spoil their fantasies a little. Or would it?

❖

The subject of the murder came up again later, while Annette was with a customer. It was the one called Jack, who had first showed up a few weeks before and now appeared to be making it a habit. He seemed to have relaxed a bit since his first visit. She had expected him to choose Candy, but he had chosen her, even though Candy was free at the time. Maybe she could cultivate him as a regular. He seemed a lot more personable than some of them.

'I was beginning to think I had horns,' she said, when they were settled in the cabin.

'Sorry?'

'You've never chosen me before.'

'Oh, sorry.'

'I'm only kidding. We don't bother about things like that.'

'At least you remembered me. That's nice.'

'I never forget a face.'

'The other week, Candy came into the pub where I work. I don't think she recognised me.'

'Did you have your trousers on?'

'The boss usually insists on it.'

Annette laughed. 'That explains it. Our boss takes a slightly different line.'

'So I've noticed.'

She continued to massage his back. She didn't feel like hurrying things along. It wasn't her normal policy, and in any case there hadn't been a queue of customers waiting.

Neither of them spoke for a few moments. Then he said, 'Did you hear about that murder?'

Annette was taken by surprise. Should she say anything? She didn't immediately reply.

'The guy battered to death in his house. I recognised him. I met him in here the week before last.'

What was the point of denying it? It was just a coincidence that the man had been a customer. 'I know. I gave him his massage. It was a shock when I saw the news.'

'Did he come here often?'

'Every time, as far as I know.'

'I walked right into that one.'

'You certainly did.' She paused. 'I suppose we shouldn't joke about it. I feel sorry for his wife.'

'I know. It's a bummer.'

It also brought the conversation to a halt. Annette finished massaging his back and got him to turn over. She was still taking her time, when the silence was broken by the sound of Candy faking an orgasm in the next cabin. *She* certainly didn't hang about: she'd still been in the lounge when Annette had gone off with Jack. Left to it, Candy was capable of getting through the afternoon shift single-handed. Time to get things moving.

'Well,' she said, 'I've really enjoyed the chat. Was that all you came here for?'

❖

While she was settling up with Edna at the end of her shift, she mentioned the murder, just to see what Edna would say about it. Her boss was a good-looking woman of forty who had been in the profession most of her life and had now graduated from worker to employer. Not all girls could have made such a transition. As Candy characteristically put it, Edna had her head screwed on as well as her arse screwed off. Annette doubted whether a blacker pot had ever maligned a kettle, but why let that stand in the way of a good piece of bitchiness?

'You've had a good day,' said Edna.

'It picked up towards the end.'

'Candy did even better, though.'

'Give us a break. She does better than everyone.'

'Apart from Miranda.'

'Keep my shifts away from that pair and I'll do better too.'

Edna sighed. 'You'll have to join the queue. Still, your weans should get fed this week.'

'They always do.' Annette hesitated, then said, 'Did you hear about that murder?'

'What murder?'

Am I the only one who ever stays at home and watches the telly? Annette thought. Then she realised that Edna probably wouldn't have recognised the victim. Apart from the occasional spell at the door, she only appeared twice a day to collect and count her cash. Annette told the story again and Edna listened in silence, apparently with interest. Maybe she was a real human being after all.

Then Edna said, 'This has got nothin' to do wi' us. Make sure you keep your mouth shut about it, OK? I'll tell the other girls.'

I might have known, thought Annette. And I thought she was feeling sorry for the poor man's wife.

8

A Work of Art

I think the second murder was a great success. Not quite perfect, but a considerable improvement. Even more satisfying than the first one and a lot less risky.

Not that I mind a certain amount of danger. It helps to get the adrenaline flowing. But I can't afford to be too careless, not when there's so much left to do.

I keep reliving my triumph again and again, savouring every moment. It helps keep me subdued until the next time. Gives me the patience to complete the long and careful planning.

Waiting in the street until his wife and her nurse come out of the building, making sure they don't see me, hanging on until they're out of sight, checking that the street is empty before pressing the buzzer.

Getting the lift to the top floor without meeting anyone. If I'd run into another person, no matter who, I'd have postponed it. Frustrating, but necessary. Can't have any witnesses. Luckily, there was no need.

Waiting until he opens the door, then moving quickly, taking him by surprise, hitting him with the hammer, pushing him back into the hall, slamming the door behind me. Checking he's unconscious, hauling him into the nearest room. Then – and here's the masterstroke – going into another room, taking off all my clothes, before returning to him and unleashing my frenzy with the knife. Half an hour later, washed in his shower, dressed again, completely free of bloodstains, I'm trotting down the stairs to an empty street.

Murder two was a triumph of careful preparation. My ground rules are developing well.

One, select the subject. Note the careful choice of word. He's not a victim, but a criminal receiving justice. The choice isn't easy when the list's so long. Some of them will have to wait, but I'll get to them eventually.

Two, watch the subject and know his movements. This was where the last killing scored so heavily over my street attack. After a week's observation, I knew that he'd be alone in the house in the morning, that the wife and nurse would be gone for an hour, possibly more. That I'd have time to clean up afterwards, not only myself, but any traces I might have left in the house. I don't think the police forensic team will find anything useful.

Three. A new rule, to be followed next time, if possible. Having a chance to talk to the subject. Letting him know that he's about to die and the reason for it. This could be tricky. They're all grown men, and so far I've relied on the element of surprise in order to overpower them. In a fair fight, I might well lose. Still it's an important point. Not being able to talk to them spoiled my pleasure – just a little bit – in the first two kills. Maybe I can get a gun to threaten him with. Or I could knock him out, tie him up, then let him regain consciousness . . .

I'll think of something. This is more than justice, it's an art form.

9

An Interesting Day

On the week following the murder, during Annette's Monday shift, two customers got into a fight over Miranda. At least it added a little excitement, almost as much as dealing with drunks at the end of an evening shift.

The two customers were rather alike, sharing similar objectionable qualities. Both were in their thirties, good-looking in a smooth sort of way, beginning to show the effects of good living and self-indulgence. Annette didn't know what they did for a living, but could imagine either of them driving a flash company car and conducting much business on the golf course. One of them called himself Martin and the other John; some customers gave their real names, but these were probably pseudonyms. The book at the front desk was half full of johns called John.

Annette's character assessments were not based on first impressions; they were both regular customers, though they had possibly not run into each other before.

They arrived in the early afternoon, and spent some time sweating off their business lunches in the sauna and steam room respectively. Probably not a very healthy practice, Annette reflected optimistically. Martin was first to arrive in the lounge, but John was only a few moments behind him. Sylvia served them both with cold drinks, following it up with the usual attempts at small talk. Annette was disinclined to make the effort.

After a very short time, John gulped down the last of his drink and turned to Miranda. 'Can I have a massage?' No 'please' or 'are you free?', Annette noted.

Miranda rose to her feet, giving him her special smile, the one that mesmerised the customers and enraged the other girls.

Then Martin said, 'Hang on, mate. I was here first.'

John regarded him coolly. 'Too bad. I asked first.'

'That's got nothing to do with it.'

'I don't see the problem. There are two other girls here. You can have them both together, if you've got the cash. And the stamina.'

'I want Miranda.'

'Fine. You can have her after me.'

'Why the hell should I hang about for half an hour, waiting for your leftovers?'

Miranda had stopped on the way to the door. She said nothing, but continued to smile, in stand-by mode.

Sylvia said, 'Why don't you toss for it?'

'I suppose you'll want to do the tossing,' John said with a sneer. 'Seeing as it's one of your specialities.'

'It takes one tosser to know another,' said Martin.

By now they were both on their feet, facing each other, about a yard between them. They seemed about to resort to fisticuffs.

'Now, now, gentlemen,' said Annette, in what she hoped was a placatory tone. 'Why don't you try to settle this amicably?'

Neither of them replied, but both cast the same contemptuous look in her direction. It seemed to say, 'Shut up, whore. What's this got to do with you?' Annette felt her face flush, equally from anger

44

and humiliation. She resisted the temptation to reply and, like Sylvia, withdrew from involvement.

It was clear that it could only be settled by Miranda herself. This had been apparent for some time, but only now did she seem prepared to do anything about it. 'Oh dear,' she said, 'it looks as if it's up to me. I wish I could keep you both happy, I really do. But you came in at more or less the same time, and John *did* ask first.'

Martin had little alternative but to accept this decision, though he did so with bad grace, not helped by John's beam of triumph. 'I'm sure Annette or Sylvia would love to help you out,' Miranda said to him with a parting simper. 'Or you can have another drink and wait for me, if you like.'

Martin said nothing until she and John were out of the room. Then, still flushed with anger, he turned to Annette. 'I'm fucked if I'm waiting till he's done. You'd better give me the massage instead.'

Fuck you, thought Annette, about to refuse. Then she drew upon the waning reserves of her professional cool. 'I'd love to,' she said smiling, and led him to the cabin.

It was hard work, but she managed it. She wasn't sure if she'd been entirely successful in disguising her feelings, but could see that he was too insensitive to notice.

When they were finished, she waited in the cabin until she was sure he was out of the way. Then she had a shower before returning to the lounge. There she found the customer called Jack, sitting between Miranda and Sylvia and waiting for her.

Immediately, she began to feel better. She had stolen two customers in a row from Miranda. Did she see awareness of this register in her rival's Barbie-doll features? She hoped it wasn't just her imagination. Also, it was a relief to get a customer she liked. After Martin, Jack seemed like the nicest man in the world.

45

Annette's shift was due to end at five o'clock, but she didn't finish with her last customer until twenty past. When she went to Edna's office to settle up, she found her boss having an argument with Miranda.

'It's ridiculous,' said Miranda. 'I only want to use the phone. I can afford to pay for the call, if that's it.' She didn't actually sound angry, but this was the nearest to it that Annette had ever witnessed, a slightly exasperated, ultra-reasonable tone.

'You're no' phonin' the police fae here,' said Edna. 'And that's final.'

'But my car's been stolen. What am I supposed to do?'

'Phone the police. Fae a call box, or fae home. Or go to the station.'

'But I only want to use the *phone*. The sooner I report it, the better chance they have of finding it. They won't know where I'm phoning from.'

'They can check the number.'

'Why should they? The police *know* what we do here. They're not going to raid the place just because I report a stolen car.'

'Maybe not,' said Edna. 'But there's nae point in lookin' for trouble.'

Miranda's face was now slightly flushed, her tone of exasperation a little less mild. So she *does* have emotions, thought Annette. Maybe she comes from this planet after all. However, though it wasn't her natural instinct to side with Miranda, she had to agree that Edna was being a little unfair. She also decided not to get involved. Edna's memories of their profession went back a long way, to a time when the police were less tolerant. She was acting from a deep-rooted instinct.

Miranda said nothing more, obviously sensing that it was a waste of time. 'I'm sorry,' said Edna. 'But it's a basic rule of this business. You don't draw attention to yoursel' beyond what's needed to get the punters in. It's bad enough our customers gettin' murdered, withoot phonin' the cops to remind them where we are.'

This diverted Miranda's attention from her immediate problem. She looked startled. 'What do you mean our customers getting murdered?'

She doesn't *know*? thought Annette. It showed you how often the other girls spoke to her. 'That accountant who got murdered last week,' she said. 'Battered and stabbed in his own house. He was one of our regulars.'

'But that's *awful*,' said Miranda. 'I didn't know anything about it.'

'It's just a coincidence,' said Edna, now looking sorry that she'd mentioned it. 'It's got nae mair to do wi' us than if he'd got knocked doon in the street. But it's better if we don't mention it, especially to the other customers.'

'Fair enough,' said Miranda. It was clear that she still couldn't see why this should prevent her from using the phone, but was past arguing. She took her leave.

'She thinks I'm being unreasonable,' Edna said to Annette when Miranda had gone. 'But I've been in this game too long tae take unnecessary chances.'

'I'm sure you're right,' said Annette tactfully.

In the street where she'd parked her own car, Annette ran into Miranda again. She was talking to a man who had just got out of a blue Ford. But wasn't that Miranda's car? Annette had seen it quite a few times, parked near her own. Miranda and the man were too deep in conversation to see Annette approach.

'Did you find it then?' she asked.

Miranda looked round. 'Oh, hello, Annette. What do you think? It wasn't stolen at all. Derek had just borrowed it and hadn't brought it back in time.' She didn't seem particularly annoyed with Derek, whoever he was. Her usual poise had returned.

'Just as well you didn't phone the police after all,' said Annette.

'I *know*,' said Miranda. 'After all that fuss too. Still, it would have served him right, giving me a fright like that.'

'I got stuck in traffic,' said Derek, coming round from the other side of the car. 'Aren't you going to introduce me?'

'Oh, sorry,' said Miranda. 'Annette, this is my husband, Derek. Annette works beside me.'

Presumably Derek knew what the job was, but no indication of this showed in his manner. 'Nice to meet you, Annette,' he said, shaking her hand warmly. He seemed much more open and forthcoming than Miranda. He was possibly a few years older than her – early thirties maybe. He was handsome, stylishly dressed, and slight in build, only marginally taller than his wife. They looked like a perfect match.

Annette chatted inconsequentially with them for a few moments, then took her leave. Until then, she had not even known that Miranda was married. Annette wondered what Derek did for a living and what he thought about the way his wife earned hers. He seemed very relaxed about it. Maybe he thought they both really were *bona fide* nurses in a private clinic.

As she slowly eased her car through the rush hour traffic, negotiating her way around pedestrian areas and one-way streets on her way to the motorway, she forgot about Miranda. Normally she'd have put her work entirely out of her mind, as she crossed the line between the two quite different worlds she inhabited.

Instead, she found her thoughts turning to the customer called Jack. It looked as if he might be developing into a regular. She liked him: he was easy to talk to and had a good sense of humour. And he had preferred her to Miranda, a sure sign of intelligence . . .

And next week he might be back with Miranda or Candy or with one of the other girls. Or off to another sauna. He was just another customer, no more reliable than any of the others. It was time to forget about her work for another day.

She reached the motorway and soon was speeding back towards her home and her children.

10

A Stranger in Town

'See that wee guy sittin' over there?' said Morag. 'No, not that table, the one next tae it. Drinkin' the half pint of lager. *Don't stare at him, he'll see you.*'

Jack looked across at the customer, trying not to make it obvious. He couldn't see anything particularly unusual about the man. Not the expected midget: only from the perspective of a heftily-built woman of five foot nine would he have been described as 'wee'. And in the West End, an area packed with more eccentrics and actual lunatics than the rest of the country put together, it would take more than short stature to get you noticed. A complete circus act would have been accepted as routine. Maybe it was the fact that he was only drinking a half pint. In Byres Road that *was* unusual.

'What about him?' asked Jack. 'He looks ordinary enough. It's not compulsory to be a nutter in this area, it just seems that way.'

'I think he's followin' you.'

'Following me?'

'I think he might be a private detective.'

'You're not serious. Why would anyone put a private detective on to me?'

'You tell me.' Morag looked at him appraisingly, a sly smile on her lips. 'You're somethin' of a mystery man, Jack Morrison. All the girls think so.'

'I'm flattered,' said Jack. 'I lead a quiet life, that's all. I'd planned to spend the winter in the Caribbean on my yacht, but my wages wouldn't stretch that far.'

Morag laughed. 'If they did, I'm workin' in the wrong pub.' She was a barmaid in Tennent's and was spending her break in the Centurion. 'Maybe your wife wants a divorce.'

Jack sensed a fishing exercise in progress. Maybe Morag liked him more than he realised. 'I'm sure you've heard from the local bush telegraph that I'm already divorced. Anyway, it was my wife that needed to be followed, not me.'

'Sorry,' said Morag. 'I didnae know. Honest.'

'It doesn't matter. What makes you think he's a private eye?'

Before Morag could reply, a customer appeared at the counter. While serving him, Jack managed to sneak a glance at the supposed detective. Medium height and build, youngish, casually dressed. Quite unremarkable, but of course that was how a detective would want to look; a pipe and deerstalker might give the game away, even in the West End. The stranger saw Jack looking at him, finished off his drink and left the bar.

Back with Morag, he said, 'Well, that's him away. What made you notice him?'

'He was in Tennent's while you were on your break. He kept lookin' at you.'

'You never said anything about it at the time.'

'I never thought anythin' of it. Then, as you were leavin' the bar, he took a photo of you.'

'He *did*?' Jack remembered the camera flash, but hadn't realised that he was the subject.

'Then he follows you in here, has another half pint and buggers off. What more do you need?'

'Not a lot,' said Jack. 'It can't be a coincidence. But would a trained detective blow his cover like that?'

'He wasn't to know that we'd have our breaks in each other's pubs. That was just bad luck.' Then she had a new thought. 'Maybe he isnae a private dick, maybe he's an undercover cop. You shouldnae have robbed that bank.'

'You shouldn't have had that second drink,' said Jack. 'You've your work to go back to.'

As the pub got busier during the build-up to closing time, Jack kept a look out for the stranger, but he didn't reappear. There was probably no reason why he should. He had no idea why anyone would want to have him watched, and became more and more convinced that nothing unusual had taken place. It was quite common for people to do pub crawls of Byres Road, and if you stuck to half pints in each place you might have a fighting chance of waking up next morning. He may just have been photographing the interior of Tennent's bar – whose architectural merits, admittedly, had escaped Jack before – and Jack had got caught in the shot accidentally. Maybe he was just a tourist, a timid Southsider sampling the heady pleasures of the Wild West. In that case he should have waited until the weekend, when an impromptu cabaret was certain to develop, staged by that week's volunteer troupe of drunks.

When he left his work just after eleven thirty, Jack had almost forgotten about the incident. Then, a few yards down Byres Road, he saw the stranger again.

He was standing in a shop doorway, beside a bus stop. At first Jack wasn't sure, then, while walking past, he turned his head and briefly looked the man in the eye.

It was him. The nearest street light was close enough for the man's face to be clearly visible. The man returned his gaze impassively, with no hint of recognition. Jack walked on down the road, his eyes fixed in front of him. With any luck his interest would be attributed to the idle glance of a stranger, or someone who thought he had recognised a friend.

As he made his way towards the end of the street, Jack became convinced that he was being followed, but forced himself not to look round. A couple of blocks from the junction of Byres Road and Dumbarton Road, he stopped in order to cross the road, first checking for traffic in either direction; this enabled him to look back the way he had come without it appearing obvious.

There were people scattered about, at intervals. But there was no one he recognised, or who appeared to be following him. He crossed the road and proceeded down the side street that led to his home.

As he was opening the security door at the close mouth, he again glanced back the way he had come. Nothing unusual. He went up the stairs to his flat.

Jack's flat was on the edge of Partick, where the inflated West End prices were less prohibitive than in Hyndland or North Kelvinside. This was not only due to the location, but because the houses tended to be smaller, built towards the end of the nineteenth century for the less expansive needs of the working class. The building had been stone-cleaned and refurbished during the grant-financed clean-up a few years previously, and the dirty grey Glasgow tenement of fifteen years ago was now (in the estate agent's words) a 'handsome, blonde-sandstone block of flats'. All this, of course, was reflected in the price Jack had paid when he bought the flat the year before. The owner who had coughed his way through the sand-blasting probably now lived in Hyndland or Bearsden.

The flat was comfortable, handy for his work and the university where he was a student. Though much more modest than the semi-detached Southside villa where his ex-wife Margaret still lived, it was sufficient for his needs, and Margaret's buy-out of his share in their former home had given him enough money to buy the flat on a low mortgage. It had also provided him with enough capital, along with his barman's wages, to see him through his university course. If he didn't squander it all first.

He made himself some supper, watched TV for a short while, then went to bed. He wasn't particularly paranoid by nature, and by now the mystery man was almost forgotten as his mind wandered into other areas.

He thought of Morag. What had happened tonight? Casual flirting, or was there more to it than that? She was quite attractive, if you liked big women. A few years younger than him, but not a teenager. Did she fancy him?

Did he fancy her? Possibly, but not as much as he fancied Annette. Nor was he yet fully recovered from his split with Margaret. He didn't like the idea of entering into a relationship he was lukewarm about, just for sex. That was the advantage of paying for it. It was an honest commercial arrangement between consenting adults. There was no deceit, there were no false declarations of love. No commitment and no guilt.

And no money in your bank account.

Before it came to that, the situation would have to be resolved. He had now been with Annette four times and, since the first time, had never chosen anyone else, or felt the need to. Candy was sexy and good fun, but that was all there was to her and once had been enough. He had tried Miranda a couple more times, but once he had got over being dazzled by her beauty and the realisation that such a lovely creature was there for the asking, she had proved somehow unsatisfactory. She was always perfectly pleasant and proficient at her job, but otherwise seemed a little remote. You didn't feel that you had made contact with another human being, except on a purely physical level. That was no doubt enough for many men, and had satisfied him at first. But with Annette he felt that he had made some human connection. He enjoyed her company and she seemed to like his. And how had he ever thought her less attractive than Miranda or Candy? He didn't think that now.

What was he doing? Ignoring the possibility of a normal monogamous relationship for another, strictly limited, monogamous union that was certain to bankrupt him? Was Annette worth the loss of his capital and his future career prospects?

At times like this, lying alone at night in his single bed, he sometimes thought that she might be. But by daylight he would see it differently. He would have to slow things down, think it all through. Soon.

11

Justine

From the beginning, Annette wasn't sure what to make of the new girl. She was very good-looking, not quite in Miranda's class – who was? – but, bearing in mind the constant craving for novelty shown by some customers, quite attractive enough to make the other girls want to keep clear of her shift. It was nothing personal, just that the competition was already stiff enough.

It wasn't the girl's appearance that caused Annette to wonder about her. That only happened when she opened her mouth.

Edna had told Annette about the new start the day before. 'Claudia wanted moved to an evening slot, so I'm puttin' her on wi' you and Candy. I'd like you to look after her, show her the ropes. You've got a bit more sense than Candy.'

As well as more free time, thought Annette. Trust Edna to make it sound like a privilege. Take on the job of training officer, for no extra pay, and show the newcomer how to steal your customers. Just the sort of perk she needed.

'Has she worked anywhere else?' Annette asked.

'No,' said Edna. 'She's completely new to it. Remember an' tell her that the condoms are free.'

Edna bought condoms in bulk and supplied them to the girls free of charge, an uncharacteristic act of generosity which she liked to remind them of from time to time.

The new girl arrived the following morning, promptly at eleven, just after Annette herself. She seemed a little nervous, but that was understandable. She looked no more than twenty-one, damn her.

'I'm Annette,' said Annette. 'Have you made up your mind on a name?'

The girl looked puzzled. 'How dae ye mean?' As soon as she spoke, Annette noticed the discrepancy. She obviously took care over her appearance, and was clean, well groomed and carefully made-up, quite classy in fact. However, she had obviously dropped out of finishing school before the elocution lessons.

'Most of the girls use a false name. I don't bother myself.'

'I never thought about it. What's the point?'

'The customers like you to have a name that's a wee bit exotic. What's your name anyway?'

'Effie.'

'I'd change it.'

'You think so?'

'Only for in here. You don't have to alter your birth certificate or anything. Some of the girls think it helps them to keep their work and their personal life separate.'

'I'm only daein' this for a wee while, till somethin' else turns up.' Where have I heard that before? thought Annette. 'You see,' the girl continued, 'my man walked oot on me. Just like that. Nae warnin'. No' a word. I don't even know where he is. An' I've got a wee one tae look after an' a mortgage tae pay. It's a nice hoose, I don't want tae give it up. I wouldnae normally do a thing like this. It's just for a wee while, till I get back on my feet.'

A wee while on your back to get you on your feet, Annette thought. She shouldn't be cynical. The girl seemed to mean it.

Now that she had started talking, Annette couldn't get her to stop. She told Annette all about her man Joe, and what a great guy he was, until he did his Houdini impersonation. His folks had seen him since, so she knew he was OK, but they claimed not to know where he was staying, though she didn't know whether to believe them. She told Annette all about her nice new house, in a good area, and all the lovely furniture she had. All about her wee girl Moira, who was eighteen months old, who was being looked after by her mother, who'd murder her if she knew what she was working at. All about her pal Lizzie, who'd done this job for a wee while, and who said it wasn't all that bad and that the money was good. All about a score of other things, and then the same ones again, and then again, in a different order. Above all, about how Joe had so suddenly vanished, and how she still couldn't understand why. It wasn't long before Annette began to form her own theory.

Eventually, Annette managed to steer her back on course. Already the first customer had arrived and gone off with Candy, a trend that could too easily continue for the rest of the day. They discussed names for a while, and finally settled upon Justine. It was a nice name, she'd heard it on some TV programme or other, and Annette was able to assure her that none of the other girls were using it. Then Annette gave her a brief rundown on some basics: the prices to charge, the amount of Edna's cut, the importance of keeping her cabin tidy so that customers would find no distasteful traces of their predecessors, plus a few other tricks of the trade picked up from trade with the tricks. Justine sat through it all with a look of slight puzzlement, as if she didn't understand any of it, or couldn't quite believe it.

Candy returned and added some characteristic wisdom of her own. 'The mair ye tease them, the quicker they'll come. It helps you keep up the turnover an' keep doon the wear an' tear.'

'She's the last of the romantics,' said Annette.

Justine still looked bemused. Another customer arrived, one whom Annette recognised, though he wasn't stuck on any particular girl. He was reasonably young, presentable and, as far as Annette could remember, a quiet and pleasant guy with no abnormal tastes. As good a choice as any to break in a new girl. Annette and Candy let Justine look after him and, after a short session of strained small talk, he obligingly chose her.

Annette and Candy watched them go off. Justine had been abnormally quiet from the time the customer had arrived, probably a good move, though she hadn't planned it that way. However, the customer's action in choosing her seemed to pull the cork out. She was already yattering non-stop before they had left the lounge. 'You know this is ma first day an' you're ma first customer? I've never done this before. I'm only daein' it for a wee while tae get some money, because I'm on my own wi' a wee one tae look after. Are you married, have you any kids? You know I wouldnae do a job like this if it wasnae . . .'

Annette couldn't make out any more, but felt confident that Justine would be halfway through her autobiography before they reached the cabin.

'Is she half daft or what?' Candy asked.

'She's nervous. She's never done it before.'

'Never at all? Is that why her man left her?'

'You know what I mean. Anyway, he'll probably find it a turn on, knowing he's her first customer.'

'Maybe,' said Candy. 'Looks to me like she's a coupla cans short of a party pack.'

'You just don't like the competition.'

'There's nae competition. You wait and see.'

Another customer arrived, and Candy spirited him off in record time, as if to prove her point. Then a third appeared, while the other two girls were still engaged, and Annette was able to make a start.

Justine seemed to settle in fairly well – at least there were no major crises as far as Annette could tell. Her looks and novelty value made her popular, but it was a busy day and Annette reckoned that she lost fewer customers to Justine than Candy did. At any rate her takings weren't noticeably down. Candy's probably were, but Annette didn't waste any time worrying about that. Glasgow's licensed traders would survive the unexpected dip. Justine's daughter and her nice house were probably a better cause.

Candy herself accepted the competition with good humour. She was too good-natured to get seriously bitchy and, Annette suspected, didn't expect that there would be any long-term threat.

❖

Annette didn't see Justine again until the same shift on the following week. Since then, Justine had done one other daytime shift along with different girls; Edna had confined her to two shifts until she settled in, though she was also kept in reserve to fill in for absentees.

She was still proving popular, though mainly with customers who hadn't met her before; Annette noted at least one who'd chosen her the previous week, and who now reverted to Candy. Annette didn't have much time to speak to her until the mid-afternoon lull, between the business men on extended lunch hours and those who sneaked off work early; presumably they had to spend some time earning the money to pay for their expensive habits. Candy was working, but Annette and Justine were waiting in the lounge. Annette had already noticed that Justine's loquacity was undiminished.

'How are you getting on?' Annette asked.

'Fine,' said Justine. 'You know, that's a really nice big guy, that last one I had. I was tellin' him all about Moira, my wee girl. He's got one the same age. We had a right good laugh, talkin' aboot the things they get up to. You know what it's like, though yours are older, aren't they? Anyway . . .'

I'm surprised you remembered I had kids, thought Annette. I must have got a word in more often than I realised.

'. . . I says to him, what are you daein' spendin' your money in a place like this when you've got a wife an' a wee girl tae look after?'

'You said *what*?'

'Just kiddin' him on, like, you know. Anyway, he says, I've got a good job, they don't go without. That's good I says, that means you're lookin' after two wee girls, yours an' mine.'

Jesus Christ, thought Annette.

'We had a good laugh over that. What are you lookin' at me like that for? It was just a joke.'

'They may not like you talking about their family. You're better letting them bring up the subject.'

'I don't see the harm in it,' said Justine.

'If he's married, he might feel guilty about being here. He doesn't need you to remind him about it.'

Justine frowned, as if she found coping with this idea something of a struggle. She said nothing for a few moments. Annette enjoyed the silence and didn't interrupt. Was it possible that her advice was beginning to register?

Then Justine said, 'There's one thing I wondered about . . .'

'What's that?'

'It's just that, it might no' be anything but . . .'

She hesitated, apparently having at last found a subject delicate enough to stem the verbal flood. Annette had to coax it out of her. It seemed that an unduly high proportion of her customers had opted for oral sex, and she wondered if this was normal. 'It's no' that I mind that much, I mean I've done it before, my man Joe used to like it . . .'

'I wonder why?' Annette said, half to herself.

'What's that? It's just that I like a right good blether wi' them and . . . What's she laughin' at?'

Candy had returned and was listening to the conversation with interest.

'Never mind her,' said Annette, trying to avoid Candy's eye. 'Don't you think . . .' She paused, trying to be tactful. She noticed that, for once, she had Justine's full attention. 'Don't you think maybe they're trying to tell you something?'

'I don't understand what you mean.' She turned to Candy. 'What's the joke?'

'Nothin',' said Candy. 'I'm just happy at my work.'

'I mean,' said Annette, 'it's OK to have a chat with the customers, getting them to relax. But that's not the main reason they're here, is it? There comes a point where you've got to let the body language take over, if you know what I mean?'

It was clear that Justine was still having difficulty with the concept, but a customer took her away before they could discuss it further. Annette saw no evidence of Justine acting on her advice; if anything, she seemed to have speeded up her verbal assault on the customer, as if she was determined to get through the maximum amount of material before the rude interruption.

When Justine had gone, Candy said, 'Tell me, is she thick, or is she *really* thick?'

'I'm beginning to wonder,' said Annette. 'I'm sure part of it's nerves.

I don't think she's properly settled into the job yet. Maybe she's not cut out for it.'

'Who is?'

'You are. I'd say you were born to it.'

'Fuck off.'

'I'll have a good talk with her. Maybe that'll help.'

'Tell her bugger all,' said Candy. 'You've already said too much.'

'I thought you weren't worried about the competition.'

'I'm not. But if she takes one punter from me, that's my fag money for the week.'

'And if she takes more of your customers,' said Annette, 'she might save your liver as well as your lungs. You should look on the bright side.'

'I always do. By the way, not all her punters go for oral. You know that guy I had earlier, the one who took her last week? She gave him a hand relief.'

'What did he say about her?'

'Nothin' much,' said Candy. 'He wanted tae know if she'd ever been a tattie howker.'

12

Out to Lunch

'Cigarette?'

'No thanks, I don't smoke.'

'Do you mind if I do?'

'I'd prefer it if you didn't, Mr Archer.'

'Sure,' said Steven Archer. 'No problem.' He replaced the packet of cigarettes in his pocket, wishing that he'd smoked another one in the car before meeting this bugger. Somehow he'd thought that, lunching with a journalist, it wouldn't be a problem. Obviously this guy wasn't typical. That became even clearer when Steven consulted the wine list.

'Nothing for me, thanks,' said his guest. 'I don't drink. Go ahead yourself, if you want.'

The words were polite, but the tone a little condescending, as if he was making a significant concession. Damn the man. Steven would have risked a bottle between the two of them, but not one on his own when he was driving. He knew that he could drive quite capably after a bottle of wine, but the cops wouldn't see it that way if he failed a breath test. He couldn't afford even the slightest chance of losing his licence. The car was essential to his work.

Steven eyed the waitress with interest as she returned for their order. She filled that old-fashioned maid's uniform very nicely, like something out of a period erotic fantasy. Pity she wasn't on the menu herself.

'Have you decided what you want, gentlemen?'

'Yes,' said Steven, looking her directly in the eye and smiling. 'But we'll settle for ordering a meal.' He looked across at his guest, to share the joke with him, but got no reaction. The waitress continued to smile, also ignoring the innuendo. But she knew what he meant all right. Whether the other man did was another matter. It might have been the waitress's grandmother who had served them, for all the effect it seemed to have on him.

It wasn't as if his guest was all that old. He could be little more than thirty-five, Steven's own age, but his conservative dress style and old-fashioned mannerisms made him seem much older. His appearance was obsessively neat, from the manicured fingers to the highly polished black shoes and the well-cut business suit. His short hairstyle was undoubtedly a throwback to earlier days rather than observance of a new fashion: somehow Steven couldn't see him as a long-haired youth in the 1970s. An uptight, humourless bastard if ever he'd seen one. Steven regarded himself as a man's man, who found it easy to get along with the normal male. But he felt no rapport with this guy at all.

After scoring nil for smoking, drinking and casual lechery, Steven expected him to be a vegetarian as well, but he ordered a steak. So that they could establish at least one thing in common, Steven asked for the same. He also ordered a single glass of red wine while his guest settled for mineral water.

'I'm sure they could pour it from the tap and we wouldn't know the difference,' he said. 'But since you're paying . . .'

Was that actually an attempt at a joke? Steven reluctantly redirected his eyes from the waitress's departing rear. 'Absolutely, Mr Washington.'

'Robert.'

'Robert. Be my guest. Go wild and drink as much water as you like. I'm sure you're going to make it worth my while.'

So maybe he was susceptible to at least one deadly sin. Could his last remark have been an indication of avarice? It was routine for Steven to assess new business acquaintances for weaknesses, in case some form of inducement proved necessary. As far as Washington was concerned, a case of whisky or a night with a hooker seemed unlikely to be effective, but a bundle of used banknotes might just work. Though God only knew what he would spend them on.

Right now it was a hypothetical exercise. This was likely to be a straight business deal, with no need for inducements. Such transactions still occurred sometimes.

'I'm sure I can be of service, Mr Archer. Or can I call you Steven?'

'Of course.' Here we were, almost the twenty-first century, and this guy still seemed to be struggling his way out of the nineteenth.

'I understand you were thinking of a centre-page spread, Steven?'

'That was the general idea.'

'It'll cost you.'

'How much?'

Washington told him. Bloody hell, thought Steven. He supposed he could just about afford it, as long as it did the job. But there would be no more free lunches, not even teetotal ones.

'That's a lot of money,' said Steven. 'What did you say your circulation was?'

'A hundred thousand.'

'As much as that?'

'That's the beauty of a free newspaper, Steven. You don't have to sell it. Your circulation is what you can afford to print and distribute.'

'You should be able to print a few from the cost of a centre spread.'

'That's the way it works.'

'And what's your distribution area?'

'The north side of the city, from Yoker to Dennistoun and as far north as Springburn. That's why we're called the *North Clyde Advertiser*.'

'You include the West End?'

'Of course. That's our heartland. Also the city centre, so the paper can be picked up by people from other parts of the city, and from out of town. In restaurants and pubs and suchlike.'

'You don't have any moral objection to distributing in pubs?' He shouldn't have said that, not before the deal had been struck. But Washington didn't appear to take offence.

'Not at all, Steven. Neither do the Salvation Army. It doesn't mean that either of us approve of hard liquor.'

Steven felt he was beginning to get the measure of Washington. His strict moral outlook wasn't allowed to interfere with business. He probably paid his distributors Third World wages, exploiting under-age kids and the unemployed. Not that there was anything wrong with that.

While they were consuming their starters and main course, Washington quizzed Steven about his new housing development – the subject of the proposed advertisement feature – while recording the conversation on a portable tape recorder. Steven had almost expected him to produce a shorthand notebook, but he seemed up to date as far as business was concerned. They discussed the general shape and content of the article, and Steven handed over a number of brochures and photographs.

'Have you a copy of your paper?'

'Have you never seen it?'

'Off and on. But I'd like to examine it a little more closely.'

'Of course. I thought you would.' Washington opened his briefcase and brought out a small bundle of newspapers. 'These are the last six issues.'

Coffees were ordered, and Washington looked through the brochures while Steven scanned the newspapers. At first they seemed much as he expected, being dominated by the adverts which financed the whole concern, along with a smattering of news and features of local interest. All very predictable. Then, in the most recent issue, the headline of a leading article caught his eye:

A FIRST BLOW FOR THE MORAL MAJORITY

In this issue, we take a small but important step in the endless battle against permissiveness, that modern plague undermining the structure of Christian society.

In the past we have indicated our support for the residents of Partick in their fight to excise a cancer from the streets where their innocent children play. I refer of course to the brothel calling itself the Rosevale Sauna. It is scandalous enough that such havens of vice should infest the commercial areas of the city, in some cases even being awarded licences by the council. But when they appear, like the eruption of a boil on healthy skin, right next door to the homes of decent working people, it is time to act.

The authorities tell us they are taking steps to close down this evil cesspit. In order to give them a much-needed nudge in the right direction, we have regularly been stationing a photographer on the street outside. Every week, beginning today, we will let the public see what the patrons of this vile establishment look like.

Fornicators and adulterers take heed. You can no longer hide your shame.

Beside the column, a large photograph showed a small shop unit, on the ground floor of a tenement block of flats. Behind the plate-glass window drawn blinds concealed the interior from view. A man was emerging from the doorway, his features clearly identifiable.

Steven realised that Washington was watching him. 'I see you're reading my leader,' he said. 'Don't you agree with it?'

'No . . . well, I mean . . . yes. It seems a bit strong.'

'Are you a family man, Steven?'

'Yes.'

'I'm sure you wouldn't like to have your children playing outside such a place. Don't you think the families in Partick deserve the same consideration? Isn't it bad enough that their children already buy sweets from shops whose top shelves are full of pornography?'

'Oh, absolutely. I see what you mean.'

'And while I abhor the conduct of women who sell themselves, I believe the time is overdue for an attack on the men who use them. After all, they're the cause of the problem. Without them, the women would have no market.'

'Yes. Yes, you're right.'

It was Steven's practice always to agree with business contacts, to tell them what they wanted to hear, though in the present case it was becoming something of a strain. The man was obviously a fanatic, a complete nutter. Was he himself a family man, like those whose interests he was so keen to protect? More probably he was an overgrown mother's boy, raised in some strict religious sect, still a bachelor. Or maybe he was married to some harridan who kept a padlock on her knickers. Steven briefly wondered whether he should go ahead with the deal, but the newspaper seemed successful enough, despite its owner's obsessive crusade.

He realised that the photographs of sauna customers probably wouldn't put readers off, but would be an attraction. The public might not go along with Washington's extreme views, but they'd still want a look, to see if they recognised anyone.

They finalised their arrangements and Steven paid the bill for the lunch. At last he got free of the man and returned to his car.

He lit a cigarette and sat for a moment, before starting the ignition. What next? The business lunch had taken up much less time than the usual convivial affair, and he had time in hand before he needed to be back in the office. It had earlier occurred to him, since he was in the area, to give the Rosevale Sauna a try, but that now seemed like a bad idea. Fuck the man! Just as well he'd found out in time.

What was wrong with Washington, for God's sake? His idea of an evil cesspit represented, for Steven, the essence of modern, civilised living. No more need for a messy extramarital affair, fending off demands to leave your wife, worrying about being found out, when all you wanted was your leg over on the side. No need to go kerb-crawling, risking police interference or HIV infection from some junkie. Instead, you just nipped down to the nearest fast-fud shop, then back to work with no one the wiser.

As long as that bastard Washington didn't have a photographer posted outside.

It wouldn't take long, he decided, to drive across town to the Merchant City. Maybe that blonde bird Miranda would be on today. Now there was a really high-class piece of pussy, far too good for that place she worked in. Why did she do it? Probably too thick to make the same money doing anything else.

Maybe he wouldn't have to fight over her this time. Not that it mattered. He had sorted out that wanker all right, and would do the same again if he had to.

13

How to Clean Up in the Sex Business

Jack managed to keep clear of the Merchant City Health Centre for three weeks, his best record since discovering the place. In the intervening period he did his job as a barman, worked at his studies, and watched with relief as the haemorrhage in his savings came to a stop. He worked out a budget and reckoned that he could afford an occasional visit without eroding his capital. After the novelty had worn off, this would surely be enough for him.

Having reached this decision, it wasn't very long before he convinced himself that the first such occasion was due. It was a Tuesday, and a phone call confirmed that Annette was there on her usual shift, along with Candy and a girl whose name he didn't recognise.

He was no longer nervous about entering the dingy close in the back street. That had quickly been superseded by a feeling of illicit excitement. He experienced that now, intensified by his three-week absence. In a perverse way, the seediness of the place added to the pleasure. It was probably the influence of his religious upbringing, from which he had long since lapsed; if you wanted to enjoy a relapse into sin, it helped to do it in the right surroundings.

On the first floor, he had to push past a queue of people waiting for the pawnbroker to reopen after lunch. He kept his head down as he went by, wondering if they knew what was on the floor above. Unless he began to show more self-control, it wouldn't be long before he would be joining them in the queue, before going straight upstairs with the cash.

'Hello, Jack,' said the woman behind the desk. 'Haven't seen you for a while.' She took his money, noted his name and time of arrival in her book, and handed him a towel, locker key and wallet. 'Still know your way about?'

'I think so.'

He made his way down the hall to the changing room. The air of seediness no longer ended at the front door. At the time of his first visit, the place had seemed clean and somewhat luxurious; later, with familiarity, it seemed less so. It would have benefited from redecoration and more regular cleaning. It was common to find at least one of the showers out of order, sometimes the toilet as well, and many of the robes and towels were wearing thin. Some of the locker doors were bent out of shape, mainly (according to Annette) due to drunken customers, unable to work the lock, or reduced to vandalism after parting with their money only to discover that their desire had exceeded their capability.

As he was making his way from the shower area, Annette came out of the lounge with a customer. 'Hi there, Jack, how are you?'

'Fine. Yourself?'

'Fine. I'll see you later.'

She continued on her way to the cabin, chatting to the customer as she went. Jack recognised some of her patter, which she had used on him in the past. What did she mean that she would see him later? She was taking a lot for granted, wasn't she?

There was only one other person in the lounge, a girl whom Jack hadn't met before. It didn't take him long to notice that she was the best-looking girl he had ever seen in the place, with the possible exception of Miranda. She was younger than the others, in her early twenties at the most. She had long, dark hair and a slim but full figure, which the regulation white coat couldn't entirely conceal. She gave Jack a smile that was friendly, a little bashful and quite endearing.

'Hello,' she said, 'I'm Justine. What's your name?'

'Jack.'

'Would ye like a drink, Jack?'

'Thanks. I'll have a coffee.' Her speech, unfortunately, didn't quite match her looks in sophistication. 'I don't think I've met you before.'

'I've only been here a fortnight. What do you take in it?'

'Milk and one sugar, please. Where did you work before?'

'Naewhere. This is my first place.'

So she was completely new to the job. Jack thought about this as she was pouring out his coffee. She handed the cup to him and sat down beside him. Unlike most of the girls (apart from Annette), she didn't immediately light a cigarette. As she sat down, the flap of her coat fell aside and she immediately pulled it up again. Apparently she was a little more modest than Candy. That was refreshing.

She chattered on in an inconsequential way. She was over-garrulous and seemed a bit naive, but in a way that added to her charm. He sipped his coffee, which he had chosen in preference to a cold drink because he had been expecting to wait for Annette. But now he was less sure. Why should he wait? It would be at least half an hour before she was free. Meanwhile, she was in a cabin with that other guy and Justine was sitting right beside him, seeming more and more desirable by the minute.

'Are you free for a massage?' he asked her.

'Aye, of course. We're in Cabin Three.'

He put down his unfinished coffee and followed her through to the cabin.

'Make yoursel' comfortable an' I'll be back in a minute.'

Jack lay face down on the narrow bed, after taking off his robe and placing it along with his towel and wallet on the floor beside him. The bed was mounted on a solid plinth and was just wide enough to serve its main purpose while still doubling as a massage table. There was a pillow at the end and a large towel served as a top sheet.

He turned over on his side, admiring himself in the wall mirror then glancing briefly at the pornographic video showing on the wall-mounted TV.

Justine returned and began to massage his back with oil. None of the girls, he was sure, were professionally trained masseuses, but they generally had a light touch and showed some awareness of the procedure's erotic possibilities. Not Justine. She absent-mindedly pummelled his body, in a rough and perfunctory way, as if it was merely a way of keeping her hands occupied while she chattered.

'What did you say your name was again?'

'Jack.'

'Oh aye. I'm Justine. That's no' my real name of course. The girls nearly all use different names. Annette says . . . You know Annette that works here?'

'Yes, I know Annette.'

'Annette says the customers prefer it. She doesnae bother aboot it hersel', she uses her real name.'

'Is that right?'

'Aye, though I cannae really see the point. I'm only workin' here for a wee while, because I need the money. I've got a hoose to pay for an' a wee one tae look after. My mother takes care of her while I'm workin'. She doesnae know what I'm doin', she'd murder me if she found oot. Still, if ye need the money, what can ye dae?'

'I know,' said Jack, wondering why he needed to know all this. He was aware, of course, that she was doing it for the money, rather than an irresistible desire for his body, but it was nice to pretend otherwise instead of having the reality spelled out for him. It struck him that he knew practically nothing about Annette's personal circumstances, despite all the times he'd been with her. And now he already had half of Justine's life story, with the rest sure to follow. He was beginning to find her prattle a little less endearing.

'Are you married, Jack?'

'Divorced.'

'Oh, that's a shame. Have you got any kids?'

'No.'

'Aw well, maybe it's just as well. You've still got time. Maybe you'll meet somebody nice an' then you'll no' need tae come here. Would ye like tae turn over?'

With some relief, Jack turned face up. The massage of his back generally took a little longer, but usually it was more enjoyable. Now they could get down to the real business. He waited for her to raise the subject, but she carried on as before, with hardly a break, now mauling his chest instead of his back.

'You know, there's a lot of married men come here, but I don't think that's right. I mean, I know we wouldnae have so many customers if it wasnae for them, but I still don't think it's fair of them. There was one in the other day an' I just says to him . . .'

'Do you do extras?' Jack asked.

Justine looked a little upset. Presumably she wanted to earn the money, but not if it meant being interrupted mid-sentence. 'Oh aye, of course,' she said. 'What would ye like?'

'What do you do?'

She seemed a little embarrassed by the request, but dutifully reeled off the usual price list and he made his choice. At this point, now that the real nature of the transaction was out in the open, he expected her to take off her clothes before resuming the massage, a normal part of the foreplay in a commercial encounter like this. But Justine carried on as before, every button of her white coat still in place.

'You know,' she said, 'this place is all right, but I think they could keep it a wee bit cleaner, know what I mean? I like to keep my hoose really clean. I think that's important. I've got a really nice hoose, did I tell you? If you ask me this place could do wi' a good hooverin'. I've just got a new hoover, I bought it oot my first week's wages.'

The wages of sin, Jack thought, is a clean carpet.

'It's a really good one. It sucks the dirt up really well, right up tae the edges. I could do wi' bringin' it in here, givin' the place a good clean oot, but that's no' my job, is it? But it's a really good one. It's a Hoover Turbopower.'

'That's the kind I've got,' said Jack, feeling the need to say something.

'Is that right? That's really amazin'.' She appeared astonished and delighted at the coincidence. 'It's a really good one, isn't it?'

'It certainly is.'

On she enthused about the formidable cleaning properties of the Turbopower. Jack realised that his passing remark had been all that was necessary to convince her of his interest and bring about her second wind on the subject. Then, just as he was about to ask her if she had forgotten something, she finished pasting oil on to his legs, wiped her hands clean with a tissue and began to unbutton her coat. At last she stopped talking and looked at him shyly as she continued to undress. Underneath the coat she only wore a bra and panties, which she proceeded to remove as well. She had a beautiful body. She really was a stunning-looking girl. As Jack's nerves began to recover from her continual yattering, he entered a more forgiving mood. It was good to have a chat with the girl, for them both to be at their ease. She had overdone it a bit, overdone it quite a lot in fact, but now it would be worth it. She brought out a condom from her handbag and tore open the covering foil.

Then, as they changed places and she lay down on her back, she said, 'The only trouble wi' thae Hoovers is gettin' new bags for them. There's that many different kinds, I cannae understand why they need that many. When you go intae a shop, they never have the right one. Mind you, there's a good wee place in Partick, I don't know if you know it? They say you can use a bag more than once, but I don't like tae, it goes a' soft an' clatty. An' see gettin' the bag fitted properly? Why do they make it that difficult? The first time I tried tae fit a new bag, it wasnae on properly an' it blew dirt all ower the place. What a mess it made! I'm tellin' you . . .'

Jack felt his desire fade and wished that he'd waited for Annette.

❖

Annette returned to the lounge, expecting to find Jack waiting for her as usual. Instead she found Candy sitting on her own.

'What happened to Jack?' she asked, trying to sound casual.

'Your boyfriend, you mean?'

'My *regular*.'

'Whatever you say. Why, was he here?'

'I met him in the corridor earlier.'

'I never saw him. He musta gone aff wi' Mary Poppins.'

'The bastard. All right, don't tell me you told me so.'

'I told you so. What are you worried aboot? Naebody's gone back to her for seconds yet. Edna's bound tae catch on.'

'I suppose so.'

More customers arrived and Annette didn't see Jack leave. When she thought about it later, she was surprised at her reaction on finding out that he'd gone with another girl. He was paying for that privilege after all. What right had she to expect him to sit there faithfully while she was screwing another customer?

Normally it wouldn't have bothered her at all, but this time it did.

14

The Way Ahead

I need blood.

It's too long since the last killing. My research continues, my list grows longer and longer. But what's the point if I'm not doing anything to shorten it?

I still take some comfort in reliving the first two murders. I remember every detail and regularly play them back to myself. I read through my newspaper clippings again and again. As I expected, the police have no leads and public interest has already begun to wane.

I get a great deal of satisfaction from all of this, but it's not enough. The problem is finding a way to improve my procedure. The more I think about it, the more essential it seems that the subjects should be given a chance to know their fate and the reason for it. But so far I haven't thought of a way to do that. I could send them anonymous letters, telling them of my intention. But this would put them on their guard, and some might even take my letter to the police. No, that's a stupid idea; it could lead the cops straight to me.

But how do I get them alone, under my power, safe from outside observation and interference? Last time I was able to kill him in his own home, but that won't always be practical.

There are several contenders for first place on the list. They need to be dealt with urgently.

Then at last I get the break I need. I see the way ahead, how to trap one of the offenders. And he's one of the worst, fighting for top place. Nailing him would be a triumph.

And the method is ideal. It has been given to me, gift-wrapped, out of the blue.

15

The Subplot Thickens . . .

The more Jack thought about his situation, the more it seemed to him that there was only one solution. He should put his relationship with Annette on a more conventional basis. He should ask her out on a date.

This had occurred to him before, but it had seemed like a bad idea. She would certainly refuse. He would only succeed in spoiling a perfectly good professional relationship. He had felt that a rapport was developing between them, but that might only mean that she was very good at her job.

Then several things happened to help him reconsider the idea.

The first was his encounter with Justine. There could not have been a better counter-example to confirm his attraction to Annette.

He was given further cause for thought after a night out with some of his fellow students. He'd had the occasional drink with them before, usually in the students' union or in the city centre, near the university. But now there was a move to celebrate the end of their exams more daringly by 'hitting Byres Road'.

Jack regarded this as less of an adventure than did some of his classmates, who were still enthusiastically learning many of the adolescent lessons that he had mastered years before. But they put pressure on him to go along, particularly young Alison Steele who was one of only three girls in the class and looked upon Jack as her protector. Jack knew that she had a regular boyfriend who lived out of town, and he had no illusions about his role.

He gave in and, realising the implications of being the only one who lived locally, even gave his Turbopower a workout.

After a couple of drinks elsewhere, they settled in Tennent's. There were eight of them altogether, Alison being the only female, and Jack being the only one over twenty. Jack had bought a round earlier and it was some time before it was his turn again. Before then, Alison, feeling the effects of trying to keep up with the boys, decided to rest her head on Jack's shoulder. Jack didn't object, finding it much more enjoyable than listening to the nonsense coming from the others.

He was suddenly roused by a loud clinking of glasses, a few inches from his ear. He looked round to see Morag, who was collecting pint tumblers from a table behind him. He had noticed that she was working that evening, but so far hadn't had an opportunity to speak to her.

'Hi, Morag,' he said. But she was already on her way back to the bar, a cluster of glasses in each hand.

He thought nothing of it until he went up to the bar to buy his round. Morag was the only member of the bar staff free, but he seemed to have some difficulty in attracting her notice. Eventually, after he had called her name several times, she came slowly over and took his order. Jack was feeling the effect of the drinks, but nevertheless detected a definite coolness in her manner.

'Havin' a nice night?' she asked. She was smiling, but it seemed to be costing her some effort.

'Not bad,' he said. 'They're all from my class at the uni. The exams have just finished.'

'Oh, I see.'

'It's hard work keeping up with all these young ones.'

'You seem to be doin' all right. I never thought of you as a cradle snatcher.'

'What?' said Jack, the drink making him slow on the uptake. 'No, you've got the . . .'

But Morag had already gone off to the till with his money. She returned with his change and he ferried the drinks back in several journeys. She could have given him a tray, but this possibility seemed to have escaped her.

Back at the table, he resumed his role as Alison's pillow. Then, after another couple of drinks she revived and began to flirt with him. He responded, and soon they had settled into a prolonged kissing session, like a pair of teenagers. It was all very innocent, but Jack rather enjoyed it, including the reaction of the other male students. In the back of his mind, he realised that Morag couldn't have failed to notice, but so what? There was nothing between them. He wasn't accountable to her.

By closing time, Alison was having to cling to him in order to remain on her feet. Outside, they flagged down a taxi and Jack helped her into it. One of the other students went with her, promising to see that she was safely dropped off.

Jack just wanted to go home to bed, but the others clustered round him. Two of them, who hadn't bought a second round, had bought a carry-out. He gave in and led them down the road to his flat.

❖

Jack didn't drink much more, but next morning lack of practice and the age gap between him and the others had taken their toll.

After checking that the bodies on his couch and floor were still breathing, he went back to bed until his minimal duties as host required further involvement.

Fortunately, he wasn't due at work until six o'clock, and after seeing off the last of the stragglers around midday, he cleared away the fish-supper wrappers and empties, and settled down to an afternoon of intensive rest. He had no energy left to do anything, but plenty of time to think.

The previous evening's events had helped to put a few things into focus.

He'd had an inkling that Morag fancied him, but now he was sure. She had been jealous. He could see why Alison might cause that reaction. Morag was attractive enough, but so was Alison, as well as being younger and more economically built. Of course Morag's reaction was quite misplaced. There was nothing between Alison and him, nor would there ever be.

The situation between him and Morag could easily be put right. There was no need for him to pay for sex. But he didn't want Morag. He didn't want Alison. He wanted Annette.

The flirtation with Alison had pinpointed what was wrong with his commercial relationship, apart from its ruinous effect on his bank account. He wanted to be seen with Annette, to show her off, kiss her in public, sleep with her, instead of just having sex. He enjoyed her company and wanted more of it.

By the time he got to work he was feeling a little better. During a brief lull mid-evening, young Les Wilson handed him a newspaper, folded open at an inside page. 'Have you seen that?'

Jack noticed that it was the *North Clyde Advertiser*, a free newspaper circulating in the area. A copy was delivered to his home every week, but more often than not he threw it out unread.

He looked where Les was pointing and saw half a dozen photographs showing different men coming out of what seemed to be the same shop doorway. Some of the photographs had been taken by day and others at night, by flash. Each showed a close-up of the man's face, the features clearly identifiable.

'They're tryin' to close that sauna in Partick. You'd better watch out, or you might get your photie in the paper.'

'What do you mean?' said Jack, a little too quickly. Les was only joking. He couldn't know.

'Only kiddin'. He seems to have a bee in his bunnet, the owner of that paper.'

Les went off to serve a customer, and Jack read the article beside the picture, trying to make his interest seem casual:

THE TRIUMPH OF DECENCY

Since the start of our campaign, our photographers have noted a distinct drop in the number of degenerates indulging their vice at Partick's Rosevale Sauna. We are not surprised to note that exposure has bred repentance, however reluctantly, and this week we are publishing even more photographs of those for whom the message has yet to sink in.

We propose to continue this policy until the Rosevale Sauna is no more than a dirty memory, fast fading in the minds of Partick's decent citizens. We do not think that will be long.

We have been encouraged by the many letters of support for our crusade. Such has been the success of our campaign, that we intend to target another of these cesspits in the near future.

To those it may concern: we are watching you. And so are thousands of our readers.

'What do think of that?' said Les, when Jack gave him back the paper. 'These guys must be havin' to dae a bit of explainin', eh?'

'The man must be a nutter.' Though this was undoubtedly true, Jack realised that the campaign would probably be commercially effective. He doubted if he would ever again throw away a copy of the paper unopened, and the same probably applied to most other people, whether or not they were in danger of seeing their photograph.

'Oh aye,' said Les, 'but it's a laugh, isn't it?'

'I don't see the joke. I think it's a gross invasion of privacy.'

'Only for guys who pay for nookie. You'd never catch me doin' that. I'd cut it off first.'

Jack was unsure why such a choice would ever be necessary. But Les's reaction was typical of most men. If they were all telling the truth, it was a real mystery how so many women made a living selling sex.

'Anyway,' said Les, 'why are you gettin' so hot under the collar? If I didnae know how many women you're fightin' off, I'd think you had somethin' tae hide.'

'What women?'

'Oh, come on! What about your neckin' session last night, wi' some bimbo young enough tae be your daughter?'

'How'd you hear about that?'

'You were in Tennent's, for God's sake! Probably everybody in the world saw you. Was Morag there?'

'Oh aye.'

Les shook his head. 'Two women after your body an' you take one of them into the pub where the other works. Either you're daft or spoiled for choice. You couldnae point some of your leftovers my way?'

'I'll think about it,' said Jack. 'Let me know if you're in danger of amputation.' Not being prone to sexual boasting, he had been about to explain the truth about Alison, then decided against it. He wouldn't be telling any lies, and it was unlikely to get back to Alison. Better to be mistaken for a Romeo than be suspected of frequenting saunas.

Also, having such a reputation was something of a novelty. He found that he was quite enjoying it.

16

. . . And Thickens

Jack returned to the Merchant City on the following Monday, having first carefully checked the street for lurking photographers. At first there was no sign of Annette, though he had phoned to make sure she was working that day. On his way to the lounge he passed Miranda leading a customer to the cabin.

'Hi there,' she said, giving him her usual dazzling smile, which he had once found so irresistible. Now it had less effect. He responded politely.

The only other person in the lounge was the woman called Claudia, who had been replaced by Justine on the Tuesday shift. Now she seemed to have taken Sylvia's place on Mondays. She responded to Jack's nod with the sort of look that she might have given a plague-bearing rat. He sat down on the sofa, keeping a safe distance from her. There was a silence while she looked him over. Jack felt somewhat nervous in her company. He got the feeling that in a moment she might threaten to beat him up if he didn't choose her. She could probably manage it too.

Then she said, 'You waitin' for Miranda?'

'For Annette.'

Claudia nodded, as if this confirmed his rodent qualities, and turned towards the television, ignoring him. Any of the other girls would have offered him a drink, even knowing that he was waiting for someone else. But this didn't seem to be Claudia's policy.

Even without the lesson of his previous visit, Jack reckoned he would still have waited for Annette, though Claudia was sexy enough in her own way. Alone among the women, she seemed to be excused the regulation white medical uniform. Instead she was dressed entirely in figure-hugging black – a low-cut top, tight leggings and shiny high-heeled shoes – that matched her short black hair and dark eye shadow. She was a big-boned woman, with a full figure, though not particularly tall and with no trace of surplus fat. She looked about Jack's own age.

Another customer arrived, a skinny, nervous-looking man in early middle age. Claudia gave him the same reception as she had given Jack. At least it seemed to be nothing personal.

The newcomer sat between Jack and Claudia, legs pressed together, hands clasped round his knees. Claudia didn't even speak to him and, after her initial disgusted inspection, ignored him completely. After a short silence, during which the man seemed to be summoning his small reserves of courage, he said, 'Could I have a drink, please?'

'Help yersel',' said Claudia, without looking round from the television.

The man got up and poured himself a cold drink. He resumed his place and there was a further silence. Jack got the impression that he was in a quandary, unsure whether Claudia was intimidating him into choosing her or into leaving her alone. Eventually, he said meekly, 'Can I have a massage, please?'

'Go through to Cabin Three,' said Claudia, again without looking round. 'I'll be there in a minute.'

He did as he was told. Claudia continued to watch the TV for at least five minutes, then got up and left the lounge.

Jack was now in even less doubt that it was worth waiting for Annette. He poured himself a coffee and sat on his own for a further ten minutes. Then Annette arrived.

She seemed pleased enough to see him. 'Hi, Jack.'

'Hello, Annette.'

'All on your own?'

'Yes,' he said. 'Sitting here, waiting for you.'

She seemed about to say something, but didn't. 'Good. Are you ready to go through?'

Jack drank the last of his coffee and put the cup down. 'Lead on.'

'We're in Cabin Four.'

While he was waiting, he listened for sounds from the cabin next door, but could hear nothing. Claudia had probably rendered her victim unconscious already.

Annette soon returned. *She* didn't keep her customers hanging about, Jack noted.

She began the massage and, unusually, there was silence at first. They usually chatted for a while, though Annette knew when to bring it to a close. Eventually she said, 'How did you like the new girl?' Jack fancied that the remark wasn't as offhand as she tried to make it sound.

'Oh, fine.'

'Good.'

'We've got a lot in common.'

'Oh?'

'Oh aye. We've got the same make of Hoover.'

There was a pause, then Annette burst out laughing. 'We've all heard about that wonderful machine. You must have a really clean house.'

'I wouldn't go that far.'

After that, the atmosphere was more relaxed and it was like old times. At one point, the silence from next door was briefly broken by a loud, shuddering moan.

'Is she murdering that poor guy or what?' Jack asked.

'Probably.'

'Not my idea of a good time.'

'I'm glad to hear it.'

Annette seemed to make a special effort to please him. When they'd finished and he had paid her, she leaned forward and gave him a brief kiss on the mouth. It was only the second time that he'd been given this privilege. He knew that some of the girls didn't like kissing their customers, wanting to hold something in reserve for real lovemaking.

What was the significance of Annette's brief peck? A friendly gesture for a good customer, or something more? He wasn't sure, but he felt encouraged.

He had put his robe back on and was ready to return to the shower room. Instead, he stood opposite her as she pulled up her stockings and put her white coat back on. She looked at him a little curiously.

'I was wondering...'

'Yes?'

He hesitated. 'The thing is,' he said, 'I really like you. I won't be trying any of the other girls again.'

'That's up to you.'

'I mean, I think we get on well together. We've got the same sense of humour. I get the impression that you ... well ...'

'You're a good customer.'

If there had been some reserve between them earlier on, it was nothing compared to the gulf that had now opened. Jack's anxiety

94

increased. 'What I was thinking . . . I was wondering if you would like to go out with me sometime? For a date. Away from here.'

Annette said nothing, but stared at him as if his words hadn't registered.

'What I meant was . . .'

'I heard what you said,' said Annette. 'I know what you meant.'

17

Citizen Kane

Martin Kane's day started off badly over breakfast, when his wife gave him his daily instructions. After that it continued to deteriorate, until late afternoon when he managed to fit in a visit to the Merchant City Health Centre. That proved to be interesting in a way he hadn't expected.

Such little pleasures were all the more enjoyable because of the difficulty in bringing them off. His father and his wife between them had such a tight grip upon both his daily schedule and his finances that it required much ingenuity to skim off enough time and money for an undetected piece of self-indulgence. Luckily his wife and his father didn't actually collaborate on a daily basis regarding the times when custody of Martin passed from one of them to the other; this was because they didn't like each other, otherwise they would certainly have plugged such an obvious hole in their coverage.

'You'll need to be home by six o'clock at the latest,' his wife Rose told him over breakfast. 'I've got to be at Mary's for half past. I'll make Sheena's tea if you clear up.'

'Do I get some as well?'

'Is that supposed to be a joke? You could always get your father to loosen his grip half an hour earlier, and we could eat together as a family. But that would be too much to expect. Oh, and make sure

Sheena finishes her homework before the TV goes on. You're far too soft with her.'

'No, I'm not.' Martin tried to catch his daughter's eye, but Sheena sat looking down at her breakfast cereal, collaborating in her parents' practice of discussing her as if she wasn't there. 'How's Kathleen getting on?' he asked his wife.

'You mean when will she be well enough to come back? Probably next week. Meanwhile, between us I'm sure we can look after our own daughter for a few more days.'

'Absolutely,' said Martin, no longer putting up even a token resistance. Direct confrontation never worked with Rose. Cunning and subterfuge were the only ways.

'Oh, and you'll have to take Sheena to school. I've got an early meeting.'

'So have I.'

'Not before you see your father at ten,' said Rose. 'I checked your diary. You can think up the excuses for your latest piece of incompetence, whatever it is, while driving Sheena to school. You don't need to do it in the office.'

Sheena was unduly quiet in the car. Martin tried to strike up a conversation several times, then gave up. What did his daughter make of these humiliations, he wondered, which her mother daily heaped upon her father without any concern for their possible effect upon an impressionable child? Did Sheena even notice? Who knew what went on in a kid's mind?

In his own way, Martin loved his daughter. She was the one good thing in a world where he was constantly having shit flung at him. But he had little expertise in dealing with a paternal emotion like this, and there always seemed to be a gap in communication between him and Sheena. At times their relationship seemed as formal as that between him and his wife; both were symbolised by the home Rose had created for them, which bore more resemblance to an antiques showroom than a place to live in. Sometimes he thought that Rose thought more of her house than of him; in fact there wasn't really much room for debate about it.

Delivering Sheena to her private school in the south side of the city didn't involve a major diversion in his journey from Newton Mearns to the factory in Dennistoun. However, it caused him to be slowed down in traffic which he usually managed to avoid.

He passed the time, and eased the frustration a little, by working on the plan to murder his wife. He tended to alternate between this and the scheme to do away with his father. He knew that both of these projects were impractical, and he would never in any case have the courage to do anything about them. But thinking about it gave him a great deal of pleasure. Maybe he could devise a way of setting them against each other. Then he could just stand back and let them fight it out to the death. It would be close, but his money would be on Rose.

Wouldn't it be wonderful if she were simply to keel over, from some unexpected, fatal disease? Nothing that could be pinned on him, of course. No matter what she put in her will, she couldn't avoid leaving him some of her money. He had checked that with a lawyer. He hoped that this advice, bought for the price of a drink in the golf clubhouse, was sound.

And once the old man had popped off, Martin was sure he'd really be able to do something with the family business. He was fed up being held back by his father's caution and then blamed for everything that went wrong. The elder Kane claimed that, single-handedly, he had built up the business to what it had been ten years ago, and that with Martin's help it had then slid back to the position it occupied today.

He arrived at work just after nine thirty. The factory was an old building, erected before the segregation of industrial estates, and a group of post-war council houses faced it across a main road. On both the front of the building, facing the yard, and on its side wall, facing the road, there was the same large notice:

KANE'S LEMONADE
Quenching the thirst of successive generations.

On the wall facing the road, there was also a smaller notice, a garish red in colour. By contrast, it lent the main notice considerable dignity:

KANE'S KOLA
The Kool Alternative

Martin parked his car in the yard and bustled into the office suite in his usual businesslike fashion, as if he were hurrying back from an important meeting.

'Morning, Martin,' said the painted old cow behind the reception desk.

'Morning. I got held up. Anyone looking for me?'

'No.'

'Oh. Never mind, send me in some coffee.'

'OK, Martin.'

There was something insolent about her manner, he was sure of it. Who the fuck did she think she was talking to? Just because she'd been with the company for the last thirty years it didn't mean she owned the place. *He* did. Or he would do, one of these days.

He went to his father's office a little early, just before ten.

With anyone else he would have been deliberately late, just to remind them of their place in the pecking order. But not with his father.

Kane senior was on the phone, and waved Martin towards the seat in front of his desk. The old man was really showing his age these days, Martin thought. Still not quite sixty, but he looked a lot more. How much longer was he going to insist upon running the place? Until he dropped, probably. Though with any luck that wouldn't be too long.

Andrew Kane replaced the receiver and regarded his son wearily. He looked as if he might agree with Martin's diagnosis. 'Martin, Martin,' he said finally. 'What am I going to do with you?'

'How do you mean?'

'I mean, how can I use you in a way that'll justify the exorbitant salary you draw, without giving you enough power to push the company under?'

'Hang on, what are you . . . ?'

His father silenced him by lifting up a brightly-coloured presentation folder from his desk. 'I'm talking about this feasibility study. The one that you ordered and somehow forgot to tell me about.'

'Uh, I knew you were busy, and . . .' How had the old man found out? That little bastard Anderson had told him, he was sure of it.

Andrew Kane opened the folder. 'Let's see what we've got here. "Kane's Krunchy Knuts. The snack that keeps you chewing between meals." Krunchy *Knuts*? With a *K*? That isn't a misprint, is it?'

'No. We've agreed before that we need to diversify.'

'Oh yes, that was when I was still stupid enough to listen to you sometimes, the time when Kane's Krisps were launched.'

'They're doing all right.'

'They're just about breaking even, as long as we keep bribing half our soft drinks customers to keep taking them as part of a package deal. If we start pushing nuts at them as well, we'll end up losing them altogether. Soft drinks are still what make our profit, reduced as it is. We're basically a soft drinks company, always have been and always will be. We actually know how to make the stuff. Apart from the Kane's Kola disaster.'

Glasgow's answer to Coca-Cola. As it turned out, the sales didn't even come remotely near those of Barr's Irn-Bru, the answer Glasgow had already thought of. But the old man had gone along with it at the time. Why did it have to be Martin's fault? 'I don't agree,' he said. 'I think we should . . .'

'I don't care what you think.' Kane senior lifted the report and dropped it into his waste bin. 'That's where this nonsense belongs. How much did it cost us anyway? No, don't tell me.'

As usual, Martin didn't bother to argue further. His time would come. 'Is there anything else?'

'No, get back to your work. What have you got on this afternoon?'

'I'm giving some of the West End pubs another try, see if we can . . .'

'OK then, get on with it,' said Andrew Kane, waving him away.

That was typical of his father, to treat Martin's sales efforts as a waste of time. Did he think their products sold themselves, for Christ's sake?

Back in his room, he called in Dave Anderson. It was time this upstart was put in his place. His father listened to him too much, was even thinking of making him a director, for God's sake!

'The old man thinks your idea's shite,' he told the little bastard.

'What idea was that?'

'The Kane's Knuts proposal, what the hell do you think?'

'I thought that was your idea.'

'Don't get cute with me. He's thrown it in the bin, where it belongs. I don't know why I bother listening to you.'

Anderson said nothing, but gave him that look that so infuriated Martin. The look seemed to say, 'It's because you don't have any ideas of your own.' The insolent bastard! Martin filled with rage, as if the words had actually been spoken. 'Have you got nothing else to say?'

'No.'

'Well, I have. I'm fed up with your fucking attitude. It's time you realised who runs things here. *I* do. It's *my* name on the letterhead, *my* name on the wall outside. Got that?'

'Oh yes.'

'Well, it's about bloody time.' Martin continued to rant on for several minutes. Anderson just stood there and said nothing.

When Martin eventually paused, Anderson said, 'Is that all?'

'Yes, yes, I've got work to do if you haven't.'

After all the shit he had to take from Rose and his father, it was good to find someone he could let loose on. It was a pity that Anderson didn't react more, instead of just keeping his mouth shut in that smug, smartass way. He thought he had the old man in his pocket, that was it. Well, Martin would see about that! Just wait until his father retired, or croaked, then the bugger would find out who was boss.

He got more satisfaction later on by yelling at the sixteen-year-old intern and reducing her to tears. By the time he was ready to set off on his afternoon rounds, he was almost content. Then, on his way out he went to the toilet and found that someone had written a message on the plaster wall, in big letters, using a felt-tipped pen:

That bastard Anderson! Except that it didn't look like his hand-writing. Martin realised that it could have been any one of half a dozen men from the factory floor. One of them came in as Martin was still trying to obliterate the message with his ballpoint. 'What the fuck are you looking at?' Martin snarled at him.

He was still in an evil mood as he drove off. If it wasn't Anderson, how did anyone else know about his secret project? Even his father had just found out about it. Whoever it was, Anderson must have put him up to it. He'd get to the bottom of it all right and sort the bugger out.

He had left sharply, shortly after twelve, and for lunch made do with a snack en route so that he could start early on his rounds. This was his usual way of stealing some free time for himself later in the afternoon.

The first half of the afternoon was frustrating, with several West End pub managers remaining obstinately blind to the merits of Kane's Kola and Kane's Krisps. But what did you expect when the old man kept refusing to let them extend into tonic water or ginger ale, or any of the other soft drinks you needed for the licensed trade market? The problem was, his father wasn't really interested in that market. He didn't see its potential, as Martin did.

Then, when he was about to give up the afternoon as a dead loss, he managed to find a corruptible manager in a Byres Road pub. In return for an envelope of banknotes, which Martin had in readiness, he took a trial order of Krisps and Kola. The day was beginning to improve.

It was still only three thirty, and out of the slush money that would appear in his expense account under a suitable euphemism,

Martin had saved a little for himself. Money that Rose, with her formidable mastery of the family finances, would never know about. It was time for some well-earned relaxation. He set off for the Merchant City.

❖

The woman at the front desk confirmed that there were three girls working that afternoon: Annette, Candy and Justine. The first two he'd had before, but the third was a new name to him. Candy, he knew, was definitely tasty, but she was with a customer. He'd had Annette last time; she had a certain appeal, with her innocent, nice-girl-next-door looks, belying the fact that she was just a bloody whore like the rest of them. But when he entered the lounge Annette pointedly ignored him, continuing to stare at the TV as if no one had arrived. Rude bitch!

But this all became irrelevant when he saw Justine. She was easily the best of the three. Younger than the other two and definitely a cut above them. The best-looking girl he'd ever seen in the place, with the possible exception of the one called Miranda. And there were no other customers around to jump in before him, like that bastard last time.

She even acknowledged his arrival with a nice smile and got him a drink, chatting away as she did. That was a pity, as she was more impressive with her mouth shut. He drank his juice quickly and went off with her before any rivals had time to appear.

She continued to talk crap as she took him to the cabin and after she had returned to give him his massage. He should have known better. Some of them might seem classy, but you had to keep remembering that this was an illusion; they couldn't be quite normal, or they wouldn't be working in such a place. In her case it was obviously because she was too thick to do anything else.

She rubbed oil into his back as if she were kneading a piece of dough. Didn't she know that a massage was supposed to be an erotic experience, for Christ's sake? As she punished his body, she gabbled on and on, telling him about her fucking daughter and her fucking house for about the third time. Then she said, 'Are you married, Martin?'

'Yes.'

'Have you got any kids?'

'I've got a daughter.'

'Is that right? That's amazin'! Just like me.'

'I don't think so.'

'What's that?'

'I mean, she's a bit older.'

'Oh aye. Would ye like to turn on your front?'

He turned over, and she put more oil on her hands, beginning to pummel his chest. 'What age is your daughter, Martin?'

'Ten. Can we talk about something else?'

'Oh aye, if ye like.' With hardly a pause, she switched into another routine of shite from her seemingly endless repertoire. Martin felt the annoyances and frustrations of the day, which had earlier begun to ease, descend upon him fourfold.

Eventually, interrupting her in full flood – there was no other way to get a word in – he said, 'Are you going to take your clothes off?'

She looked taken aback. 'Oh aye, of course, if you like. Were ye wantin' somethin' extra?'

'No, I just came in for the massage. You've got such a nice light touch.' She regarded him uncertainly. 'What the hell do you think?'

106

She looked at him blankly. God, she was dim. At least he had shut her up for the time being. Then she said, 'What would ye like?'

He thought of asking for oral – that would muzzle her for a while – but then thought better of it. If she showed the same degree of skill as she did with the massage, she'd probably bite it off. 'How much do you charge for a fuck?' he asked.

She was looking increasingly unhappy, but gave him a price. 'OK,' he said, and gave her a nice smile, a reward for shutting off that godawful babble. 'Why don't you take your clothes off, there's a good girl.'

She smiled happily, pathetically reassured by his apparent change of mood. She began slowly to unbutton her white coat.

Then – would she never learn? – she started up all over again. 'A lot of married men come here, you'd be amazed. I cannae understand why, do they no' get it at home? Is that the case wi' you, Martin? Does your wife know you come here? I don't suppose she does. You know I don't think that's fair, wi' you havin' a daughter an' all. What'll she think when she grows up if she finds out that . . . ?'

Justine broke off as Martin pushed himself up into a sitting position, swinging his legs over the side of the massage table. 'What the fuck's that got to do with you?'

Justine took a step back, her coat half unbuttoned. She now looked seriously alarmed, the fact that she had overstepped the mark having at last registered. Unfortunately, she reacted by resuming her babble, now speeded up and tinged with hysteria.

'I'm sorry, I didnae mean anythin' by it, I was just tryin' tae be friendly. I like tae have a good blether wi' the customers, it's nice tae be nice, I didnae mean tae be rude, honest, I'm sorry, I mean—'

Martin drew his arm back, and slapped her face hard with the back of his hand. 'For Christ's sake, shut up!'

She did.

Martin felt a surge of elation that he had not expected. He imagined that it was his wife Rose in front of him, and hit Justine again, and again, this time using his fists. Then, before she could recover from the initial surprise and begin to scream, he put his hand over her mouth.

'If you make a fucking sound, I'll kill you. Got it? *Got it?*' Justine nodded, and he took his hand away. She whimpered a little but otherwise was quiet. He found that he was sexually aroused. What do you know? He took hold of her white coat and pulled it fully open, ripping off the buttons.

'Take off the rest of your clothes and lie down on the table.'

He hit her a few more times for good measure, then he pinned her down, climbed on the table and yanked her legs apart.

18

Consequences

'Did you hear about Sylvia?' Annette asked.

'What about her?' said Candy.

'Edna gave her the push. She found heroin in her handbag.'

'Stupid bitch. When was this?'

'Sunday. I doubt if the stuff was even for her. It would be for that arsehole she lives with.'

'Still, she shoulda known better. She knows what Edna's like.'

It was true. Edna's practice of periodically searching her employees' effects was not one of her more endearing qualities, but it was well enough known. Not that they entirely blamed her. The presence of drugs was the one thing guaranteed to attract the police, and no one wanted that.

'What do you think she'll do?' asked Annette.

'Mibbe she'll get a job in the Boiler Hoose. I don't suppose Edna found anything on Miranda?'

'No such luck.'

'What does she dae wi' all that money she earns?'

'What do you do with all yours? I guess Miranda's husband gets some of hers.'

'She's married?'

'Oh aye. I've met him.'

'Does he know what she does?'

'He certainly does. She says he's cool about it.'

'You mean he doesnae like it?' said Candy.

'No, he's relaxed about it. He doesn't seem to mind.'

On their first shift together after Annette had met Miranda's husband, Miranda had briefly confided this much, as if she felt some explanation was necessary. Then she had resumed her usual reticence, and her husband Derek had not been mentioned since.

'What's he like?' asked Candy.

'Just like her, only male.'

'Fucksake,' said Candy. 'Well, at least she's better aff than Sylvia. If ye're gonnae be stuck wi' an arsehole, he might as well be a high-class one. Who got Sylvia's place on the Monday shift, by the way?'

'Claudia.'

Candy laughed. 'Well, that's good news. You should pick up mair of Miranda's leftovers.'

'Thanks a lot. Claudia does all right.'

'Aye, but fae her regulars. She knows they'll follow her tae the new slot. They'd show up at five on a Sunday mornin' if she told them to.'

'She'd probably get a bigger turnout,' said Annette. 'She's a strange one, Claudia. I don't know what to make of her.'

'Dae ye understand Hitler?'

'Obviously some punters like her style. The trouble is, with her it isn't an act. She really does hate the customers. All of them. Why do you think that is?'

'Who knows?' said Candy. 'Maybe she was abused when she was a wee girl. Maybe she's a butch dyke an' she just hates men. Who cares?'

'I mean the punters are just human beings, like the rest of us. They're all different. Some of them are bastards – like that one who's in with Justine. Some of them are just pathetic. But there's nice ones as well.'

'Why do I get the feelin' that this is leadin' up tae somethin'?' Candy asked.

Candy could sometimes be quite astute. Annette realised that she was blushing. 'You know that guy Jack who comes in here?'

'Your boyfriend?'

'Aye, well . . . He's asked me out. On a date.'

'Great. Will I get an invite tae the weddin'?'

'Don't be daft.'

'I don't think I'm the one bein' daft,' said Candy. 'Has he got money? Is he gonnae whisk ye away tae a life of luxury?'

'I doubt it.'

'So he's just fed up payin' for it. He thinks he can get you tae do the business for nothin".'

'It's not like that.'

'Or you could offer him a cheaper rate if you cut oot the middle woman. Just as long as Edna doesnae find oot.'

'You make it sound really sordid.'

'No, just stupid. At least you'll no' need tae worry aboot him findin' out what you do. I think he might have twigged already.'

Annette was wishing that she had never raised the subject. She was supposed to be the sensible one, Candy the scatterbrain, and now *Candy* was giving *her* advice. It was probably good advice too.

A customer arrived and soon had gone off with Candy. It was now after four thirty. Annette hadn't noticed any other new arrivals. Maybe she would get one more customer, maybe not, but either way it hadn't been a bad day. She made herself a cup of coffee and sat down opposite the lounge door, which gave her a view down the corridor.

She wondered how Justine was getting on with that bastard, the one called Martin. She had disobeyed one of her own rules that afternoon and totally ignored him. Normally she did her best to make the customers feel welcome: it was good manners as well as good business. But in his case she was happy to make an exception.

Just then she noticed him appear from the direction of the changing room and hurry off down the corridor. That was odd. If he'd had time to get dressed, maybe even have a shower, then Justine should have reappeared by now. Maybe she was taking a shower. That had been her own impulse after a session with Martin.

A few moments later, when Justine still hadn't showed, Annette decided to investigate. She checked the shower area, the toilets, even the sauna and steam room, but they were all deserted. So was the changing room. Maybe Justine had met a punter in the corridor and gone back into the cabin with him. That sometimes happened, but if so she should have told Moira at the front desk. Annette went down the corridor to check.

'Did Justine go in with another customer?' she asked Moira. 'Apart from the guy who's just left?'

'No. Why, did you think she was skippin' the queue?'

'No.' Annette couldn't be bothered explaining and went back up the corridor to the cabins. Why was she hesitating? Damn it, if Justine was with a customer, the door would be locked.

She knocked on the door of Cabin 2. 'Justine?'

There was no reply. She tried the handle and the door opened. She went in.

Justine was alone in the cabin. She was squatting on the floor, naked, her back to the wall, her hands clasped tightly round her knees, weeping quietly. Streaks of mascara ran down each cheek, like some kind of primitive war paint. Blood was flowing from her nose

112

and her mouth. The room, which Justine normally kept in a state of tidiness unequalled by any of the other girls, was in a mess: her white coat lay on a heap on the floor, with half the buttons missing; her underclothes and shoes were scattered about; the towel on top of the massage table was crumpled and bloodstained. On the table, obviously flung there in a hurry, were several banknotes.

For a moment Annette stood in shock, taking in the scene. Then she went into the cabin, having the presence of mind to shut the door after her. In case Candy's customer should hear anything, she thought, hating herself. 'Oh, Justine!' she said, sitting down beside the other girl. At first Justine shrank back, then she let Annette put her arm around her. She winced in pain at the contact and Annette loosened her grip. Justine's sobs grew louder. 'Oh, Annette!' she wailed. 'Oh, Annette! What am I gonnae dae?'

'It's all right,' said Annette. 'It's all right.' Why do we say such things, she wondered? Obviously it *wasn't* all right.

'He . . . He . . .'

'It's all right.'

'He hit me. He kept hittin' me. He wouldnae stop. Oh, Annette . . .' She resumed her sobbing, and winced again when Annette gave her a hug. Obviously a number of bruises would soon be showing. 'He . . .' Justine lowered her voice, as if afraid to say the next part. 'He *raped* me.'

'The bastard!'

'Oh, Annette, it was awful!'

'I know. I know.' Annette reached up to the nearby table for a box of tissues. 'We'd better get you cleaned up.' She gently wiped the blood and make-up from Justine's face. The bleeding had slowed down but hadn't quite stopped.

Then she got up. 'Just sit there for a minute.'

113

'Don't leave me!'

'I won't. I'm just going to get help.'

Annette opened the door. By a piece of luck, Candy was in the corridor. She must have brought her customer to fulfilment in record time, no doubt encouraged by the approaching end of her shift and the many open pubs outside.

'Where is everybody?' Candy asked.

'Justine's in here. Her last customer gave her a doing.'

'Bloody hell. Is she all right?'

'She's not great. Could you see if Edna's there?'

The magical hour of the shift change – and the first cash hand-over – was almost upon them, and Edna was on the premises. She hurried through to the cabin, full of concern, some of which might have been for Justine. She fussed over her and then, with Annette's help, got her on her feet and back into her clothes. They had to take it carefully, as every move caused Justine pain. After Candy had been dispatched to check that the coast was clear of customers, they half carried her to the girls' changing room. Edna produced a first aid box and Justine was cleaned and patched up some more. Then they helped her into her street clothes, a slow and painful procedure.

'You're going to be sore for a while,' said Edna. 'But I don't think there's any permanent damage.'

When did she get her medical qualification? Annette wondered. But she said nothing. Edna was probably right. But from the bruises that were already developing, it was clear that Justine was going to look a mess for some time, with a couple of black eyes, swollen nose and mouth, and many other marks that couldn't be kept hidden from view in her line of work.

'Who was the man that did this?' Edna asked.

'His name's Martin,' said Annette. 'He's been here before.'

'He'll no' be back in a hurry. And that'll no' be his real name.'

'It might be,' said Annette. 'Some of them use their real names.'

That clearly wasn't the answer Edna wanted to hear. 'How do you know? Anyway, we don't know his surname, or anythin' else about him. Do we?'

'No,' said Annette.

'He's married,' said Justine meekly, 'and he's got a wee girl of ten.'

'That's really nice for him,' said Edna. 'But it doesnae quite pin him down.' It was obvious that she regarded the subject as closed. 'Could you do me a really big favour, Annette?'

'What?'

'Take Justine home. She doesnae drive, does she?'

'No. Of course I will. Can I use the phone?'

Edna immediately looked suspicious. 'What for?'

'I'll need to tell my childminder that I'm going to be late.'

'Aye, of course. You can use the phone in my office.'

Edna left Justine in Candy's care and accompanied Annette while she made the call. Then she helped smuggle Justine and Annette from the premises, after tactfully finding a way to relieve each of them of the money due to her.

'Now you take care,' she told Justine solicitously. 'I'll see that your shifts are covered until the end of next week, and we'll take it fae there. I'll keep in touch.'

Annette's car wasn't far away, and they got there without meeting any customers. Then, before starting the engine, Annette turned to Justine. 'What do you want to do?'

'What dae ye mean?'

'You were raped and beaten up. Do you want to go to the police?'

Justine looked terrified. 'The polis? Edna would be furious.'

'The hell with Edna. I'll take you there now if you want to.'

'What do you think?'

'I don't think the bastard should get off with it,' said Annette. 'On the other hand, you offered sex for money and he paid you. That would make it difficult for a rape charge to stick.'

'He *raped* me.'

'I know, I know. But a court might not see it that way. And even if he was just charged with assault, what you were doing for a living would come out in court.'

'Oh no!' said Justine. 'It might get in the papers. Everybody would know.'

Annette started the car. 'Anyway, Edna's probably right. They would never catch him. I just wanted to make sure you'd thought it all through.'

She drove to Ingram Street and turned right.

'Where are you goin'?' asked Justine. 'This isnae the way to—'

'We're going to A&E at the Royal Infirmary. I'm sure there's nothing too serious, but you need to be checked over, just to be on the safe side.'

'But what'll we tell them?'

'We'll think up a story. We'll say you fell downstairs, something like that.'

Justine began to cry again. 'Oh, Annette, you're the only friend I've got in that horrible place. I'm never goin' back there again.'

'It's all right,' said Annette. 'It's no bother.'

Justine's gratitude made Annette feel guilty. If ever a girl had needed a bit of guidance, it had been Justine. Annette had given her some support, but could have done more, if she hadn't let Candy influence her.

If Justine did return, Annette decided, she would try and make it up to her.

19

A Quiet Night
on the Western Front

'You've certainly got plenty of women chasin' after you,' said Les. 'She's not bad. Not bad at all. Where'd you dig her up?'

'None of your bloody business.'

'Just as well it's Morag's day off.'

'Is it? I didn't know that.'

'That'll be right. Still, I wouldnae take this one intae Tennent's. Word gets around.'

'I'm grateful for your advice,' said Jack. 'Why is it never *your* day off during my shifts? Now, if you've finished in that bloody fridge, maybe you'll let someone else in.'

Jack picked out a bottle of beer and served his customer. When he had finished, several more were waiting. It was the middle of the five o'clock rush, the last flurry of activity before the end of his shift. As he hurried to get the orders, he remained self-conscious about the presence of his visitor, sitting by herself on a bar stool at the counter. He knew it was stupid of him. Apart from Les, no one was interested, or had even noticed.

For a while all they could manage was an exchange of smiles as he went past. Then there was a lull and he was able to fit in a brief exchange.

'It won't be long till I'm finished.'

'There's no hurry. Who's that other barman? He keeps looking at me as if I was a plain-clothes cop.'

'Don't worry about Les. It's just simple lust.'

'I suppose I should take that as a compliment.'

'He's harmless. Would you like another drink?'

'I'm driving, remember.'

'What's that you're on?'

'God knows. It's absolutely disgusting. I asked for a Coke.'

'I think I know the problem. I'll get you another one.'

Jack got her a real Coke, then tackled the new queue of customers that had begun to form. Annette sat and sipped her fresh drink, abandoning the previous one, which Jack poured down the sink. At the first opportunity, he said to Les, 'Would you mind not serving that shite to friends of mine?'

'Aitken said we had to shift it.'

'Try it on people you don't like. There's plenty to choose from. This is the West End.'

'OK, OK,' said Les. 'I can see you want tae impress your bird. When I served her I didnae know she was with you.'

'If you stop gaping at her, I'll maybe forgive you.'

He was kept busy until the end of his shift, but remained aware of Annette's presence all the time, snatching a few words with her when the chance arose. Les's reaction was understandable. Seen out here in the real world, she had no competition. If Morag had entered the bar now, he would not have given her a second glance. Annette, as well as being the embodiment of sexiness, looked fresh and wholesome, good enough to take home to his mother, if she'd still been around.

He made a quick escape at six o'clock, getting out ahead of Les, whose shift was also ending. Annette took his arm as they made their way along Byres Road. 'Where now?' she asked.

'Are you hungry?'

'Definitely.'

'Since you're on the wagon, I thought we could go straight to the restaurant. If there's time before the film, we can have a quick drink later. Where are you parked?'

'Near the cinema.'

They went down Ashton Lane, to an Indian restaurant. It was a few yards from the cinema and a couple of minutes' walk from Annette's car.

Over the meal, they continued the process of getting to know each other. This was their third date. The first two had been in city centre bars, near Central Station, where Annette could get a train back to Paisley. This was the first time he had got her into the West End, an area of many amenities, including his flat.

He told her more about his marriage and its failure, about his university course and his plans for the future. He heard more about her children, the house she was now buying, something of her earlier life. She mentioned her ex-husband, but that was still a subject on which she was a little reticent. Mainly he heard about a world that was completely different and separate from the one in which he had met her.

They also discovered that they had a number of common interests, including the cinema. After the meal and the film they found themselves back in the street at ten thirty. Jack felt that the evening had been going well.

A few yards from the cinema, the lane reached a junction. They could turn left to Byres Road or carry straight on to Annette's car. They slowed down to a halt. Annette seemed to be leaving it up to him to make a suggestion.

'What do you fancy?'

'I don't know. What do you suggest?'

Jack hesitated. 'My flat's not far from here.'

'I know.'

'We could . . . I mean . . .'

'I know exactly what you mean. Have you got real coffee or only instant?' He was reduced to silence and Annette laughed. 'I told the babysitter I'd be home by midnight. Maybe another time.'

The cinema crowd had dispersed and it was dark. For the moment, they were alone in the lane. Annette put her arms around him and gave him a long kiss, her body pressed closely against his. In a way, it was their most intimate contact so far. 'I hope you're not too disappointed.'

'No. It's just that we seem to be doing things the wrong way round. I'm not sure what the rules are.'

'Neither am I. We'll just have to make them up as we go along.' She took his arm and steered him round the corner, towards the main road. 'Come on. We've time for a nightcap in your pub.'

They made their way back along Byres Road. The Centurion was moderately full, but they found a table to themselves near the counter. There were two barmen on duty: Vince, the assistant manager, and Arnold, a law student from Glasgow University.

'What would you like?' Jack asked.

'My round. What's yours?'

'A whisky.'

As Annette returned to the table, another customer came up to the bar. As he stood at the counter, he was only a few feet away from Jack and Annette, and they were able to hear all of the subsequent exchange. He was a man in his forties, whose complexion suggested that alcohol was a regular part of his diet. Jack recognised him: he had one of those faces that seemed able to be in every Byres Road pub simultaneously. By the look of him, this evening had been no exception. He called Arnold over, waving an opened packet of potato crisps in front of him.

'What's this shite?'

'Sorry?'

The customer stuck the packet in front of Arnold's face. 'This garbage. What do you call it?'

'I'd call it a packet of crisps.'

'Would you? I'd call it a packet of shite. Except that it's worse than shite. In fact, shite tastes better than this.'

'I'll have to take your word for that,' said Arnold.

Jack exchanged glances with Annette and winced. It wasn't always easy to deal with drunken idiots, but getting smart with them was unlikely to help. Arnold, who was new to the job, was still learning this.

Fortunately, the remark was lost on the customer. 'Who makes this crap? Kane's Krisps. Is that the same jokers that make Kane's Kola?'

Arnold appeared to give the matter consideration. 'The name would seem to suggest that.'

'My wife tried that the other day. It tastes like piss. Their cola tastes like piss and their crisps taste like shite. Where the hell do they make the stuff? In a public lavatory?'

'I'm not familiar with their manufacturing methods. Anyway, did you just come up to chat or was there something else?'

'I want a packet of decent crisps. Or my money back. I should ask you to pay for gettin' my stomach pumped at the Western Infirmary.'

'As far as I know, you can still get that done on the National Health.'

'Don't get cute wi' me, son. Fuckin' student, are you?'

Jack got up and stood at the bar beside the customer. Throughout the exchange Vince, the assistant manager, had been serving a succession of customers, managing not to notice that there was a problem.

'I think you should give him his money back,' Jack said. 'These crisps are pretty bad. I've tried them myself.'

Arnold looked at Jack a little resentfully. But he followed the suggestion and the customer, after a few more grumbles, went back to his seat.

'There was no need for you to butt in,' said Arnold. 'Just because you want to impress your lady friend.'

'I saved your life, but don't bother to thank me.'

'Is that right?' said Annette, when Jack had returned to his seat. 'What?'

'That you were just trying to impress me.'

'Of course.'

'Well, I'm impressed. I think you also saved your pal from getting a sore face. Is it always like this here?'

'You've caught us on a quiet night. The cabaret's even better at the weekend.'

The diversion over, there was an awkward silence for a moment. 'So,' said Jack, 'I really enjoyed the evening.'

'Me too.'

'Are we going to do the same again?'

'I hope so. How are you placed at the weekend?'

'I'm off Saturday evening.'

'Good. I've got a suggestion . . .'

On their way out, they passed a table where the drunken customer was still proclaiming loudly about the excremental qualities of Kane products. Fortunately, he didn't see Jack and they made it safely to the street.

20

Best of Three

'I think you've let this become an obsession,' he says. 'Can't we talk about it?'

That's exactly what we're doing. Talking about it. But on my terms, which is the part he's unhappy about. That, and being tied to the chair. Though it's not particularly warm in the room, a film of sweat glistens on his brow, reflected from the ceiling light. Apart from this giveaway sign, he seems remarkably unruffled. I can admire his nerve, but what I really want is to hear him beg for his life.

I bring out my knife and test the sharpness of the blade with my finger. His eyes follow my movements closely, but he shows no other reaction.

There's plenty of time. We're in the large dining kitchen at the back of the house, where the light can't be seen from the road. And there's no nightwatchman. I checked that out.

I did my homework carefully. Already I can see how well it's paid off.

The problem: how to get the subject, a man bigger and stronger than me, into a position of helplessness before I finally kill him. In a location where we are free from interruption, so that I can explain to him at length why he deserves to die. A difficult problem, which I mulled over for some weeks.

Then the solution was presented to me, gift-wrapped, in a two-page advertisement feature. Botanic Court, a small development of luxury flats, now nearing completion. Built by Archer Homes Ltd, owner and managing director Steven Archer. For the first week after it opens, the show flat will be manned personally in the evenings by Mr Archer himself, to demonstrate his faith in the project and answer personally any queries from prospective purchasers. Also – this part *not* in the advert – to save the miserable bastard from having to pay any of his employees overtime. A cost-cutting exercise that will prove fatal.

It takes an effort of will not to show up on the first night, at six o'clock prompt. Instead I hang on until Wednesday, a dull and rainy night, when legitimate enquirers are less likely to bother turning out. I wait until nearly half past eight, by which time the trickle of visitors has run out. Then I make my move, in case he shuts up shop early.

The security door is hooked open and I close it behind me as I make my way directly into the building. The show flat is on the ground floor. Convenient for the public and allowing any flaws in the unfinished development, like a leaking roof, to remain hidden from the public. Maybe I'm being unfair to him. For all I know, he may be a very good builder. That's not why he's being held to account.

I rattle the letterbox and the man himself comes to the door. As soon as I see him, my hatred swells up, but I control it and return his smile.

I follow him around the house, listening to his sales patter, asking the right questions, waiting for my chance. While we're in the bathroom I note with relief that the water is on. I wasn't sure if it would be, but now I know that I'll be able to clean myself up properly, as I did last time. There won't be any hot water, but no scheme is perfect.

My opportunity comes, conveniently, as he's showing me round the dining kitchen. The kitchen, he explains, comes fully fitted, cooker, fridge freezer and washing machine all included. I show a particular interest in the fan-assisted oven. Obligingly, he bends over to open the oven door. For a moment, his back is to me.

A hefty push and he loses his balance, falling face down on the floor, his head narrowly missing the oven door. I perch on his back, keeping him pinned down. Once recovered from his surprise, he'd be able to throw me off, but I have thrust the cloth under his nose, holding it there. His struggles gradually lessen as the chloroform takes effect.

Leaving him for a moment, I quickly go round the house, switching off the lights in all the other rooms, then shutting the kitchen door behind me. It's now nearly nine o'clock, it's unlikely that any more visitors will show up, but if any do they'll find a house in apparent darkness, its sole light visible only from the empty back court.

I push one of the dining chairs in front of the central heating radiator, beneath the window. Then, with an effort, I haul him over there and sit him on the chair. From my innocent-looking M&S plastic bag I bring out the rope and truss him up securely, legs together, hands behind the chair, then several loops tightly round his chest and the chair frame. I tie the chair itself to the radiator pipe, so that he can't pull it away or knock it over. Then I sit down at the dining table, patiently waiting for him to regain consciousness.

It takes a while, but I don't mind. I'm not in any hurry. Eventually he begins to stir, opens his eyes. I give him time to get his bearings, a few moments to struggle with his bonds and realise that it's pointless.

Then, seeing that I've got his full attention, I introduce myself and tell him why he has to die.

After I bring out the knife, he makes a final attempt to reason with me. 'I understand how you feel.'

'No, you don't.'

'But I think you've got things out of proportion. Can't we come to some arrangement?'

'An *arrangement*? You think you can *buy* your way out of this?'

'That's not what I mean. I can give you money, no problem about that. But I don't think that's what you want. If you let me go, I promise I won't go to the police. Why should I? I don't want my wife to know about this. And you've got my word that I'll never . . .'

I interrupt by jabbing him in the arm with my knife. He gives a yelp of pain and looks down in horror at the blood. I cut him again, this time in the leg. Nowhere fatal just yet. At last he begins to show his fear.

I don't know how much longer I'll be able to contain my rage. But first I mean to have some fun with him.

Things are working out well. This promises to be my most satisfying effort so far.

21

The Talk of the Steam Room

'I'm telling you,' said Annette, 'it can't be a coincidence. Three of our customers murdered. All in the same way. All by the same guy.'

'Hang on,' said Cleo. 'What d'you mean three? OK, that last one looks familiar. I may have had him once, or maybe twice.'

'Or three times, or four,' said Claudia.

Cleo ignored her, affecting the air of disdain she normally reserved for the customers. She was probably Claudia's biggest rival for the 'treat the punters with the contempt they deserve' corner of the market.

'You wouldn't know the others,' said Annette. 'You've only been here a month. They were killed before that.'

'Well, that puts me in the clear,' said Cleo. 'Far as I know, the Manchester punters are all still alive.'

'Recoverin' well fae their injuries,' said Claudia. 'Since you came up here.'

'Fuck off.'

Annette listened to the exchange with some surprise. This wasn't like Claudia. Was it her idea of good-natured banter?

'Look,' she said, pointing to the tabloid laid out on the coffee table. The other girls obligingly clustered round. The first customer had still to arrive and they had to pass the time somehow.

BUILDER SLAIN IN SHOW FLAT
THIRD LINKED MURDER?

Glasgow builder Steven Archer (35) was found brutally
murdered yesterday morning, in a way that suggests a link with
two unsolved killings in the city earlier this year. Horrified
foreman Joe MacFarlane (45) arrived at the new luxury
development yesterday morning to find his boss tied to a chair
in a pool of his own blood.

TURN TO PAGE TWO

The remaining space on the front page, sandwiched between the
huge headline and the brief text, was filled by a large photograph of
the murdered man and two smaller pictures of the earlier victims.
The latter were identified as Richard McAlpine, a solicitor, and
Arnold Bell, an accountant.

The murderer seemed to be concentrating on the middle classes.
Or maybe only those who could afford expensive vices, like the one
that linked all three.

Am I the only one to realise the significance of this? Annette
wondered. 'You must know them. This one, the accountant guy.
I gave him a massage only a few days before he was killed. I thought
it was just a coincidence at the time. But now there's this new one,
and the first one as well. I didn't know about the first one at the
time. There couldn't have been much publicity. But look at him.
Who could forget that face?'

'Aye, he does look familiar,' said Claudia. 'I havenae seen him
about lately.'

'For Christ's sake, Claudia!' said Annette. 'He was murdered in

130

February!' Then she noticed Claudia's grin. 'Aye, OK . . . So what about you, Miranda? You must know them.'

'I don't know,' said Miranda. 'I think so. It's just so *awful*.'

'You must know that last guy, Steven Archer. He used a different name. He had a fight over you, remember? With that bastard who beat up Justine.'

'Was that him?' Miranda shuddered. 'Oh no!' She looked ready to burst into tears.

The first customer of the day arrived, and the conversation was stopped for a while. To no one's surprise he went off with Miranda, who seemed to have made a quick recovery.

All the same, Annette thought, she had at least shown some reaction. Claudia and Cleo just didn't care. If someone had been killing off the girls, they might have taken notice. But it was only the customers, and there were still plenty of them left to part with their cash.

'I suppose I'd better tell Edna,' said Annette.

'What's the point?' said Claudia. 'You know what she's gonnae say.'

Annette did have an idea, which would be proved right. Meanwhile the day progressed in a normal fashion. Annette was kept reasonably busy, even though there were four girls on instead of the usual three. Miranda had asked for an extra shift – an offer her mercenary boss had found impossible to refuse – and Edna had thought that the Friday trade could probably stand it. So in fact it proved. As well as stealing the other girls' customers, Miranda tended to bring in additional ones. It seemed as though the punters, phoning on the off chance, would hear Miranda's name and head for the Merchant City like flies to a jam pot. It didn't turn out too badly for Annette. Claudia mainly had her own customers; as for

Cleo, the punters seemed evenly divided between those who looked on a black girl as a novelty and those who weren't interested at all. This left Annette with more than her fair share of Miranda's leftovers, a slightly humiliating but profitable situation.

A couple of her regulars also turned up. Though not, of course, Jack.

But she was seeing him the following day. A bridge was being formed between the two worlds that she had kept so strictly apart. She still wasn't sure if she was doing the right thing, but she was looking forward to it.

Edna arrived promptly at a quarter to five, fifteen minutes before the shift change. Seeing no sign of a final customer on the way, Annette went straight through to Edna's office. She showed her boss the newspaper and told her the story. It was clear Edna did in fact take the matter seriously. She read the newspaper article from beginning to end, then turned back to the front page and the three photographs.

'You're sure it's the same men?'

'Positive.'

'You cannae be that sure. Why dae you think I fit dimmer switches in the cabins? So you can lie back an' pretend it's Brad Pitt.'

'Come off it, Edna. We don't just see them in the cabins. There's no doubt.' Annette shuddered. 'It's horrible. It can't be a coincidence. There must be a link.'

Edna eyed her steadily. 'So what should I do about it?'

'We'll need to report it to the police. It's an important clue.'

'I thought you'd say that,' said Edna. 'Now listen carefully, Annette. Read ma lips. We're reportin' bugger all to the cops. We're keepin' our mouths shut. *You're* keepin' *your* mouth shut. Got me?'

Annette hadn't really expected Edna to respond to a good citizenship plea, so she tried self-interest. 'Well, it won't do us much good if all our customers get killed off.'

'Don't be stupid,' said Edna. 'They'll probably catch the killer before he does it again. At the worst, we might lose a couple more punters. But if this gets intae the papers, they'll stay away in droves.'

'At least they'll be alive.'

'If they're no' comin' here, they might as well be deid as far as I'm concerned. Anyway, it's probably got nothin' to do wi' us at all. You think this is the only place these guys came to? They're probably known in half the saunas in Glasgow. Let one of them blow the whistle. We can pick up their customers afterwards.'

'But . . .'

'End of conversation. If you want to keep workin' here, you'll keep yer mouth shut. I mean it, Annette. Who else have you told about this?'

'Just the girls that were on today.'

'Right,' said Edna. 'Let's settle up, then we'll have them all through.'

Five minutes later, all the day girls had gathered in Edna's office, along with Moira from the front desk and the first girl to arrive for the evening shift. (Cleo was doing a double shift and Candy had still to appear.) Edna briefly told them the story and repeated her edict. None of them put up an argument. When told that Annette had wanted to tell the police, they regarded her with varying degrees of surprise; Claudia looked at her as if she had gone insane.

Annette began to wonder if she was indeed making a fuss about nothing. Why should she bother, if no one else did? Edna was probably right. These men would be known in other saunas. The connection might lie elsewhere.

But they had all been regulars. In how many other places could *all three* of them be that well known? How much money did these buggers have, for God's sake? And wasn't it up to the police to decide if there was a link?

To hell with it. She had done her best. As she was leaving, the evening shift had started and it was business as usual. 'Yes,' Moira was saying into the phone, 'tonight we have Candy, Cleopatra and Chantelle.'

Annette found herself laughing. How many baby girls in Glasgow (or Manchester) were christened with names like that? Why was she getting uptight? She was going home to her family. Tomorrow was a day off and she was seeing her new boyfriend.

She met Candy on the stairs. This was her one evening shift, her liver's night off.

'Edna wants to see you,' said Annette.

'Damn,' said Candy. 'I couldnae help it. It was . . .'

'I know. You slept in. It's nothing to do with that. Another customer's been murdered.'

'Bloody hell,' said Candy. 'Was it Bob the Gobbler?'

22

Forebodings

Jack travelled by train from Glasgow to Paisley, then followed the directions Annette had given him. After a few minutes' walk from the station, he found the pub; it was just off the main street, occupying the ground floor of an old tenement, now stone-cleaned and transformed into a beautiful red sandstone building.

Inside, the period design had been preserved, subject to a few modern intrusions, including the huge television screen that looked down the long bar from its vantage point just inside the door; fortunately no football match or other communal distraction was showing, and the sound was turned down, leaving a silent display of the sports results for any who were interested. The bar was crowded, but it only took a moment for Jack to check that Annette hadn't yet arrived. She generally arrived about ten minutes late for their pub appointments. It might have been no more than unpunctuality, but Jack suspected that she felt diffident about entering pubs on her own. It was an old-fashioned attitude, but one he rather liked.

This time she was fifteen minutes late, but as soon as she appeared he forgave her. At once he felt at home in a room full of strangers. He ordered her a drink, along with a half pint to top up his own.

'I like your choice of pub.'

'It's busier than I thought it would be.'

'What do you expect at teatime on a Saturday?'

'Shows you how often I get out these days.' They were standing at the counter, jammed between bar drinkers and incomers clamouring for service. 'Are there any seats?'

'Loads, but there's an arse on every one of them.'

'Oh God!' Annette giggled. 'There are some rooms at the back. Let's have a look.'

They squeezed their way to the back of the bar. All of the rooms had people in them, but one of the larger ones had a spare table. They sat down, trying to ignore the four men who were talking loudly about football.

After a little more small talk, they fell silent. Annette had at first seemed to be her usual self, but now Jack sensed that something was troubling her.

'You're a bit quiet.'

'Sorry. There's a reason for it.' She lowered her voice. 'But I don't want to discuss it here.'

'Have I done something wrong?'

Annette laughed, then leaned over and kissed him on the cheek. 'A man who admits the possibility that something might be his fault. That's really refreshing. But don't worry, you're in the clear.'

'But very curious.'

Annette glanced at the other table, then opened her handbag and brought out a folded newspaper. She unfolded it, revealing the front page. She held it at an angle, between the front of the table and their laps, keeping its contents out of the other table's view. 'Did you see that story?'

'I saw something on the telly. Horrible.'

Annette pointed to one of the three pictures. 'And do you remember him?'

Jack glanced at the picture, then took a second look. 'God.

136

They said the new one might be linked with previous murders, but I never . . .'

'That's not all.' Annette looked up at the other table, but the men were engrossed in their discussion, paying no attention to the couple in the corner. 'I recognised the other two as well,' she said, in a lower voice. 'From the same place.'

It took a moment for the information to register with Jack. 'You mean . . . ?'

Annette leaned across and spoke in his ear. 'They were all regulars.'

'Jesus Christ!'

'Not him, only the other three.'

'It's not funny.'

'You're bloody right it's not.'

Jack took the paper, read the article in full, then returned to the front page and examined the photographs again. He remembered meeting the second victim, though the other two were strangers to him. But that meant nothing: the first one had been killed before Jack had even set foot in the Merchant City Health Centre. And it would have been something of a coincidence if he'd run into both of the other victims.

But Annette recognised all of them. It couldn't be a coincidence. He was too confused to think beyond that.

He refolded the paper and returned it to Annette, who put it back in her handbag. 'Have you told the . . . ?'

Annette put her finger to her lips. 'Not here. We'll talk about it in the car.'

The conversation lapsed again, any small talk unable to compete with what had gone before. They finished their drinks and Jack said, 'Do you want another one?'

'It's my turn, but I thought we'd get on our way. I don't have a babysitter, I just got Norah to sit in with the kids for an hour.'

'Norah?'

'My next-door neighbour.'

They left the pub and made their way down the street. 'By the way, don't say anything to Norah about . . .' Annette hesitated. 'She doesn't know what I . . .'

'Don't be daft. So where *did* we meet?'

'You were a patient at the private clinic where I work. It's almost true.'

'A patient falling for his nurse. It sounds trite enough to be plausible.'

A short walk took them to the multi-storey car park where Annette had left her car. When they were seated in the car, Annette put the key in the ignition, but didn't turn it on. 'I don't know what to do. I had to tell somebody.'

'You haven't told anyone else?'

'Only the other girls. And Edna, the boss.'

'What did *she* say?'

'She told us all to keep our mouths shut. If it gets into the papers, we might as well close down.'

'So she's not going to the police?'

'You don't know Edna. She's got a thing about the police. It goes back to her time as a working girl, in the bad old days. She wouldn't even let Miranda phone them when she thought her car was stolen.'

'Someone's got to tell them.'

'Don't look at me. Edna would sack me on the spot. She told me.'

'You could phone them anonymously. She wouldn't know it was you.'

'Oh aye, she would. None of the other girls give a damn about it, at least not enough to stand up to Edna. I've already stuck my neck out.'

'So you do what you're told and keep quiet. How are you going to feel when the next guy gets the chop? What if it's me?'

Annette shuddered. 'Don't say that!'

'Why not? I may be next on his list. I seem to have the right qualifications.'

'No, you haven't. You don't go there any longer.'

'Maybe the murderer doesn't know that.'

'Jack, you've got to promise me you won't tell anyone!'

'You should've asked me that at the beginning.'

'*Promise* me!'

There was a pause. 'All right, I promise. But only if you do something about it yourself.'

'OK, OK.' Annette turned the key in the ignition. 'I'll think about it.'

They spoke very little during the short journey to Annette's house. Within ten minutes, they had left the centre of town, passed through a suburban area and were in the housing estate where Annette lived.

She parked beside an end terrace house, at the bottom of a cul-de-sac. It had a small patch of garden at the front and a larger grassy area at the side. The whole garden was bounded by a three-foot-high hedge, recently trimmed. A footpath ran along the side boundary, and at the other side of the path a high wooden fence and some trees separated them from what looked like a private housing estate. Directly across from Annette's house, children were playing football in a large, open area with a scattering of young trees.

Annette switched off the engine and turned to him. 'Jack, let's drop that other matter for the moment. I don't want it to spoil tonight.'

'Fair enough,' he said. 'Neither do I.' But it did.

She kissed him lightly on the cheek and they got out of the car.

Their arrival had been spotted and Annette's children came running out to meet them. Norah was waiting for them at the door. From then on, everything was much as Jack had expected. The children were lively but well behaved, curious about Jack, but not hostile. The same could be said about Norah. She was friendly, and she and Jack took to each other immediately; he also felt that he was under scrutiny, as if Norah was standing in for Annette's absent mother.

She waited while Annette prepared the meal, and the interrogation continued. Loosely disguised as a casual conversation, Annette's cover story was presented and seemed to pass muster. He felt a little more disconcerted when young Andrew came up to him and said, 'Did Mummy cure you when you were sick?'

'Yes,' said Jack, 'she certainly did.'

'That's what she does. She cures sick people. She's cured lots and lots of people.'

'Those that can afford it,' said Norah. 'I'm surprised you could manage it on a barman's wages.'

'I've got a bit put by. Left me by my parents.'

Norah looked as if she wanted to ask more questions, but perhaps felt she had been nosy enough for the time being. Just as she was looking as if she might have found her second wind, the kids recruited Jack to play a video game with them, and ran off to set it up.

'They're great kids,' said Norah. 'A real credit tae her. They want for nothin'.'

'I can see that.'

'They must be the best-dressed weans in the whole scheme. And toys . . . you name it, they've got it. An' they're no' cheap nowadays. They've even got a computer; well, it's Annette's, but she lets them have a go at it. They want for nothin', but she's no' soft wi' them. She's bringin' them up well. I don't know how she does it on her own. Mind you, her man wasnae much help. A complete waste of space, but there's nae need tae go intae that.'

Jack couldn't think of anything to say, but Norah seemed able to manage for both of them. 'She's even bought this hoose fae the cooncil. And now she's thinkin' aboot gettin' a garage. Of course, she's lucky tae have such a good job. But she's done well, just the same.'

'I know. She certainly has.'

'I've got a lot of time for Annette. It would be nice if she found someone. Somebody a bit better than . . . but I don't want tae speak ill of the brain dead.'

Jack got the impression that he had passed the test, at least provisionally. The children returned and for a while they were all diverted by the game.

When dinner was ready, Norah took her leave. Her husband hadn't yet returned from the pub and she seemed a little reluctant to leave the company. Annette thanked her profusely for her help, but Jack was relieved to see that her gratitude didn't extend to a dinner invitation.

Things went well during dinner and for a while afterwards, while the children were still around. They seemed to like Jack and to be quite happy that their mother had brought home a friend; Jack got the impression that their father had been out of the scene too long for any awkward comparisons to arise.

After a while, he was left alone watching TV while Annette put the children to bed. He watched the end of a film, then the national news was followed by a brief local report. The shadow over the evening, which had lifted for a while, now fell once more.

'Police are still baffled by the savage murder of Glasgow builder Steven Archer, which has been linked with the similar recent killings of Richard McAlpine and Arnold Bell. All three died of multiple stab wounds, in a frenzied attack, but although it seems likely that the same killer is responsible, no other link has been established between the victims.'

The scene switched from studio to police station, where a senior police officer, identified in a caption as Detective Chief Inspector Matt MacDermott, continued the story: 'So far we've been unable to identify any motive for these senseless killings. They don't appear to be random attacks; Arnold Bell was attacked in his own home and Steven Archer in his show flat. There must be a connecting link. If any member of the public has any information, no matter how trivial it might seem, please get in touch with the police.'

The scene changed back to the studio and another news item came on. Only then did Jack notice that Annette was in the room. She came round and sat beside him on the sofa.

'How much of that did you catch?'

'Enough.'

'Well?'

'I don't want to talk about it. Not tonight.'

But the damage had been done. They changed the subject, but the conversation became a little strained. Earlier, Jack had gained the impression that he was going to be asked to stay the night. However, before much longer, Annette was phoning for a taxi to take him to the station. It seemed appropriate. The atmosphere was no longer right.

At the door he kissed her, and she clung to him tightly, as if she feared that he was escaping from her life.

'I'll phone you,' he said.

'Make sure you do.'

As the taxi drove away, she was still standing at the open door. He waved to her and she waved back.

23

Next on the List?

'By the way,' said Morag, 'the cops want tae talk to you.'

'*What!*'

'The cops want tae talk to you. You know, the pigs, the filth, the fuzz, whatever you want tae call them. They'll likely be poppin' in later.'

'You can see he's got a guilty conscience,' said Les. 'He nearly jumped ower the counter.'

'I always thought he had some dark secret. A real mystery man. Now it's all gonnae come oot.'

'Dae ye think he's the murderer?' said Les. 'Or is he just another bank robber?'

'What the hell are you talking about?' said Jack.

'Keep yer hair on,' said Morag. 'It's one of your best features. But they really do want to see you. And it is about the murders.'

'Fucksake,' said Les.

'But I don't think you're a suspect. Only a witness.'

'How do you mean? How am I a witness?'

It was Morag's mid-evening break. She seemed to have forgiven Jack for his flirtation with Alison. Sufficiently, at least, to resume spending her breaks in the Centurion, though she still liked to make him suffer from time to time. At any rate, she didn't seem to have heard of Annette's visit to the West End. Not that it mattered. Jack had decided that he wasn't interested in Morag.

'Remember that wee guy?' she said. 'The one that was followin' you? The one we thought was a private detective?' She looked at Les, who still stood beside Jack, taking in every word, and smiled at him sweetly. 'In Tennent's we don't leave customers standin' at the bar wi' their tongues hangin' oot.'

'What?' After a moment, Les took the hint and slowly went off to serve the customer.

'What about him?' asked Jack.

'I saw him again. On the night of the murder.'

'Where? In here? In Tennent's?'

'No, in the street. Just up fae the new flats, where that last guy got done in. I live just up the road fae there. He walked past me in the street.'

'My God! You sure it was the same man? I don't think I'd know him again.'

'I'm positive. I got a really good look at him that first time. Better than you did.'

'Did you see him go into the flats?'

'No, but he was in the area on the night of the murder. And he was definitely actin' suspicious that first time we saw him. Anyway, the cops said they wanted any information they could get, no matter how trivial. So I thought I'd better give them a ring, before all the men in the city get bumped aff. I wouldnae want that.'

'There's still plenty of us left,' said Les, now back in place, his ears tuned.

'I said men, no' boys.'

'So when do they want to see me?' asked Jack.

'I've to go doon tae the station the morra, tae look at some mug shots. They said they'd probably want you as well.'

'I'll never recognise him again. I only got a glimpse.'

'It's probably nothin'. There's nae need tae look so worried.'

'I told you he had a guilty conscience,' said Les.

Jack shouted at him. 'Shut the fuck up!'

Les looked startled, and did as he was told. Morag also looked taken aback, but made no comment. 'I'll need to get back,' she said, finishing her drink. 'See you at the clink.'

It was Tuesday night and the bar was quiet. However, only the two of them were on duty and they were kept fairly busy. Jack was able to avoid talking to Les for the time being. He regretted having shouted at him, but sometimes the little bugger needed sorting out. He'd get over it.

But Morag's news *had* shaken him, for reasons neither she nor Les could guess at. Three customers of the Merchant City Health Centre had been murdered. Jack had been one of their customers. And a man seen near the location of the last killing, on the very evening it had taken place, had earlier taken a mysterious interest in Jack.

Maybe it was all a coincidence. But was it one he could take a chance on?

He had spoken to Annette on the phone the day before, and they had arranged a date for later that week. When he asked her if she had thought any further about going to the police she had stalled him, talking round the subject. Probably the children had been within earshot. But they would have to discuss it further.

Meanwhile, as Morag had predicted, the police came to him. He was spared the embarrassment of two uniformed officers marching into the pub and asking for him; instead they phoned the bar and asked him if he could go down to the station the following morning, to look at some photographs.

When he hung up, he saw that Les was looking at him. 'Yes,' he said. 'It was the cops.'

'I never said a word.'

Jack smiled at him. Les was all right. A daft little bugger, but you couldn't stay angry at him. 'It's OK,' he said. 'I'm not under arrest. You won't have to finish the shift on your own.'

❖

When he arrived at the police station, he met Morag coming out. 'Nae joy,' she said. 'Maybe you'll have better luck.'

'I doubt it. I think they're clutching at straws.'

'Maybe that wee guy had nothin' tae do wi' it. I hope no'. He didnae seem to like you.'

'What are you talking about?'

'I didnae like to say at the time. The looks he was drawin' you. It made me wonder if he really was a private detective. He seemed to be takin' it more personal.'

'Thanks a lot,' said Jack. 'That really makes me feel good.'

'I'm no' tryin' tae wind you up. I thought you should know. Just take care, OK?'

'OK, thanks.'

'See you tonight, if you're still with us.'

'It's my night off, so don't go jumping to conclusions.'

He was shown into an interview room by a policewoman and left with a bundle of photographs. He looked through them several times, but didn't see a face he recognised. After a while he was joined by a young plain-clothes officer, who introduced himself as Detective Sergeant Madigan.

'Any luck?'

'Nothing, sorry. I didn't really get a good look at him.'

'So there's nobody there you recognise?'

'No. Who are these guys anyway?'

'Some of them are convicted criminals. The rest are private detectives. Can you think of any reason why a detective would be watching you?'

'None. I'm already divorced.'

Madigan sighed. 'OK. I don't really think this is taking us anywhere, but you'd better tell me what happened.'

Jack told him about the man being in the Centurion, what Morag had told him, and about seeing him in the street afterwards. 'I thought at first he was following me home, but I think it was just my imagination.'

'OK,' said Madigan. 'It was a long shot. But every lead's worth following up.'

He rose to his feet. The interview seemed to be at an end.

Jack hesitated, continuing to sit where he was.

'Was there something else?' Madigan asked.

'Morag said the guy didn't seem to like me.'

Madigan laughed. 'You know the West End. Full of nutters. You probably served him a bad pint the night before.'

'Yeah, maybe.'

'You don't sound convinced. Is there something you haven't told me?' Jack said nothing. 'Mr Morrison, if there's anything else, any reason for you to suspect you might be in danger, I think you ought to tell me. I'm sure you've heard what this maniac does to his victims. It's probably a false trail, but if it was me, I don't think I'd take a chance on it.'

Jack was thinking quickly. He had wanted to discuss it further with Annette, to persuade her to go to the police. But if she didn't agree, *someone* would have to tell them.

If she did go forward, he would probably be interviewed again.

One way or another, he was likely to end up having to explain why he'd initially said nothing.

'It's a bit embarrassing,' he said.

'Go on,' said Madigan. He was looking at Jack intently. This was no longer a routine interview.

'Is it likely to get into the papers?'

'We don't tell the press any more than they need to know. Sometimes we give them information if we need their help. I can't give any guarantees, especially when I don't know what you're going to tell me. You *are* going to tell me something, aren't you? I'm becoming intrigued.'

Jack took a deep breath. He couldn't go back now. 'Yes,' he said. 'I do know something else. Something you've been looking for. A link between the murders.'

Until then Madigan had remained impassive. Now a faint smile intruded. Did he smell promotion?

'Go on,' he said.

24

Hitting the Fan

The news broke on Friday. It appeared first as an exclusive in a morning tabloid, and by evening was on the TV news, local and national. Jack missed the newspaper story, and so the shock was even greater when he switched on his TV and saw a familiar back street in the Merchant City: the squat, three-storey stone building, nestling like a younger sibling against the gable of the taller tenement beside it; the dingy close beside the old-fashioned pub; the first-floor windows painted with the name of the Blackfriars Pawnbroking Company; their top-floor counterparts curtained and anonymous. Into this discreet byway a searchlight had now been aimed. The national item showed only a glimpse of this, along with a brief statement from DCI MacDermott; however, in the local bulletin, it was the lead story.

This time the Merchant City location was given more coverage. Suddenly Jack saw Annette coming out of the building, her face in full view as the cameras took her by surprise. Too late, she fended off the questions and hurried off down the street. 'The connection between the murders,' said the commentary, 'was first noticed by sauna girl Annette Somerville, who recognised all of the victims as former clients. Ms Somerville, who is helping the police with their inquiries, tonight declined to comment.' The last part accompanied a picture of Annette, evidently having been pursued halfway across the Merchant City, trying to hide her face as she got into her car.

There followed an interview with sauna proprietress Edna Brady, who maintained that the Merchant City Health Centre was a respectable establishment and the apparent link with the murders was a coincidence. She stated these outrageous propositions with such deadpan gall that Jack almost believed her. A more extended statement from the DCI ended the bulletin.

Several other news items passed unnoticed as Jack tried to collect his thoughts. The enormity of what had happened to Annette was too much for him to properly grasp. And how had the press managed to get hold of the story? Surely the police wouldn't have released it? DS Madigan, after hearing Jack's story, had thought it unlikely that they would make the information public. It could only put the murderer on his guard.

After his interview with the police, he had tried without success to warn Annette. On Wednesday the phone had been answered by her childminder, and on the following evening her number was continuously engaged. He was due to meet her later that evening. Would she turn up? If she did, what sort of reception would he get?

She did show up, only five minutes late. She wore dark glasses, no make-up and what looked like her oldest clothes; either she had failed to take the usual trouble with her appearance, or was deliberately trying to cultivate an image that would attract less attention. She looked nervously around her, as if unable to believe that she wasn't the centre of attention.

Jack bought her a drink and they retired to a quiet alcove. They were in a dimly-lit basement bar in Sauchiehall Street, a discreet enough location. It had been their original intention to go to the cinema, which now seemed unlikely.

She took off her glasses. There were dark rings under her eyes and she looked exhausted. 'I wasn't sure if you'd have the nerve to show up,' she said. 'What the fuck did you think you were playing at?'

'Hang on, I don't think that's . . .'

'Did you see the news?'

'That was nothing to do with me. I never told them.'

'But you spoke to the police. Don't deny it; they told me.'

'They came to me.' He told her about the man who had been following him, the one spotted by Morag. 'He could be after me. I may be next on his list. The police had to be told.'

'You could have warned me.'

'I've been trying to get hold of you all week.'

Annette sighed. 'I spent Wednesday evening at the police station. Since then, the press have been hounding me and I left my phone off the hook.'

'I'm sorry, but I didn't tell them. Do you think I want *my* name in the papers?'

'You've managed to avoid it just the same. It's all right for you.' She covered her face with her hands and began to cry. Jack tried to comfort her, but she pulled away from him. She recovered quickly, seeming determined not to show her weakness. 'And Edna's fired me.'

'What the hell for?'

'What do you think? She thinks I told the cops and went to the papers. I denied it, of course, but she wouldn't believe me. I was the one who wanted her to go to the police in the first place.'

'Would you like me to talk to her?'

'What good would that do? It would just confirm that I was involved.'

'Oh God,' said Jack. 'I don't know what to say.'

'And because Edna threw me out early, they had enough time to get my face on the evening news. Wonderful, isn't it?'

'How did they know your name?'

'Who knows? Maybe Edna told them, maybe they checked my car registration. The damage is done.'

They sat in silence for a while. 'What are you going to do?' Jack asked eventually.

'I haven't had a chance to think about it. I won't get a job – any kind of job – until this blows over. If it ever does.'

'It will.'

'I've got some money put by. I can hold out for a little while. Meanwhile I've got to face the neighbours and my family. And God knows what they'll put my kids through at school.'

She broke down again. Jack watched her, feeling useless. After a while she recovered a little. 'I'm sorry.'

'It's all right.' He hesitated. 'I was thinking . . . It might be for the best. I mean, you could . . .'

She looked at him sharply. 'What?'

She seemed to sense what he was going to say, daring him to go ahead. Jack was wishing he'd kept quiet. 'Why don't you . . . I mean . . . Have you ever thought of doing anything else?'

'Get a *respectable* job, you mean?'

'I didn't say that.'

'But that's what you thought.'

'Well . . . you can't do that work for ever.'

'That's right. Whores are like footballers, they've got an early sell-by date. I didn't think I'd reached mine just yet.'

'I didn't mean that. Just that maybe you should get out before . . .'

'Before what? Before I'm only fit for a job in the Boiler House?'

154

'Where?'

'Never mind. And meanwhile I suppose you'll keep me and my kids on your barman's wages, in the style to which we're accustomed. But your offer's got a time limit, in case the goods get too damaged.'

Jack said nothing. Every time he opened his mouth he seemed to make matters worse. At the moment she seemed to need a punch bag rather than a confidant; that was probably the only reason she had turned up. Maybe he deserved it.

'I wondered when this subject would crop up. Well, let me tell you this, Jack Morrison. I'm not ashamed of what I do. And you don't have the right to lecture me. You don't know me well enough. And considering where we met . . .' She finished her drink and started to put her coat on. 'I think it's time I went. I only came to see what you had to say for yourself.'

'I'm sorry. Stay and have another drink.' He grabbed hold of her arm, but she pulled it free.

'I don't drink and drive. I'm a respectable, law-abiding citizen.' She suppressed a sob, and blew her nose. Her appearance had deteriorated further. Her eyes were puffy, her nose red. She looked angry and miserable, but evidently there was nothing he could do to help. 'I don't want to see you again. Not right now, anyway.' She got up and walked quickly out of the bar.

Jack sat on for a moment, then went up to the counter and bought a drink. He stood at the bar until he had finished it. Then he bought another.

❖

Annette left the pub and walked along Sauchiehall Street, past the McLellan Galleries and the Glasgow Film Theatre, where she and

155

Jack had intended to spend the evening. Her car was in a multi-storey park above a shopping centre, the next block along.

She brought out her dark glasses, then put them away again as she saw that no one was giving her a second glance. It had been the same in the pub. Most people wouldn't have seen the news bulletin, and those who had were unlikely to remember her after only one glimpse. Apart from those who already knew her. They were the main problem.

Had she been too hard on Jack? She still couldn't think straight about that. She only knew that her life was in pieces, and that he had started off the process. At first she'd been driven by the need to confront him, then by an even more compelling desire to escape from him and from that bar. She'd felt closed in, unable to breathe.

The evening was cool and dry, and there was an hour or more of daylight left. Annette slowed her pace and enjoyed the fresh air. Her tension began to ease a little. She carried on past the car park, having decided to walk for a little longer before driving home. She'd paid Linda for the whole evening, an arrangement made earlier in the week when she'd still expected a cinema date.

She hadn't yet experienced the full consequences of the publicity: Linda didn't seem to have seen the news, and she hadn't met Norah yet. The evening at the police station had been enough of an ordeal, mainly because of the attitude shown by her interrogators. It hadn't helped that she'd failed to come forward on her own. She'd tried to make up for it by answering all their questions honestly, but it wasn't enough. Beneath the superficial courtesy she could sense their contempt. She was only a whore. What was her word worth? She hadn't given a damn about helping to catch a murderer, about saving lives, only about safeguarding her sleazy living. That, at any rate, was the way the police seemed to see it.

Was that the way Jack saw it? Or was she only projecting on to him her own self-image, which the events of the last few days had shattered?

She left Sauchiehall Street, skirted the side of the shopping centre, and crossed Bath Street. Now she had reached the crest of a hill. A long straight road, flanked by office buildings old and new, stretched down before her almost to the River Clyde, invisible at the bottom of the urban valley. In the distance, she could see the tops of buildings on the south side of the river. She continued downhill for several blocks, then turned right into Waterloo Street, intending to complete a wide circle back up to Sauchiehall Street.

At once she realised that she had inadvertently wandered into the red light district. Women were spaced out at intervals, singly or in pairs, in shop doorways and at street corners, waiting for business. Annette quickened her pace. This was an unwelcome reminder of her predicament.

'Hello, Annette.'

She stopped and turned to face the girl who had addressed her. 'Sylvia!'

'You workin' this area?'

'No,' she said. 'No, I'm not.' She at once regretted the haste of her reply and joined Sylvia in her shop doorway. 'It's good to see you. How are you doing?'

'I suppose I've been better.'

On closer examination, Annette could see that this was an understatement. Always thin by nature, Sylvia now looked almost anorexic. The evening wasn't particularly cold, but she was shivering under her flimsy coat. Her face was pallid, her hair untidy and she wore dark glasses. There had been a marked deterioration in a very short time. Had she acquired her boyfriend's habit?

'You fancy a cup of tea somewhere?' Annette asked. She wanted to talk to Sylvia, but didn't want to hang about at her stance. If a photo of *that* were to get in the papers . . .

'Aye, all right,' said Sylvia. 'There's a wee place round the corner.'

This proved to be a pub on Argyle Street, a few hundred yards further downhill. On the way, Annette noticed that Sylvia was walking a little stiffly, as though in some pain, but she said nothing. They passed from the city's commercial area, with its gleaming glass-and-steel office blocks, into a neighbourhood where gap sites and semi-derelict remnants of old Glasgow had only partly been replaced by new development. They went into a dingy corner pub where the likes of them would not attract attention. Annette bought a double vodka for Sylvia and a soft drink for herself, and they sat down at a corner table. For the first time Sylvia took off her dark glasses.

'Jesus Christ!' said Annette. 'What happened to you?'

Sylvia had two black eyes and, now that Annette examined her more closely, several other partially healed bruises that she'd attempted to conceal with make-up. 'I got a doin' last weekend. This is ma first night back.'

'That bastard! I don't know why you still . . .'

'It wasnae Charlie. He's a bastard right enough, but he's no' violent.'

'A punter?'

'Aye. One you know an' all.'

'A Merchant City punter?' Sylvia nodded. 'Don't tell me. Fair-haired, early thirties, business type. Calls himself Martin.'

'Aye,' said Sylvia. 'That sounds like him. Him and another guy had a fight over that stuck-up cow, Miranda. You were there.'

'That's him all right. What the hell were you thinking about?' Then Annette realised that Sylvia had been sacked before the attack on Justine, and wouldn't have been aware of the danger. She told Sylvia the story. 'Sounds as if he got a taste for it.'

'The bastard. How is the lassie?'

Annette was ashamed to realise that she didn't know. 'She hasn't been back. I took her to the hospital for a check-up.'

'You're a gem, Annette.' Sylvia looked as if she was about to cry. 'I've missed you.'

'Anyway,' said Annette, quickly changing the subject. 'Have you heard about the carry-on at work?'

It turned out that Sylvia had seen neither the newspaper story nor the TV reports. Annette told her all about it. It was good to have someone to confide in, someone already in on her secret.

'Jesus Christ!' said Sylvia eventually. 'Somebody bumpin' aff the punters? Pity they didnae get that cunt fae the other night.'

'That would've been a public service. But how about this? The last guy to get done in was the one he had the fight with. You know, over Miranda.'

'This is gettin' really weird.'

'You could say that.'

'An' that bitch Edna gave you the push? I cannae believe it. You were her best girl.'

'I don't know about that.'

'You were always the best-hearted, an' that's the truth. Never mind, Annette, you'll get another job nae bother. You're no' like me. This is all I'm fit for.'

'Don't be daft,' said Annette, trying to sound convincing. 'Anyway, I'll maybe be able to pick something up when it's all blown over. You want another drink?'

'I wouldnae mind, but I'd better get back. I might get some business once it's dark enough.'

There was still some daylight left as they made their way back to Waterloo Street. Sylvia clung to her tightly as they hugged goodbye, even though it was clear that her injuries still hurt. 'It was good tae see you, Annette.'

'You too, Sylvia. Take care.'

But as she walked quickly up the street, Annette realised that the appeal was likely to be in vain. Meeting Sylvia had put some things into perspective. If her life had reached a crossroads, she was now clear about the direction she didn't want it to take.

At the next junction she decided it was time to cut back up to Sauchiehall Street and return to her car. As she stood waiting to cross the road, a car drew up and stopped beside her.

Annette was going to walk on, then, on an impulse, bent down to face the driver as he lowered the window. She treated him to one of her best professional smiles.

'Are you looking for business?' the driver asked.

Annette opened her handbag and briefly flashed her driver's licence. 'Yes,' she said. 'Police business. Would you mind stepping out of the car, sir?'

The driver crashed into gear and stamped on the accelerator. Annette made a show of staring after him, as if she were memorising the registration number.

She crossed the road and carried on up the hill, already beginning to feel better. She hoped she hadn't lost Sylvia a customer.

❖

She didn't see Norah until Sunday. Before that, Annette got the impression that Norah was avoiding her. In the case of neighbours who lived independent lives, who didn't seek out each others' company, it was of course possible to go for days, or even weeks, without even a chance meeting. But not with Norah.

And so when the whole of Saturday and half of Sunday went by without a sighting of her neighbour, Annette drew the appropriate conclusion. By that time the press attention had waned and her phone was back on the hook. She had reckoned that it was better to endure a few calls than risk a physical invasion of her home. So far she had been spared a personal visit by a representative of the tabloids, but she didn't fool herself that she was in the clear just yet.

At twelve thirty on Sunday she saw Norah's husband George leave for the pub. If he followed his usual timetable, he'd be back some time after three o'clock, looking for his Sunday dinner. Normally, Norah would have been in Annette's house or vice versa by one o'clock, but by ten past there was still no sign of her neighbour. Realising that she would have to take the initiative, Annette went out and knocked on Norah's back door.

There was a delay before Norah appeared, and at first it looked as if she wasn't going to answer at all. Then, just as Annette was about to knock again, the door opened about a foot and Norah peered out cautiously.

'Hi,' said Annette, trying to sound normal. 'Where have you been hiding?'

Norah said nothing. Annette fancied that she was holding the inside door handle with both hands, ready to slam it in her neighbour's face if she took a step further forward.

'I saw George go off,' Annette said. 'Want to come in for a cuppa? The kids are out playing.'

'I don't know,' said Norah. 'I've got the dinner to make.'

'Come on. Are you going to avoid me until one of us moves out of the neighbourhood? George doesn't need to know.'

As if she didn't know what else to do, Norah came out and followed Annette into her house. She sat silently in the living room while Annette made tea in the kitchen. She still said nothing when Annette returned to the living room.

Annette first of all looked out of the front window to check on Andrew and Lisa. They were still in the grassy area opposite the house, playing with their friends. So far there was no evidence that anything had been said to them about their mother; that was what she feared most.

She sat down opposite Norah. 'I take it you've seen the news?'

Norah nodded. She seemed about to speak, then stopped herself. Then she said, 'How could you?'

'I don't know what to say. I'm sorry if it was a shock. I've had a few of them myself recently.'

'So it's true. You really work in . . . in that place.'

'Yes, I did.'

'But it's . . . From what they were sayin' aboot it . . . It sounds as if . . .'

'It's a brothel.'

Norah seemed to be finding it difficult to speak in her usual plain manner. 'That means . . .' She took a sip of her tea and almost choked on it. 'What you do . . . You're . . .'

'A prostitute.'

Norah shook her head and fell silent again. She had been hoping, Annette sensed, that a mistake had been made, that she would be given some alternative, more palatable explanation. And she would probably have accepted one, however improbable, even an endorsement of Edna's brazen statements to the press. But now the truth was out.

After a while, Norah said, 'You told me you were a nurse.'

'I am. I gave it up.'

'So there's no need . . . If you wanted, you could . . .'

'Get a job as a nurse? Right at this moment I doubt it. But you're right, if I'd wanted I could have kept on working in a real hospital. Or maybe in a shop, or behind a bar. Working twice the hours for half the money. By the time I'd paid the mortgage and the extra childminding costs, there might have been enough left to feed my children on pie and chips.'

'Other people manage.'

'I don't want to just manage.'

'What about their father?'

'I've never had a penny from him. He can't even keep himself. Unlike him, I don't want to live off the taxpayer. I prefer honest work.'

The last statement was enough to take the wind out of Norah for the time being.

Eventually she said, 'I feel I don't know you at all.'

'I'm still the same person.'

'What would your parents have thought? What about your children?'

'My parents are dead. They won't think anything. And it's because of my kids that I do it.'

'And what about that young man you brought back last Saturday? He seemed really nice. Does he . . . ?'

'Jack?' A couple of days earlier, when she'd been really angry at Jack, she might have told Norah where they'd met. Now she didn't want to. 'He knows what I do.'

Norah shook her head again. Obviously, she now felt that there were two people she'd badly misjudged.

'Look,' said Annette. 'We're from different generations. I know it's hard for you to understand, but I'm not ashamed of what I do.'

This was becoming something of a refrain. 'If I've told lies, it's because other people don't see it the way I do. It was the only way I could have any kind of normal life. I'm sorry if you're disappointed in me. I wish this had never happened. But I hope we can still be friends, or good neighbours at the very least.'

Norah was still unconvinced, but she did stay for a second cup of tea. Annette couldn't blame Norah for her reaction. In part, she now realised, it was due to the unrealistically high regard in which her neighbour had held her. Annette felt that in the last few days her life had suddenly disintegrated, but in Norah's eyes her fall had been even greater. Their relationship might recover, but it would never be the same.

Shortly after two, Norah went off to prepare her husband's dinner. Also to cover her tracks. Before leaving for the pub, George had told Norah that she was never to speak to Annette again.

25

Some Expert Views

'Of course I don't condone the murder of these men,' said Robert Washington. 'As well as being morally wrong, murder is still, I believe, against the law.' He smiled, as if he had been responsible for a great witticism. 'I'm merely objecting to the description of the dead men as innocent victims. They weren't innocent. They were moral degenerates.'

'Are you saying,' asked the interviewer, 'that they deserved to die?'

'I'm saying that they'd still be alive if they'd been true to their marriage vows.'

'Anna Grant, what do you think? Did they deserve to die?'

'No, of course not,' said Anna Grant. 'I don't think that's what Mr Washington means either. At least, I hope not.'

'Excuse me,' said Washington, 'but aren't you on record as saying that it's always the women involved in prostitution who are punished, rather than the men who use them? That the balance is wrong?'

'I meant that we should stop picking on the women. Not that we should start clobbering the men as well.'

'So, instead of being even-handed in the punishment of sinners, we should let all of them go unscathed?'

'I think we should leave out religion and the moral high ground,' said Anna Grant. 'Prostitution is a social issue, one that support groups like mine try to deal with. Murder is a crime, and that's a matter for the police.'

The interviewer said, 'And what about Robert Washington's campaign of photographing the sauna customers?'

'Silly and pointless. Apart from the fact, of course, that it's an excellent marketing ploy. A few more people may actually open his rag instead of chucking it straight in the bin, and maybe they'll notice a couple of adverts along the way.'

Anna Grant's dislike of her fellow interviewee was now quite open. They presented quite a contrast. She could only have been a year or two younger than Washington, but they looked as if they belonged to different generations. He was the odd one out. His old-fashioned and formal dress style, which went well with his opinions, seemed to lend him added years, as it did with the people in old films and photographs.

Washington didn't allow himself to be goaded by her remarks, but maintained his smirk of moral superiority. 'Maybe being publicly exposed is preferable to being murdered.'

'So you're doing them a favour? Do *us* a favour.'

'No, Miss Grant, I'm trying to discourage the evil and immoral practice of women selling themselves for money. You, on the other hand, with your so-called *support group*, obviously want to encourage it.'

'We don't encourage prostitution at all. We try to help the women already involved in it. It's not the same thing.'

'Anna Grant,' said the interviewer, 'Robert Washington, thank you both very much. We now turn to Dr Andrew MacDuff of Strathkelvin University, a specialist in criminal and deviant psychology. Dr MacDuff, what sort of person are the police looking for?

Who would want to commit such crimes? What do you think his motive is?'

'*Her* motive.'

'Sorry?'

'The killer,' said Dr MacDuff, 'is a woman.' Pausing for dramatic effect, he lifted the glass of water in front of him and took a drink. He looked about forty, was plainly dressed and spoken, and might have been plucked out of a nearby pub rather than a university.

'A woman?' said the interviewer. 'Why do you say that?'

'The physical evidence alone points strongly in that direction. In each case, the killer relied on the element of surprise to overcome the victim. Richard McAlpine was initially felled from behind by a blow on the head, attacked at night in a quiet street. Arnold Bell was caught unawares on the doorstep of his own house, at ten thirty in the morning, not exactly when you'd be expecting a homicidal attack. He was also knocked unconscious, probably as soon as he opened the door. Steven Archer was drugged by chloroform, then tied up. What do we deduce from all this? That the killer couldn't be sure of overcoming the victims by physical superiority. Exactly what you'd expect if the killer was a woman.'

'Maybe so,' said the interviewer. 'But that's hardly conclusive.'

'It's an indication. The psychological aspects clinch it. The killer is driven by an intense hatred, we know that. Each of the victims suffered multiple stab wounds, from a frenzied attack that must have continued long after unconsciousness, or even death. Who are the objects of that hatred? The clients of prostitutes. What sort of person would feel such hatred for that category of man? Most likely a prostitute herself.'

'You think the killer's a prostitute?'

'Yes. Or a former prostitute.'

'Why do you say that?'

'Let's try the following scenario for size,' said Dr MacDuff. 'It's only one possibility, but it fits the bill. A woman has been sexually abused as a child, by her father or another male authority figure. As a child, her feelings for the father figure are ambivalent. She instinctively hates the abuse, but is dependent on the man for survival and emotional support. In adulthood, when she fully realises how her trust was betrayed, her feelings flower into a deep, unambiguous hatred. By this time she has drifted into prostitution, and feels for her clients the same ambivalent feelings she once felt for her father. In one sense, they are responsible for a continuation of the sexual abuse but, on the other hand, they also provide her with her livelihood. In her mind they become associated with the father who simultaneously betrayed and supported her. Then she grows older, and what happens?'

'I don't know,' said the bemused interviewer.

'Her clients begin to fall away. They abandon her for the younger models. The men who used and soiled her don't even provide her with a living any more. Her feelings for them are no longer ambiguous. All the pent-up hatred of her father is transferred on to them. He's probably dead by now, beyond her reach, but who cares? She has an endless line of father substitutes, all offering their necks for the chop.'

'You seem very sure of this.'

'As I said, it's only one possibility. But I'd put money on it.'

'Have the police asked for your help, Dr MacDuff?'

'Not yet. So here's a wee free gift, to get them interested.

They're looking for a woman, between thirty-five and forty-five, who works or has worked as a prostitute.' He looked directly at the camera. 'How about it, guys? There's lots more where that came from. My fee's reasonable.'

26

Diversification

'Did you see that daft bastard on the telly?' said Candy. 'He thinks one of us is the murderer.'

'That'll be right,' said Cleo. 'Does he think we'd cut our own throats?'

'I never knew you watched the telly,' said Annette. 'Which pub was it in?'

'I was in here,' said Candy. 'There was fuck-all punters. What else could we do?'

Sitting alone in the lounge, they had no answer to that.

'I saw it,' said Annette.

'Loada shite,' said Candy. 'My faither never laid a finger on me. He was never sober enough.'

'You mean if he hadn't been drunk he might have?' said Cleo.

'Did I fuck mean that,' said Candy. 'It would never have entered his head.'

'Mine neither,' said Annette with a shudder. 'But I'm sure it happens.'

'Don't look at me,' said Cleo. 'I never even knew who mine was.'

Candy went up to the gambling machine, inserted a coin and pressed a button.

'You won't make your wages up that way,' said Annette.

'There's a jackpot due.'

'Aye, to Edna, when she comes in to empty it.'

'No' if I get in first,' said Candy, putting in more money. 'What time is it?'

'Four o'clock.'

'Fucksake, is that all? What d'ye think she wants tae see us about?'

'No idea,' said Annette. 'Maybe she's going to pay us off.'

'You've only just got back. Anyway why should she bother? She pays us bugger all up front an' half the girls have left already.'

'It would help if the competition was a bit more fair,' said Cleo. She glared at Candy. 'I'm on all day wi' you and all day tomorrow wi' Miranda. I'll be lucky to get a single customer.'

Annette sighed. 'Join the club.'

Annette's unemployment had lasted less than a week, though her return had so far made little financial impact. Shortly after dismissing her, Edna had discovered the real source of the press story. Chantelle had gabbed to one of her friends, a girl working for a rival sauna, and the other girl had told her boss, who'd phoned the papers. Now Chantelle was working for the other sauna, and Edna, still assuming that the police and the press leaks had a common source, had apologised to Annette and asked her back. Apart from anything else, she needed replacements for the girls who had left.

Strangely, Candy and Miranda, the two who could most easily have found alternative employment, had so far stayed on. Annette suspected that their loyalty might have been subsidised by Edna, who would certainly want to hold on to that pair until times got better. And of course they still had the pick of whatever customers were left.

Annette said, 'If the cops believe that psychologist guy, they'll be back on top of us.'

'How do you mean?' asked Candy. 'Did you have to give them a freebie?'

'Only those above the rank of sergeant. The rest had to pay the going rate. But seriously, if they think it might be one of us . . .'

Candy pressed a button on the machine and gave a yelp as it made a small payout. 'If they believed that crap they'd have been back already.'

'You think they'd want to check it out.'

'Why should they? It's shite. You know it an' so do they.'

'Are you still gettin' bothered by reporters?' Cleo asked Annette.

'Now and then. It seems to have died down.'

All of them had been interviewed by the police, but since then there had been very little contact. A few had also been pestered by reporters, though none as much as Annette. One paper had featured an interview (given anonymously) with a girl who claimed to have worked for the Merchant City Health Centre. Most of it could have applied to any sauna, and there was little that the public hadn't heard before. It might or might not have been authentic.

The police had told them to carry on as usual, in the hope of flushing out the killer. This plan had been frustrated, for the time being at least, when the story went public. The customers seemed reluctant to co-operate by acting as bait – not very public-spirited of them, if unsurprising. There was still the occasional bold (or stupid) punter who seemed to think that a fling with Candy or Miranda was worth risking his life for. And the phantom of the steam room continued to appear regularly for his celibate health kick; Candy, out of boredom as much as desperation, had made a fresh attempt to corrupt him, but without success.

'He must think this is a real health centre,' Annette had said.

'It's a pity we got rid of the exercise bike,' said Candy. 'We could've wiped the cobwebs aff it for him.'

One of the courageous survivors now appeared and took Candy away. Cleo took Candy's place at the machine, in search of the elusive jackpot. Annette sighed and went for a walk around the deserted premises. It would be nice to have at least one customer before her shift ended, to cover her petrol and part of her child-minding expenses; Linda had seemed unshaken by the discovery that she was being paid from immoral earnings, but Annette wasn't sure how much longer she could afford her.

Edna was at the front desk. One of her first economy measures had been to pay off Moira and the other woman who, between them, covered the door for most of the shifts. Now she either did it herself or got one of the girls to fill in, without payment of course. It didn't make much difference to them whether the afternoon was spent looking at an empty lounge or at a closed door.

'Still nothing doing?' Annette asked.

'You'd be the first to know,' said Edna.

'It can't go on like this.'

'I know, that's what I want to see you all about.'

'Sounds ominous.'

'It's OK, I'm no' gonnae sack you again.'

'You might as well, for all the money I'm making.'

'Just you stick wi' Auntie Edna. I've got it all worked out.'

She was prevented from elaborating upon this mysterious statement by the sound of the doorbell. So rare an event had this become, that they both jumped. Edna let in the visitor, a slightly-built man of about thirty-five. Annette immediately recognised him and her brief hope of a last-minute bonus disappeared. Edna gave him her usual false smile of welcome.

174

'Hi there,' she said. 'What can I do for you?'

'A half-hour massage, please.'

Edna took his money and entered his particulars in the book. He went off down the corridor with his towel and wallet.

'Go on,' said Edna. 'What are you waitin' for?'

'There's no point,' said Annette. 'He'll be back.'

Sure enough, he returned to the desk a few moments later, still dressed. 'Where's Miranda?' he asked.

'She's not on until five,' said Edna. 'But we have three other nice girls. This is Annette and . . .'

'I want Miranda,' said the man. 'She's always here on Monday afternoons.'

'She used to be, but now she's here on Monday evenings.'

'I phoned earlier and you said she was on.'

'I'm afraid you must have misunderstood me,' said Edna. It was much more likely, thought Annette, that she had simply lied, hoping that he would show up and accept a substitute. 'Anyway,' continued Edna, 'she'll be here soon. Meanwhile, we have a steam room and sauna, refreshments in the lounge – tea, coffee, or something stronger if you prefer. There's also TV and a gaming machine. Or,' – she treated the customer to a sly, confidential smile – 'if you'd like to retire to one of the cabins, we have a fine selection of adult films.'

Annette listened to this with some admiration. Obviously the prospect of having to return a ten-pound entrance fee had stimulated Edna into a flurry of creative thought.

'I don't know,' said the man. 'I thought Miranda would be here.'

'In half an hour. I'll tell her you're here . . . Johnny,' said Edna, picking up the name, which she'd already forgotten, from the book in front of her. 'You'll be first on her list.'

The man hesitated for a moment, then went back down the corridor.

'That guy gives me the creeps,' said Annette.

'You mean some of them don't?'

'There's something about him. All the girls feel it. He's obsessed with Miranda. He won't look at anyone else.'

'Him an' half the other punters. That's why she makes so much, or why she used to. I'm just relieved some of them still show up.'

'You should see the looks he gives the other customers, especially if they go with Miranda. As if he'd like to—'

Edna looked at her sharply. 'As if what?'

'Nothing.'

Edna didn't pursue it, but Annette had suddenly remembered Jack's story about the 'wee guy' who had followed him and taken his photograph, the one his barmaid friend had seen near the last murder scene. At the time she'd been too angry at him and feeling too sorry for herself to pay it much attention, but now . . . No, it was nonsense. Jack had never been with Miranda, had he? Once or twice maybe, right at the beginning, before he had settled on her as his favourite.

Common sense returned. In a situation like this, it was too easy to let your imagination run wild. If Miranda's customers were the target, the murderer had set himself a formidable task. His list must be a very long one. She and Edna chatted on for a while, then Annette returned to the lounge. No new customers appeared. At a quarter to five, Miranda's admirer left the sauna and came into the lounge, thereby blighting the girls' conversation. He sat opposite the door, looking down the corridor. For all the notice he took of the other girls he might have been alone in the room.

Then the evening shift arrived. At the first glimpse of blonde curls in the corridor, the customer came to life, then slumped back in his seat as Miranda vanished into the girls' changing room. 'She may be a minute or two,' said Annette, with a trace of malice. 'The boss wants to see us all.'

The man ignored her.

The girls assembled in Edna's office: Annette, Candy, Cleo, Miranda and Claudia. Annette noted that there were only two on the evening shift. This could have been a favour to Miranda, in order to leave the field even more clear for her, or it might have been due to the other girls giving her a wide berth. Claudia seemed unbothered. She had her own customers, few of whom had deserted her. Possibly it was something to do with the type of service she provided. Maybe to them a death threat was a bonus.

'You know what it's been like the last week or so,' said Edna. 'If we don't do somethin' about it, we might as well shut up shop. I've decided we should branch out intae visitin' massage.'

The air of expectation in the room turned to disappointment. 'We do that already,' said Candy.

'I know,' said Edna. 'Under the same name and the same number. The customers are still scared off. So I'm gettin' a new phone line installed, wi' a different number. Then I'll advertise a visitin' massage service, under a different name. Naebody'll know we're workin' fae here.'

It was a good idea. All of the girls looked happier. 'What name are you going to use?' asked Annette.

'I havenae decided yet,' said Edna. 'What about City Centre Escorts?'

'Boring!' said Candy. 'You need somethin' wi' a bit more oomph. I've got it. Toppers!'

'Not bad,' said Edna. Then a couple of girls sniggered and she caught on. 'Very funny. Anyway, we'll come up wi' somethin'. The beauty of it is, we can afford tae be competitive. We normally charge double for a visit, to make up for travellin' time. All the saunas do the same. But what's the point if you're all just sittin' here twiddlin' yer thumbs? We might as well undercut the others.'

'Does that include your share?' asked Claudia.

Edna looked at her coolly. 'We'll work oot a deal. One that suits everybody.'

The meeting broke up. When they re-entered the corridor, Miranda's customer rushed out from the lounge to meet her, greeting her like a shy schoolboy. 'Hello, Miranda.'

'Hi there!' said Miranda. Her enthusiasm seemed completely sincere as she gave him her special smile, the one that promised everything, or nothing at all.

❖

'I'll say this for the woman,' said Robert Washington. 'She's got some nerve. Doesn't she know who I am? Or of the campaign we've been running against people like her?' He looked again at the slip of paper, torn from a notebook, that his assistant had given him:

SINNERS VISITING MASSAGE
The Relief that Comes in the Night
287 5511

'I don't understand,' said his assistant, a skinny girl in dowdy clothes, who looked as if she should still be at school. 'I didn't know what it meant. That's why I thought I'd better . . .'

'It's just as well you did, Dora,' said Washington. 'And if a nice Christian girl like you had understood it, I'd have been very disappointed.' In the modest offices of the *North Clyde Advertiser*, his select staff made up in enthusiasm – and cheapness – for what it lacked in experience. 'You see, in this progressive age the once-respectable art of massage has become a euphemism for prostitution.'

'Oh no!' It was surprising that the girl's slight body contained enough blood to make her face go so deeply red.

'I'm afraid so. It would seem that the suppliers of these services are no longer content to have their public come to them. They want to seek them out in their own homes.'

'But that's disgusting!'

'Quite. Can you imagine how it would have looked? Our usual editorial, exposing the patrons of people like her, with that advert on the opposite page?'

'Oh, Mr Washington, I'd absolutely no idea.'

'Of course not, Dora. It's all right. She probably phoned round all the papers on the off chance. I can think of at least one vile rag that will no doubt oblige her. What did the woman say her name was again?'

'Brady. Edna Brady. I said I'd phone her back. But now I don't think I can.'

'Phoning back would be the normal courtesy, Dora. But in this case we can dispense with it.'

When his assistant had left the room, Washington lifted the slip of paper containing the advert, about to crumple it and throw it in his waste bin. Then he looked at it again for a moment or two, opened a desk drawer and placed it there instead. Upside down, beneath a bundle of other papers.

27

A Suspect?

DCI MacDermott looked at the anonymous letter and shook his head. 'I don't think it means anything. The man's obviously got enemies. It would be a wonder if he hadn't.'

'You're probably right,' said DS Madigan. 'But how many leads do we have?'

'Precious few.'

The letter was computer-printed, on a single sheet of paper. It could have originated in any one of several thousand offices, or as many homes, in Glasgow alone. The address had been similarly printed, on a sticky label, and attached to a standard white business envelope, which also bore a second-class stamp and a Glasgow postmark. A virtually untraceable communication.

Its message was succinct:

The murderer you are looking for is Robert Washington, the owner of the *North Clyde Advertiser*. He is a lunatic, who hates the clients of prostitutes and wants to kill them all.

I can't tell you who I am but, believe me, I know what I'm talking about. Look into it and you'll find that I'm telling the truth.

A Public-Spirited Citizen

'I think it's worth having a word with Washington,' said Madigan. 'It can't do any harm. Did you see that interview he gave on TV? He more or less said that the victims deserved to die.'

'If he was the murderer, do you think he'd make a public statement like that? He'd have to be really stupid.'

'But he is crazy. Whoever wrote the letter's right about that. And the murderer must be a nutter. All the indications are that he's—'

'You mean she?'

'Aye, maybe. That he or she's on some kind of moral crusade. Just like Washington.'

'So the murderer's a nutter?' said MacDermott. 'That's a big help. Maybe we should close all the pubs in Byres Road and throw their customers in jail. Hundred to one the murderer would be among them. No, I'll tell you who wrote this letter. Some businessman whose wife opened the *North Clyde Advertiser* and saw a nice clear snapshot of her husband leaving the Rosevale Sauna.'

Madigan sighed. 'That sounds plausible.'

'On the other hand, it can't do any harm to have a word with Washington. As you say, what other leads do we have? You could also pop in and see the owner of the Rosevale Sauna. He's got reason enough to have it in for Washington. Though I doubt if he can afford a computer any more.'

'It's worth a try,' said Madigan. 'Maybe I'll get offered a freebie.'

28

Becoming Restless

It's been far too long.

Reliving the last murder kept me satisfied for a long time. Or almost so. It was definitely the best one so far. To be able to take my time, talk to the subject, explain myself to him, without fear of interruption – all of that added the element missing in the previous killings. I can't go back to risky street attacks, or any other sudden assault, where he'll never know what happened to him. In future they must all know in advance that they're going to die, and why. I've been spoiled by perfection.

But how can I do it again? The show flat was a unique opportunity. The subject couldn't have made things easier if he'd deliberately surrendered to me.

It was also necessary to show caution for a while, now that the police know the connection between the killings. Better to hold back for a while until things got back to normal. Just as well that the last murder was so satisfying.

But now three months have passed and memories are no longer enough. I need fresh blood.

I've been busy enough in the interim. Maintaining my charts, updating the list, is almost a full-time job. But watching the list grow longer only adds to my frustration. I need to find a way to shorten it again.

Actually, I already know the answer. It's just that it presents some practical difficulties. But I'll find a way around them.

Basically, the concept is very simple. Visiting massage. The subject is able to indulge his disgusting vice in the privacy of his own home, or in a hotel bedroom. Instead of seeking out the girl at her place of business, the girl goes to him.

And so do I.

29

A Return Visit

On the same day that Justine returned to work, the man who had assaulted her reappeared. It was an unlucky coincidence that shattered her faltering confidence. While sitting opposite the door to the corridor, she suddenly gave a cry and ran off to the far corner of the room. Annette followed her, concerned.

'What's the matter?'

Justine was crouched, with her back to the wall, in a defensive posture. Her eyes were wide with fear and her body was trembling all over. 'It's him.'

'Who?'

'*Him*. The one that . . . He just came doon the corridor.' She grabbed Annette and held on to her, as if she were a life raft in the middle of the ocean. 'Oh, Annette, what am I gonnae dae? It's him. He'll kill me!'

'What the fuck's goin' on?' asked Claudia.

The three of them were alone in the lounge. Business had picked up, but they still had quiet periods. 'The customer who beat Justine up,' said Annette. 'She says he just came in.'

Claudia took the news with her usual calm. 'He's got some fuckin' nerve.'

Justine was becoming hysterical. 'What are we gonnae dae, Annette? What are we gonnae dae?'

'It's OK,' said Annette. 'You're all right. We won't let him anywhere near you.' Justine began to calm down a little. 'Are you sure it's him?'

Justine nodded vigorously. 'Oh aye. Aye, it is.'

Annette turned to Claudia. 'What are we going to do?'

'You know the cunt?'

'Oh yes,' said Annette. 'I know him.'

'Better take a look, just tae make sure.' Claudia returned her attention to the TV programme she'd been watching. Annette wondered what it would take to really shake her, to dislodge her from the cool contempt with which she greeted the world in general and her customers in particular. If the Yorkshire Ripper had just walked in, she would probably have reacted no differently.

And she was right. Justine was likely to see her attacker's face on just about any man who walked in the door. She'd had two customers so far, and Annette had almost needed to take her by the hand and lead her to the cabin. Luckily they'd both been well-known regulars, with no history of problems.

Annette found it took an effort for her to leave the room and investigate. As she walked down the empty corridor, there was a dryness in her throat and her heart was beating faster. She approached the front desk, where Moira was now back in place after her temporary lay-off. 'What's the name of that guy who just came in?'

'John, why?'

'Thank God.'

'What's up?'

'Nothing.' Annette went back down the corridor, feeling her tension ease. Then the customer, dressed in his robe and carrying a towel, emerged from the changing room, heading for the shower area. He nodded to her curtly as he passed.

Annette hurried back to the lounge. 'It's him. He's in the shower. We'd better phone the police.'

'You aff your fuckin' head?' said Claudia. 'You want the sack again?'

'We've got to do *something*. That bastard beat her up. He raped her. Look at the state she's in.' Justine was sitting silently on the chair furthest from the door, looking terrified and miserable, a steady stream of tears playing havoc with her make-up.

'You two go through tae the changin' room. I'll deal wi' him.'

'How do you mean?'

'I'll say you're both workin'. Just hide till I've got him in the cabin. Quick, on you go, before he gets oot the shower.'

'Are you sure?'

'Don't worry. He'll no' beat me up.'

Annette believed her. And she herself was almost as reluctant as Justine to meet that particular customer again, especially after what Sylvia had told her. She didn't argue further, but took Justine, who had almost to be dragged, out of the lounge and into the corridor. It was still empty. They made their way quickly into the small room – or large closet – that the girls used as a changing room, and sat down on the only two seats.

'I cannae believe it!' said Justine. 'On my first day back!'

'I don't know how he's got the nerve to show his face. He must be really fucking stupid.' Annette nearly told Justine about Sylvia, then thought better of it.

'I should never have come back here. I never meant tae. But I need the money. And then Edna phoned me. She was that nice. But I shouldnae have come back.' She began to cry again.

'It's all right. You've been dead unlucky. It won't happen to you again.'

Several months had passed since the last murder and business had revived. With the visiting massage venture still on the go, they were doing almost as well as before. But word of their slump had got around and Edna had been finding it difficult to get good girls. Hence the recall of Justine, whom she'd otherwise have given up on. She had entrusted her to the care of Annette, who had been asked 'tae knock some of the rough edges aff her'. An unfortunate way of putting it.

The project had got off to a very bad start.

Justine gradually calmed down again and they sat in silence, listening for sounds outside. Five, ten minutes passed and they heard nothing.

'What's happenin'?' asked Justine. 'Dae ye think Claudia's all right?'

'Oh aye.' Annette laughed, a little hysterically. Justine's mood was catching. 'She'll be fine. I wouldn't worry about that at all.'

❖

Martin Kane hadn't intended to return to the Merchant City Health Centre, but he'd felt like a change and was curious to see what the place was like these days. For a while he had indulged his new taste for violence upon street girls. It was too risky in a sauna: there were other people around, and the impracticality of escaping to the street in a bathrobe prevented a quick getaway. It was much better to pick up a girl in your car, then drive to somewhere quiet. Besides, these street hookers were just vermin, asking for it.

But after a while the novelty wore off a little, and with it revived the notion of extramarital sex for its own sake. He didn't like using street girls for that: you never knew what you might catch from them, even wearing a condom. The girls in the saunas at least had the appearance of a little more class.

There were plenty of saunas to choose from but, after sampling a number of them, he found that none suited him quite as well as the one in the Merchant City had done. Not all of them were in such discreet locations: it made him nervous to ring a doorbell then hang about in a busy main street waiting for an answer. In some the choice of girls was poor, like that place on Argyle Street that its rivals called the Boiler House. He'd never seen such a collection of hags past their sell-by date. He'd have been better off with his wife, for Christ's sake! His favourite for a while had been a little place in the back streets of Partick. It had several nice girls and, for some reason, was never too busy. Then he had found out the reason, in a free newspaper which he picked up in a pub. He hadn't featured in that particular issue, but might well have been a past victim of the paper's ludicrous campaign, which had apparently been going on for months. If so, at least neither his father nor his wife Rose had seen the incriminating issue. Otherwise he would definitely have known about it.

For a while he had still hesitated to return to the Merchant City. He might still be recognised and, apart from that, there had been something about it in the news, something about a series of murders. But all that had blown over, and the place had changed its name to the Candleriggs Sauna. It was probably under new management and, even if it wasn't, the girls would all be different by this time. There was always a large staff turnover in these places. And in any case there were only a couple of girls who could have identified him in connection with the assault; even if they were still around, even if he was unlucky enough to pick a shift when one of them was on, they probably wouldn't recognise him. Not whores like that, when you considered the number of men they met every day.

He turned out to be wrong on all counts. Who should he run into on his way out of the shower but that bitch called Annette. And, judging by the way she looked at him, she'd recognised him all right. He'd almost got dressed and walked out, but then he'd thought, fuck it. What could she do about it? She wouldn't call the police; that would definitely be fouling her nest, especially after all this time. And there would be other girls to choose from.

But when he arrived in the lounge there was only one person there, a hefty woman, dark-haired, dressed entirely in black. He remembered having seen her before, but had never fancied her. She had always been a dour bitch and wasn't exactly a teenager.

This time she seemed much friendlier than usual. Getting desperate, he supposed. 'Hi there,' she said. 'I'm Claudia. What's your name?'

'Mar . . . John.'

'Marjon?'

'No. John.' As an extra precaution, he had adopted a pseudonym.

'Would you like a drink, John? We've got tea, coffee, juice. Or would you like a glass of wine?'

'Have you any white wine?'

'Certainly.' She went up to the drinks table and poured two glasses of wine. She sat beside him on the sofa, pressed closely against him. He felt her body heat and smelled her perfume, a musky odour, faint but pleasant. 'Have you been here before, John?'

'Oh, no. No, I haven't.' Turning his head towards her he found himself looking down a cleavage like a small crevasse.

'You don't know what you've been missing.' She took a slow drink of her wine, in a meaningful manner.

'Are there any other girls on?'

That was a bit blunt, he realised, but her smile never faltered. 'What's the matter, John? Am I not good enough for you?'

'No, no, I don't mean that. I just . . . You know . . .'

She laughed. A husky, sexy laugh. 'I know. You want to know more about the field before you play it. Like all real men, you like a bit of variety. Yes, there's two other nice girls on today, Annette and Justine. They're both working just now, doing a two-girl massage. They're booked for an hour.'

Two girls for an hour? Obviously some bastard had more money (and more stamina) than anyone deserved. And he'd seen Annette on the way in. They must have just started. And Justine? He'd caught a glimpse of another girl, but hadn't got a proper look. Wasn't she the one that . . . ? Fuck!

Claudia put her hand on his thigh, began to stroke it lightly. 'You shouldn't waste your time with these young amateurs, John. Experience is what counts. What you want is a woman with years of practice in the art of pleasing men.'

To hell with it. His body had already decided what it wanted. 'Are you free for a massage?'

'Oh yes, I think so. Go through to Cabin One.'

Usually they kept you waiting, but very little time passed before she joined him. She wasn't really all that big – probably about his own height – but her presence filled the small room. She took off her dress and stood before him wearing only a flimsy bra and panties, stockings and suspenders, and knee-high leather boots. All of these black. Unlike other girls who seemed to spend half their lives under sun lamps or blowing their immoral earnings on package tours, her white skin contrasted starkly with her clothes. Her body was in excellent condition, her full figure firm and unblemished. She stood still for a moment, legs apart, hands on hips, letting him see what he was getting. She wasn't actually holding a whip, but he almost felt the presence of one. 'Right,' she said, 'lie on your face.'

He obeyed and she began to massage his back with oil. Usually they gave you a choice between oil or talcum powder, but democracy wasn't part of her act. Her touch was firm, but light, her black-varnished fingernails scampering about his body like tiny-clawed mice. Soon he wanted to turn over, for her to continue on the front of his body, for things to escalate, but she continued to massage his back long, long past that point.

Eventually, he said, 'How long . . . ?'

'Shut your face!' He did, and she carried on for several minutes more.

Then she said, 'Turn over on to your back.'

And he complied. 'I take it you do extras?' he asked.

'No.'

'What?'

'There's nothin' extra aboot ma routine. It's all mainstream.' Her voice had now coarsened from the more polite tones she had used earlier, her Glasgow accent more pronounced. For men who liked a bit of rough.

'Oh,' he said. 'What is it you do?'

'You're gonnae find oot real soon.'

'I mean, what's the choice? What do . . .'

'There's nae choice. You'll dae as ye're telt.'

'Oh. How much will it . . . ?'

She lifted out the plastic wallet from the pocket of his robe, where it hung behind the door, and flicked through the banknotes inside. 'You've got enough.'

After that he surrendered. Normally he liked to be in charge, a role-reversal from his situation at home. But this was a new type of domination, much more interesting than the kind he suffered daily at the hands of Rose. Claudia's bra and panties were now gone, though the stockings and boots remained. The massage of his front took for ever, fingers and breasts being jointly employed as implements of delicate torture. Eventually things did escalate, and then she was climbing off him, removing the condom with a tissue.

He continued to lie on the narrow massage table as she dressed and helped herself to several banknotes from his wallet.

'You gonnae lie there a' day?'

He sat up and swung his legs over on to the floor, a picture of obedience, for which he was well trained. She stood watching him as he put on his robe, her expression a mixture of friendliness and contempt. Hers was a good act.

'You'll be back for more,' she said. It wasn't a question.

'Well . . .' he said. A few minutes earlier that was exactly what he'd been thinking, fervently, with no room for argument. But as his powers of reasoning returned from the lower half of his body, he realised that this might be considerably risky. That Annette bitch *had* recognised him. Fuck!

But somehow Claudia had anticipated him. 'It doesnae need tae be here,' she said. 'We can go where there's better facilities.'

She handed him a business card. It contained a phone number and two lines of printing:

CLAUDIA'S VAULT
Strictly for Pleasure

'I don't know. I don't want anything too kinky.'

'Aye, ye do. Once you're in ma clutches, you never get free. I'll tease you tae the limit of your endurance.'

'Uh, I'm sure you will.'

'You'll phone me soon.' She opened the cabin door and stood back. 'Now get the fuck oota here.'

He did as he was told.

❖

Annette and Justine looked up, startled, as the changing-room door suddenly opened.

'Youse two still here?' said Claudia. 'Come on, there's punters waitin'.'

They emerged into the corridor, like fugitives from a priest hole. At first Justine held back.

'He's no' here,' said Claudia. 'You're a' right.'

The lounge was empty, but there was someone in the sauna and sounds of activity from the shower area. Annette had used the time to get Justine cleaned up. She was looking good, though her mask of sophistication remained fragile. She seemed less talkative these days, and that helped.

'What happened?' she asked. 'Where is he?'

'Don't you worry,' said Claudia. 'He'll no' be botherin' you again.'

Annette giggled. 'Where did you hide the body?'

Claudia smiled, but said nothing further.

Annette didn't press her. They would find out soon enough.

A customer came in from the shower. Annette knew him. He was a quiet man, who never gave any trouble. She nudged Justine and whispered in her ear. 'Go on, get the man a drink.'

❖

The shift change came, as usual, at five o'clock. Annette, Justine and Claudia were replaced by Miranda, Misty and Melanie. Annette had offered to drop Justine off at the bus station, and they went off together to the street where Annette's car was parked. Apart from the one extremely unlucky incident, Justine had got through her first day reasonably well, and had even made some money. Annette, too, had done all right. The competition was much stiffer when she was on with either Miranda or Candy.

As Annette was unlocking her car, they saw a man walking towards them. Annette recognised him, but at first couldn't place him. At the same time, he noticed her and beamed at her as if they were old friends. 'Hi there, Annette. How's it going?'

Annette remembered who he was. 'Hello,' she said. 'I'm fine. Do you know Justine? Justine, this is Derek, Miranda's husband.'

Justine and Derek shook hands and the three of them stood chatting for a moment or two. 'You two just finished?' Derek asked. Annette nodded. 'I've just dropped Miranda off for her evening shift. It's a hard life, eh?' he added, winking at them. 'The wife working, having to make my own tea.'

As before, Derek was expensively and fashionably dressed. Quite the dapper man about town.

'Have you just finished work, Derek?' Annette asked.

It was a rather pointed question, but it didn't produce the slightest dent in Derek's affability. 'No,' he said. 'I'm between jobs just now. Miranda's the breadwinner; I'm the house husband. Never mind, she keeps me in the style to which I've been accustomed.' He winked at them again. 'I'd better get going. I'm meeting some friends for a drink. See you later, girls.'

They said goodbye and watched for a moment as he carried on up the street. Annette remembered what Miranda had said about her husband, about his attitude to her work, shortly after their previous encounter. That Derek was 'cool about it'. This now seemed like something of an understatement.

Justine seemed to have reached a similar conclusion. 'Is that Miranda's man?' she said. 'He's a real smoothie.'

'You can say that again.'

'Have they got any weans?'

'I don't think so. No, they haven't. I asked her once.' That would interrupt her career, Annette supposed, and neither of them would want that.

Justine shook her head. 'I think that's terrible. I mean, you and me, we're doin' it because we've got tae, because we've got weans tae feed and we've no' got a man any more. But they don't have weans, he just lets her work as a . . . at what we dae, an' lives like a king. What kinda man would dae that?'

There was a word for it. On the other hand, Justine's attitude was rather old-fashioned. If you believed (as Annette did) that there was nothing to be ashamed of in what she did for a living; if you also believed (as she did) that it was perfectly acceptable for the woman to be the family's wage earner, then, logically, there was nothing wrong with being a man in Derek's position.

Unfortunately, they were in an area of human relations where logic didn't always rule. And did the bugger have to be so bloody *smug* about it?

'I know what you mean,' she said to Justine. 'But I suppose it takes all kinds.'

30

Another Return Visit

For several months after the third murder, Jack remained estranged from Annette. A week after their argument, he phoned her and they met for a drink to talk things over. A week after that they had their postponed cinema date. Annette had calmed down and no longer blamed him for speaking to the police. The source of the press leak had been identified and Annette had her job back. They should have been able to carry on from the point where they left off.

But somehow they couldn't quite manage it. A shadow had been cast over their relationship, a shadow caused by the nature of Annette's job. It would probably have happened eventually, but the publicity surrounding the last murder had highlighted the problem at an earlier date.

Was he being fair in his attitude? He was aware of the arguments to the contrary: there was nothing wrong with what Annette did, only the prejudice and double standards of society caused the problem; she always practised safe sex and had regular blood tests; the sex she had with customers wasn't real lovemaking, it didn't qualify as unfaithfulness to your regular partner. In any case, as a former client, what right did he have to criticise?

The reasoning was sound, but emotionally he remained unconvinced. And so their relationship lapsed. However, he found it less easy to forget her. In a way it was even worse than in the old days, when he could at least see her on a commercial basis. But he couldn't go back to that now. And she had spoiled him for other women, working ones or otherwise. Even Morag gave up on him and acquired a boyfriend. It was a frustrating period.

Meanwhile, he passed all of his first-year exams and worked extra hours in the bar over the summer. His financial position improved. Annette never disappeared entirely from his thoughts, but took enough of a back seat to let him get on with his life.

Then, one evening in late autumn, Candy reappeared in the Centurion. Once again she showed up on a weekday, with two other women, though Jack couldn't be sure if they were the same ones as before.

'See thae three over there?' said Les. 'They're on the game.'

'Is that right?' Jack said. 'How much did they charge you?'

'Very funny. Joe MacBride told me. They came intae the Aragon while I was on my break.'

'How does Joe know? Personal experience, or did somebody tell him?'

'Joe knows aboot these things,' said Les. He grinned furtively at Jack, like a schoolboy sharing a dirty joke. 'I'm telling you, they're all at it. An' they're not bad, eh? Especially that blonde. I wouldnae mind at all.'

'Stop smoking for a month, then maybe you'll be able to afford her.'

'No' me,' said Les, 'If I want my photie taken, I'll go tae a booth in Central Station. Anyway, you'll never catch me payin' for it, no' in a million years.'

It was odd, Jack thought, how many men had the same attitude, yet remained obsessed by the subject. Every time a new issue of the *North Clyde Advertiser* appeared, Les would be the first to check out the latest batch of men to be caught with their pants newly back on. By now the Rosevale Sauna had closed, but before that, as the photo opportunities outside that particular establishment had begun to dwindle, the paper had begun to target another sauna. This one occupied a small, self-contained building in a back lane off Sauchiehall Street. It wasn't in a residential area, and was located even more discreetly than the one in the Merchant City, but that didn't seem to deter the paper's self-righteous crusade. At one point their cameraman had been mysteriously beaten up – and duly awarded martyrdom in the editorial column – but this had caused only a temporary pause in their campaign.

So far Les had failed to see a photograph of anyone he knew, but he continued to be hopeful.

At that moment, Jack was concerned about a more immediate risk of exposure. Normally he'd have paid little attention to a rumour promoted by Les, but this one he knew to be true, in Candy's case at least. How was it going to look if she came up to the bar and greeted him like an old friend? Or was his face still indistinguishable among the scores of other men who passed through her life? He knew from Annette that she wasn't half as scatterbrained as she appeared.

As the girls came to the end of their drinks, he watched to see what would happen next. With any luck, they'd be on a pub crawl and would leave the bar. But no, they wanted another round, and Candy was getting up to buy it. And Les was serving another customer.

Candy arrived at the counter in her usual seductive fashion. 'Hello there, darlin', how you doin'?' She gave him the order, continuing to address him in a similar manner. Jack relaxed a little, and responded to the banter. He realised that Candy would greet an old friend, or accost a stranger, in exactly the same way. It was her natural instinct to come on to all men she met, new or familiar.

Then, as he was handing over her change, while Les was still busy at the other end of the bar, she said in a low voice, 'Why don't you give Annette a wee ring, Jack? She misses you.'

She immediately resumed her previous manner and left with the drinks, leaving Jack wondering if he'd imagined the message.

When these drinks were finished the girls went on their way. Candy waved over to him from the doorway. 'See you, sweetheart.'

'Well, you definitely seem tae be quoted,' said Les. Right then he reminded Jack of a panting little terrier.

'It's a gift.'

'For that blonde bit, I might just dip intae ma life savings.'

'If you had any.'

'If I had any.' He went on to elaborate upon what he would like to do to Candy. It was all very unoriginal, and Jack had a feeling that he'd heard it all before, the last time Candy had paid their bar a visit.

'What about your principles?' asked Jack. 'What about getting your picture in the paper? What about getting murdered?'

Les sighed. 'For her it might be worth it.'

Jack said, 'What's that guy Washington got against the punters who go to saunas?'

'Who's Washington?'

'The owner of the *North Clyde Advertiser*. He was on the telly, after that last murder.'

'He just wants more people tae buy the paper.'

'It's free.'

'OK, so he wants more people tae read it.'

'It certainly works with you,' said Jack. 'But there's more to it than that. You should've seen him when he was on the telly. He more or less said that the punters who got murdered deserved what they got. Makes you even wonder if . . . Jesus *Christ*!'

Les jumped, and looked around him. But no one new had entered, and the scattering of customers still had drinks. 'Fucksake, what is it?'

'I've just remembered. Jesus Christ!'

'You've just remembered what?'

'After the last murder,' said Jack, 'the police interviewed Morag and me, showed us some photographs. A few weeks later they had us back to look at a line-up. Washington was in it. I recognised him from the telly. We just assumed he was there to make up the numbers.'

'Bloody hell,' said Les. 'You mean he might've been a suspect?'

'Think about it. Why else would someone like him get involved in a line-up?'

'But what about the guy you an' Morag saw? The one you thought was a private detective?'

'No,' said Jack. 'That wasn't Washington. We were supposed to be looking for that other guy, but he wasn't there.'

'So maybe the paper man was just an extra.'

'Maybe,' said Jack. If he was a suspect, then the police hadn't been able to prove anything. Because now, three months later, he was still at large. Still interfering with the democratic rights of hard-working business men (and barmen) to treat themselves to a bit of clandestine sex.

31

Room Service

The Trongate Hotel had been built a few years earlier as part of the Merchant City refurbishment and, just as this renewal process had so far only partially reversed the decades of decline, so the hotel had not yet entirely realised its up-market ambitions. Had it been situated a few hundred yards to the north-west, nearer George Square and the city's main shopping areas, it might have proved more attractive to business visitors and tourists. It had excellent modern facilities, tucked behind a preserved nineteenth-century façade, part of the fine Victorian architecture that had made the area a target for renaissance. However, it was a little too near Glasgow Cross and was not quite free from the shadow of the East End, where the regeneration was proving more of a long-term project.

Denied the richest tourists and the most prestigious conferences, the hotel management had to look at other ways of attracting business. One recent initiative was a discreet arrangement with Edna Brady, proprietress of the nearby Candleriggs Sauna. Her ready supply of high-class girls, who would not attract notice in the hotel's lounge area and corridors, helped to entice some visitors away from the Grosvenor and the Hilton. It was a mutually beneficial arrangement. The high cost of visiting massage, designed to cover the expense of taxi fares and travel time to outlying residential areas, yielded a higher profit when the girl and her customer were only a short walk apart.

Perhaps Annette should have taken it as a compliment that she, along with Miranda, was a preferred choice for hotel visits. Both were such unlikely-looking representatives of their profession that the Trongate Hotel's more conventional guests were spared any distress by their presence. Annette certainly preferred the hotel to home visits: abandoning her own territory for that of the customer meant surrendering part of her control over the situation, and it made her uneasy. A hotel was more neutral ground. However, it meant working in the evenings, often on Friday or Saturday, with the extra cost of childcare eating into her takings. And the Merchant City was not yet an area where she felt happy walking about at night, even for the short distance to the hotel or to the street where her car was parked.

She was leaving the Trongate Hotel after attending to the needs of a travelling salesman from Newcastle when she noticed, not far from the hotel entrance, a man hanging about the street. It was a Friday evening, around eight p.m., and there was still some daylight left. The man attracted her notice for two reasons. The first was the way he was pacing back and forward, for short distances, as if he could not quite make up his mind, or pluck up the courage, to take a particular course of action. But this would have been only a passing observation had she not recognised him.

At first she couldn't remember where she'd seen the man before. The face was definitely familiar, but from a different context, not one where he was lurking in the street wearing a long overcoat buttoned up to the neck. Was he a former customer? She encountered so many men that it was difficult to be sure, but he had shown no sign of recognising her. He might have been deliberately ignoring her, but their eyes met briefly as she passed, and she didn't see the slightest hint of recognition. Only preoccupation with his impending decision, whatever it was.

She was almost back at her workplace before she placed him. He wouldn't have recognised her because they hadn't met in person before. She had seen him on TV.

'Do you know who I saw just now?' she said. 'In the street, outside the hotel?'

'Prince Charles,' said Cleo. 'I hope you gave him our business card.'

Miranda said nothing, but maintained her aloof pose, as if she were a film star waiting for a director's summons to her next scene.

'No,' said Annette. 'It was Robert Washington.'

'Now we know,' said Cleo. 'Who the fuck's Robert Washington?'

'He owns that free paper. You know, the one that takes photographs of the punters coming out of saunas. I've seen him on the telly.'

'Fuckin' hell. Well, he won't be phonin' us up. Did he have a camera?'

'Christ!' said Annette. 'No, I don't think so. No, I'd have noticed.'

'What good would that do?' said Miranda. 'Photographing people coming out of a hotel. It wouldn't prove anything.'

'You should've bought him a drink,' said Cleo. 'Because of all the punters he's steered our way.'

'He's a fucking creep,' said Annette. 'We could be his next target.'

'We've already suffered enough,' said Cleo. 'What with all them murders. Anyway, he won't pick us. He might photo some poor bastard who only came to pawn his grampa's gold watch.'

Even Miranda managed a smile. The pawnbroker's shop below them could be useful camouflage, though it was doubtful whether its owners reciprocated the feeling.

There was a brief respite from the quiet period and they managed to get a customer each. Then, around nine o'clock, someone else rang the visiting massage line. Annette was at the front desk having a chat when Edna lifted the receiver.

'Sinners' Visiting Massage,' she said, in her husky, sexy voice. To Annette it merely sounded tacky, but it didn't seem to put the customers off. 'What's that, dear? I can't quite . . . You phoned earlier? You're in the Trongate Hotel? No problem. We can have a girl over there in five minutes.' Edna slid into her well-rehearsed presentation, as if a tape had been put on. 'Tonight you have a choice of three lovely young girls. There's Miranda, the blonde supermodel, a real stunner, or there's Annette, the nice girl next door who likes to be naughty, or, if your tastes run to the exotic, we have Cleopatra, the African queen.' She said nothing about the queen's exotic Manchester accent, Annette noted, though that didn't seem to put the punters off either. 'What's that?' Edna continued. 'Yes, dear, no problem. Five minutes. Hang on, hang on, what's your room number? And your first name? Bye then.' She replaced the receiver. 'His name's John.'

'Now there's a surprise.'

'Sounds like a fuckin' wanker. He wants Miranda.'

'You mean there's a connection?'

'Don't be bitchy,' said Edna. 'You've had your turn.'

Annette went back to the lounge and told Miranda about the visit. Miranda left for the hotel, while Annette and Cleo waited on in the lounge for further business. Fifteen minutes later, Annette saw a customer come down the corridor.

'Oh no,' she said.

'What's the matter?'

'You'll find out.'

Five minutes later, the man came through from the shower room, wearing a robe and carrying a towel. He was a slightly-built man about thirty-five. He looked from Annette to Cleo and back again, then he said, 'Where's Miranda? Is she . . . engaged?' He hesitated before the last word, which seemed to have difficulty emerging.

'She's out on a visit,' said Annette.

'What do you mean?' asked the man. 'I phoned earlier. About half an hour ago. That woman at the desk, she said Miranda was here.' He looked on the point of bursting into tears.

'She was then,' said Annette. 'But we do visiting massage. She went out on a visit. About twenty minutes ago.'

'But that's not fair. She said Miranda was here.'

'She'll be back soon. She only went to the Trongate Hotel, along the road.'

'It's not fair,' he said again. 'I want Miranda.'

'Would you like a drink?' asked Cleo. But the man ignored her, turned round and walked from the room.

'Charmin',' said Cleo. 'Has he got somethin' against blacks?'

'No,' said Annette. 'Only against any woman who isn't Miranda.'

A few minutes later, she saw the man, fully dressed again, stride down the corridor. The front door banged.

Edna came through to the lounge. 'What's the matter wi' him? He never even asked for his tenner back.' Obviously she rated the visit as a partial success.

'He's in love with Miranda and she's away two-timing him.'

'Christ almighty!' said Edna. 'You don't half get them. She'll be back in half an hour, for fuck's sake. Where's he aff tae?'

'Who knows? Probably down to the Trongate Hotel.'

'Bloody hell, he'd better no' cause any trouble. We're supposed to be runnin' a discreet operation. Why the hell did you tell him where Miranda was?'

'Sorry,' said Annette.

But if the man did go to the hotel, he must have missed Miranda, for she returned an hour later without reporting anything untoward. Nor did the customer return that evening. Miranda, however, accepted the loss much more calmly than he had. She also failed to explain why she'd been away so long.

32

Room 123

When it comes to actually walking through the hotel entrance, into the front lobby, I find I've become extremely nervous, and hesitate for some time. So far my rage has driven me, but now it's checked by caution. This isn't like the show flat, a perfect location that will never be repeated. A hotel is such a public place, and this one isn't quite big enough for complete anonymity. And I don't like having to act on impulse: the forward planning that went into the last two killings was what made them so successful, so enjoyable. Since then, the wisdom of my tactics has been confirmed by three months of police bafflement.

Three months during which I've lost some of the momentum generated by the first three killings.

This time I've got no choice. The hotel location requires a quick reaction as soon as the opportunity arises. And this latest affront is too great to ignore.

I take a deep intake of breath, then exhale slowly. Stay calm. Look casual. To the staff I'll seem just like any other guest, one who checked in before their shift began. I walk into the recessed entrance, through the revolving door.

I don't seem to attract any attention as I cross the small lobby. The woman behind the desk is attending to a guest, a couple with their back to me are entering the bar. Resisting the temptation to use the stairs, I press the button that will summon the lift. I'm only going to the first floor, but don't want any observers to notice that.

The lift has been sitting at the ground floor and the door opens immediately. It's empty. I walk in and press the button for the first floor.

My luck holds out as I step into an empty corridor. All hesitation has now gone as I walk quickly along and knock on the door of Room 123.

No answer. Where is he? I wait for what seems like an interminable time, growing nervous again in case someone should come along the corridor. If I'm seen at this stage, I'll have to abandon the whole thing. Why doesn't he answer? The corridor is still empty. I knock again.

'Who is it?' The voice is hesitant, surprised.

'Message from the front desk.'

There is a further delay, then the door opens a fraction. Time to use the surprise element again. I quickly push the door open, putting all my modest weight behind it. It cracks him on the forehead and I jump on him as he falls back. I sit astride him, banging his head repeatedly on the floor. The blows are cushioned by the carpet, but he is stunned long enough for me to get the chloroform out.

My attack may have been planned at short notice, but my essential equipment is quite portable, carried about in readiness. It includes a knife and a length of strong cord.

As soon as he is supine, I drag him away from the door and close it upon the still-empty corridor. I've been lucky – that part was risky. Another guest could easily have seen everything on the way to the lift.

I find that the danger has added an extra excitement, one that helps make up for the lack of detailed preparation.

But now the most dangerous part is over. The situation is under my complete control. When he regains consciousness he is tied to the bed, his mouth taped.

When I surprised him, he was fully dressed. Now I've removed his clothes, so that he can be found in his full shame. However, I've left on his socks. There's something endearingly sleazy about that.

I leave his mouth taped while I explain what is to happen and my reasons for doing it. Then I remove the tape, having first put the knife to his throat and told him what will happen if he tries to shout for help. In this respect the location is much less ideal than the show flat: ungagged, he could probably summon help very quickly. It would only need an adjoining room to be occupied, or a hotel guest or staff member to be walking down the corridor. But he shows no inclination to make a noise. He seems resigned to his fate, not even in a mood to argue or plead. He's probably in shock, but there seems to be more to it than that. Almost as if he accepts the justice of what's happening to him.

I suppose that's something I should welcome, but somehow it spoils things a little.

I take off my outer clothes and fold them neatly over a chair, where they'll be well clear of any spurting blood. I keep on my underclothes. Must have some decorum. 'It's all right,' I assure him, 'I'm not after your body.' Then I realise the humour of this and laugh. 'Well, I am, I suppose, but not in the usual way.' He doesn't respond. He may have accepted his destiny, but not enough to see the funny side.

After this anticlimax, I have to work at summoning the necessary fury. But then I remind myself, over and over again, of why he has been chosen, and soon the job is done.

I take a leisurely shower in his en suite bathroom, cleaning up after me with a thoroughness that will shame the hotel maid; just as well, as she'll have her hands full with the rest of the room. After putting my clothes back on, I wipe every surface where I might have left prints. I have to walk carefully to avoid stepping on blood. After all my trouble, I don't want to leave a clear red footprint on the carpet.

The corridor is still empty as I leave the room. I pause only to wipe the door handle before taking my leave. This time I use the stairs, and soon I'm casually walking across the vestibule and out the front door. As far as I can tell, I've attracted no attention.

As soon as I'm well clear of the hotel I stop to take a deep breath. I almost shout aloud in elation. I've done it again.

And I've got away with it. I'm sure of that.

33

Helping with Inquiries

Another request for a hotel visit came through about ten o'clock. Again it was for Miranda. Business had remained slow and the girls had been hoping to leave early. But Miranda seemed reluctant to make the visit for a different reason.

'I've already done one,' she said. 'Why can't one of the others go?'

'He asked for you,' said Edna.

'He wants a member of the master race,' said Cleo.

'That's right,' said Annette. 'Young, blonde and Caucasian.'

'What the fuck are youse two talkin' about?' said Edna. 'He specifically asked for you, Miranda. He's met you before.'

'I don't want to do another visit,' said Miranda. 'Not after the last one. You don't know what that man was like.' She shuddered. 'What a creep!'

'But this one's a pussy cat. You've had him before. Go on, it'll be a dawdle.'

It took a little more persuasion, but Miranda eventually complied. 'The rest of you might as well pack it in,' said Edna. 'The night's dead.'

On the way to her car, Annette pondered over Miranda's unusual desire to turn away business. Was it possible she had just a little of the good taste that ought to have accompanied her classy looks?

By next morning another possibility had arisen.

Annette met Miranda at the police station, after they had both been called in for interview. Annette was waiting to be dealt with as Miranda was on her way out.

Her colleague seemed to be in some distress. 'It's awful,' she told Annette. 'Would you believe it? They seem to think *I* might have done it.'

'Done what?'

'Murdered that man. The one I visited at the hotel last night.'

'For God's sake!' said Annette. 'You mean there's been *another* murder?' Until then, she had thought she'd been called in about the previous one, though it had seemed a little odd after all this time.

'It's preposterous. You should have heard the way they spoke to me. As if I was nothing but a . . . but a common . . . Who do they think they are?'

Annette wondered what had offended Miranda more, the suspicion of murder or the damage to her middle-class self-esteem. The latter, by a convenient exercise in doublethink, had no doubt been kept segregated from the part of Miranda's mind that acknowledged the nature of her profession. And there was nothing, as Annette knew, like a police interview to bring the two crashing together.

'Are they letting you go?' Annette asked.

'Of course. Why should they keep me here? I haven't done anything, except what he paid me for. He was still alive when I left him.'

Annette was interviewed by DS Madigan, along with a policewoman. As before, though there was nothing specific that could form the basis of a complaint, she felt she was being regarded as a member of some sub-human species; this impression, she now

214

suspected, derived mainly from Madigan, rather than the police in general. However, on this occasion she didn't seem to be the main focus of attention. She told Madigan about having seen Robert Washington outside the hotel earlier in the evening. She also gave her best estimate, under Madigan's insistent questioning, of the period during which Miranda had been gone on her first visit. Madigan seemed anxious to determine, as precisely as possible, exactly when Miranda had left the sauna and when she had returned. After that, he seemed to be finished with her.

Annette told him about the customer who had been looking for Miranda. At first Madigan seemed uninterested, impatient to interrupt her, as if she were wasting his time.

Then she said, 'He sounds a bit like the man Jack Morrison saw, the one who was following him.'

'Jack Morrison?' said Madigan. 'Oh, of course. The barman. Your *friend*.'

Annette tried to ignore the innuendo. 'The guy I'm talking about, he's a regular customer. He's obsessed with Miranda. If he sees another customer with her, he looks as if . . .'

'As if what?'

'As if he'd like to kill the other guy.'

'Does he really?' said Madigan. 'And what's this aggressive wee man's name?'

'I don't know. He calls himself Johnny.'

Madigan laughed briefly. 'That figures. I suppose there's no point in asking if he gave you his address. So you think this might be the same man who was following your friend Jack?'

'The description sounds similar.'

'One thing about Glasgow,' said Madigan, 'is that it's full of funny wee guys, quite a few of them aggressive. And before you

215

decide to give up your . . . profession . . . and join the police force, there's one thing you seem to have overlooked. You say this man you saw last night is obsessed with Miranda, that he hates her customers?'

'That's right.'

'So why would he be interested in your friend Jack? Has he been two-timing you with Miranda? Did he ever succumb to her undeniable charms?' He smirked at the policewoman, but she remained impassive.

'No,' said Annette, a little flustered. 'Well, not for a long time. Maybe at the beginning, before we got friendly.'

'I think we're on to a red herring,' said Madigan. 'But if this man shows up at your sauna again, phone us right away. And tell your boss and the other girls the same.'

This seemed like a reasonable approach. The only apparent flaw in the arrangement was the concept of Edna phoning the police; here Annette's imagination failed her.

❖

Madigan did not like being told how to do his job by a hooker, but he thought the matter worth mentioning to the chief inspector.

'We seem to be acquiring an odd group of consultants,' said MacDermott. 'Shrinks, whores and comic singers.'

'Who's the singer?'

'I'm expecting one to show up any minute. Anyway, maybe the psychologist was right after all. What do you make of Miranda's story? Do you think she's our man, if you know what I mean?'

'She was absent from the sauna for well over an hour,' said Madigan. 'She says she was so disgusted by the punter that she went for a drink.'

'Poor, sensitive wee lassie. That should be easy enough to confirm. That she went for a drink, I mean. She's not exactly the type to go unnoticed.'

Madigan smiled lasciviously. 'I have to keep reminding myself that I'm a married man.'

'I know,' said MacDermott. 'And I'm old enough to be her father. She's not worth losing your pension over.'

'Why does a girl like that do it?'

'Probably from some deep Freudian need. Like wanting the money.'

'While we're on the subject of psychology,' said Madigan, 'the TV shrink did say that the killer was a woman, a hooker. But he also said she'd be older, beginning to lose her clients. Doesn't sound like our Miranda.'

'If that wanker got anything right,' said MacDermott, 'it was purely by accident. But you've put your finger on it, if you'll pardon the expression. What possible motive could Miranda have?'

'A subconscious hatred of her job and her clients?'

'Give us a break. We've already got one fucking shrink too many.'

'So how did the killer know the room number? If it wasn't Miranda, that is.'

'By phoning the hotel, maybe. We'd better check that out. Would they have given out that information? Did anyone actually call?'

'I'll get on to it.'

'And while we're talking to the hotel staff, make sure they've got the message. Anyone who breathes a word to the press gets thrown in jail. The same goes for the sauna team. We don't want a media circus like the last time. If we can keep a lid on it, maybe we'll just be able to flush our man out.'

'Or our woman.'

'I hope not,' said MacDermott. 'If only to prove that bloody psychologist wrong. Anyway, check out that bar she says she was in. That should settle the matter.'

'What about this guy the other one mentioned? The one who hates Miranda's clients?'

'You did the right thing,' said MacDermott. 'I don't think there's anything in it, but make sure everyone in the Candleriggs Sauna knows to phone us the minute he shows his face. And have another word with Jack the john. Maybe he's been having a fling on the side with the blonde superhooker and his girlfriend doesn't know about it.'

'We must be in the wrong business,' said Madigan. 'How much do they pay barmen these days?'

❖

'Did you see tonight's *Times*?' asked Les.

'Don't tell me you've started buying your own papers,' said Jack. 'Or did someone leave it in the bar?'

'That's just the point. I wouldnae bank on gettin' a free one this week.'

'What do you mean?' Jack took the tabloid paper from Les, then abandoned the customers to him as the front page captured his attention:

NEWSPAPER OWNER BUTCHERED
IN HOTEL ROOM
RETURN OF THE SAUNA SLAYER?

Police and hotel staff remained tight-lipped today about the death of newspaper man Robert Washington, found murdered

218

in his room at the Trongate Hotel this morning. They refuse to speculate about whether it is the work of the sauna slayer, the unknown killer of three massage parlour patrons earlier this year.

It can surely be no coincidence that the Trongate Hotel is located only a few yards from the Candleriggs Sauna (formerly the Merchant City Health Centre). That sauna became the focus of attention for the earlier killings, when it was revealed that all three of the victims had been its regular clients.

Yet Robert Washington does not seem to fit the profile of the earlier victims. He was not a patron of the saunas, but their declared enemy, regularly publishing photographs of their customers in his free newspaper, *The North Clyde Advertiser*.

Police today refused to speculate about why Mr Washington, who lived in Glasgow, had booked a room in the Trongate Hotel. Staff at the hotel and the Candleriggs Sauna have also refused to comment.

Mr Washington (35) was unmarried and leaves behind an elderly mother.

'What do you think?' asked Les. 'Really weird, eh? If you ask me, the sauna owners clubbed together to hire a hit man. They probably got a few of their customers to chip in.'

'You never know,' said Jack. 'Well, at least you don't need to worry about getting photographed any more.'

'How do you mean?'

'If you still fancy Can . . . I mean, if you've still got your eye on that blonde, you don't need to worry about your picture appearing in the paper. All you need to do is find the money.'

'Fuck off,' said Les. 'I'd never pay for it.'

'It doesn't stop you being obsessed by the subject.'

But Jack wasn't able to stay on the offensive for long. Shortly afterwards, when the local news came on the TV, the programme makers pulled out the library picture of Annette leaving her place of work, just after the previous murder. Les, already stationed beneath the screen while thirsty customers waited, looked momentarily startled, then watched the item to its end. 'I know her. Wasn't she . . .'

Jack looked up from the pint he was pouring. 'What are you havering about now?'

'That girl fae the sauna. I thought she looked like . . . No, it cannae be.'

'I wasn't watching,' said Jack, though he had been. 'I was too busy serving. I could do with a hand here.'

Les said nothing further and took an order. The evening had got off to a bad start, Jack thought.

Fifteen minutes later, he felt it deteriorate further when he saw DS Madigan enter the bar. 'Could you hold the fort for a bit?' he said to the intrigued Les. 'I think this man wants a word with me.'

34

Claudia's Vault

For several weeks Martin Kane kept Claudia's business card carefully hidden, occasionally bringing it out for inspection when he felt completely safe from discovery. Usually that was in the car, when he was stopped in traffic, and he could retrieve the card from beneath the crack in the glove compartment lining. Then he would remind himself of what was on it, and of Claudia. Not that this was really necessary, but just seeing the card brought everything back even more vividly.

He was fairly sure that his hiding place was secure. Nowhere in the house, or on his clothing, or in his wallet, would have been safe from Rose. It might have taken her some time, but eventually the card would have come to light. He tried to picture Rose's reaction if she found it. But he was a man of limited imagination, and in this he was defeated. He wouldn't like it, he was certain of that.

But the car was – almost – out of her jurisdiction. She had her own car and normally would only be in his when they were going somewhere together. It wouldn't be beyond her to give his vehicle the occasional going over, with the thoroughness of a customs officer searching for drugs, just on the off chance that she might find something incriminating. But her opportunities to do this were limited.

He had already memorised the card's contents. Soon he could

dispose of it, but for the moment he still liked to have a look at it now and then.

He still hadn't decided whether to phone Claudia. She represented new territory, unknown and possibly dangerous. But that was what made it exciting. That was why he couldn't get her out of his head.

Meanwhile the situation at work had deteriorated further. His father had actually carried out his threat and made that little bastard Anderson a director of the company. Then their next decision, easily outvoting Martin and deaf to his protests, had been to discontinue the manufacture of Kane's Krisps and Kane's Kola. 'We need to stick to the business we know,' Kane senior had said. 'The one that actually produces a profit. And that's making lemonade and the other drinks in our original range.' And the upstart Anderson had smirked his agreement, leaving Martin powerless to intervene. The contraction would take place gradually, to minimise disruption. The workers involved in the discontinued products would all be redeployed or given voluntary redundancy; his father took an old-fashioned, paternalistic view of business and liked to look after his people.

For the time being, that also included his son Martin, whose role in the company had virtually been obliterated by the decision. Gone were his ambitions to penetrate further into the licensed trade business; instead they had turned their back on that market, to concentrate on their traditional retail outlets. After the last stocks of crisps and cola had been shifted, Martin would be back trying to sell lemonade to corner shops, if he had any job at all. Anderson was probably already plotting to get him voted off the board of directors.

At the first opportunity, Martin resorted to the usual outlet for his frustration. This came on a Saturday, on his way back from the golf club, when there was a temporary gap in Rose's surveillance. He picked up a whore in Waterloo Street, drove to a quiet place and gave her a good battering. He felt he might have overdone things a little this time, but it made him feel a lot better.

Afterwards, he decided that he had better block off that particular avenue of satisfaction for a while. There had been press stories about violence against prostitutes and the police were on the alert. You'd think the police had enough real crime to deal with, without bothering honest taxpayers who were helping to clean up the streets, but that was the cops for you. It would be safer to withdraw his pest control services for a little while.

His immediate craving for violence assuaged, he began to calm down a little. His thoughts quickly returned to Claudia. Should he phone her? To hell with it, why not? He needed *some* kind of excitement in his life.

First, he needed to achieve the necessary combination of money and time. Funds he wouldn't have to account for either to his father or to Rose, coupled with a period when both of them had temporarily released him from custody. Claudia's vault, he reckoned, would require a sizeable amount of each commodity. It wouldn't be enough to leave work an hour early with a few pounds skimmed from expenses.

Ironically, the winding down of the crisps and cola business provided the finance. He was able to divert some slush money, intended for the bribery of pub managers, entirely his own way, instead of merely taking his usual percentage. Then Rose unwittingly completed the conjunction.

'I'm going to stay with Mother next weekend,' she said. 'She hasn't been keeping well. I'll take Sheena with me. The schools are on holiday the week after, so we don't need to hurry back.'

'Am I not invited?' Martin asked. He knew he was asking for trouble as soon as he opened his mouth, but sometimes he couldn't help it.

'Do you want to go?'

'Not really.'

'Well, don't ask stupid questions. Mother always likes to see Sheena; it'll make her feel better. In your case . . .'

There was no need for her to say anything more. As usual, Sheena endured her father's humiliation in silence, steadfastly looking down at the breakfast table throughout the exchange.

But while outwardly assuming martyrdom he was inwardly triumphant. Rose's mother lived on the east coast, in a small Fife fishing village, several hours' drive away. She and Sheena would be staying overnight on Saturday and Sunday. It was still only Tuesday. There was time for him to organise something.

He tried to phone Claudia three times that day before he got through. The number belonged to a mobile phone, which was switched off on the first two occasions. On his third attempt, a gruff voice answered after several rings.

'Hello?'

'Is that . . . Is that Claudia?' His throat was dry and he found it difficult to speak without stuttering. He was using his own mobile, from his car, which was parked near the premises of a customer he had just visited. He didn't trust himself to handle this call while driving or stopped in traffic.

'Yes. This is Claudia.' The voice had now changed, transformed at the use of her name into its polite, professional mode.

'I . . . I met you at the Candleriggs Sauna. You gave me your card.'

'Oh yes. When was that?'

'About three weeks ago.'

'Three weeks? You took your time. You've been a bad boy.'

'Uh, I didn't have a chance before. But my wife's going away this weekend. I don't know if that's . . . Is that too soon?'

'I'll need to look at my diary. What did you say your name was?'

'Uh, John.'

'Oh yes, I think I remember you. Hang on till I check.'

She kept him holding for so long that he thought they'd been cut off. But of course that was her style, keeping men waiting. He was beginning to worry if the battery in his phone would last out when she returned.

'Yes, I'm free on Saturday.'

That should do. But what if Rose was late in leaving? Couldn't risk it. 'Saturday's not so good. What about Sunday?'

'Really, John, you're a terrible nuisance. Hold on.'

Another interminable wait. Then, 'Yes, Sunday's OK. I've had a cancellation.'

'That's . . . That's great. Where is . . . I mean . . .'

'Where's what?'

'Your place. Your . . . your vault.'

Claudia chuckled, and her accent lapsed for a moment. 'I cannae afford a real vault. The rent would be too high. This is a visitin' massage service.'

'Oh.'

'So I'll need your address, John. And your real name.'

'Oh.' Danger signals sounded. This would mean losing control, exposing himself too much. But Claudia had to be the one in charge, that was what she was about. That was why he had phoned her in the first place. All the same . . .

'Or I could meet you in a hotel. It wouldn't be so private though. When you scream out in ecstasy, they might call the police.' She was

225

back to her professional voice, low, husky, persuasive. And very sexy. He conjured up her image and could almost feel, almost smell her presence.

'I'm not sure.'

'Yes, you are, John. You're a man who isn't afraid to reach out and take what he wants. I can tell. And you're not the kind of man who needs to hide behind a phoney name. What's your real name?'

'Uh, Martin.' There was no great harm in telling her that much. What about the rest? No, it was unthinkable. But while his brain clamoured for caution, the lower part of his body was promoting an alternative view. And the thought of doing it in the marital home, in Rose's territory, in the bed he shared with her . . . What an adventure! And forever afterwards he would know, could conjure up the memory, and Rose would have no idea. He almost laughed aloud at the thought.

'Well, Martin, what do you say?'

Fuck it. 'Yes, why not. I'll go for it.'

'Great. You won't regret it, Martin. I'll make sure of that.'

'How much will it cost?'

When she told him he almost called it off. But the project was now flying at full speed, out of control, and it was too late to apply the brakes. His illicit fund was large enough to cover it. In a moment she had his full name and the address of his house in Newton Mearns. Claudia, with her travelling vault, would be calling at two p.m. on Sunday.

It was the planned desecration of Rose's personal space that persuaded him to go ahead. For the house was indisputably Rose's territory: his name beside hers on the title deeds, his financial contribution to the expensive fittings, were only formalities. It was Rose who had chosen the house, the heirlooms were from her

226

family, it was she who had bought (though partly with his money) the many expensive antiques. He was a mere lodger in a private museum. Having sex in the house with Claudia would be like shitting on Rose's Persian carpet. Undetectably. That was the best thing about it.

❖

DCI MacDermott wondered why he'd let himself be talked into the press conference. There was so little information he was prepared to divulge that it might be difficult to keep the proceedings going for any length of time. He successfully fielded questions about whether the murder of Robert Washington was linked with the three earlier ones; so far the exact circumstances of his death and his reason for being in the hotel had been successfully withheld from the public. Whether this would achieve anything he still wasn't sure. The police knew it was the same killer, and the killer, unless he was completely stupid, knew that they knew. And if the murderer had been completely stupid they would have caught him by now.

But his instinct told him that they should avoid conducting the investigation in public, as they had last time. The more it was deprived of facts, the wilder the press speculation grew. Creating in the process, he hoped, camouflage that would hide the police's real activities. At least that was the theory.

Unfortunately, at that moment, he was having to confront their speculation in public.

'What about the theory that the killer is a woman?' asked a female reporter.

MacDermott smiled patronisingly. 'I support equal opportunities in all walks of life. But there's really no evidence for that.'

'Dr MacDuff of Strathkelvin University says that the killer is a prostitute – an ageing one, who's beginning to lose her clients. That, as a child, she—'

'I've heard Dr MacDuff's theory.'

'What do you think of it?'

'We haven't ruled out any possibilities.'

'Is it true that you've retained Dr MacDuff as a consultant?'

'No, it isn't. We already have psychological consultants and our own profiles of the killer. Several alternative ones. I'm not able to say any more at the moment.'

That should keep them confused, he thought. It might even do the same for the killer. It was worth a try.

❖

Claudia arrived at Martin's house exactly on time. By then he was in a condition of high sexual excitement and terror, uncertain which was which.

In the days that had followed their phone conversation, his feelings had pulled violently in opposite directions. At times caution prevailed and he became appalled at his recklessness. Several times he almost phoned Claudia to cancel; on two occasions he actually did call her, but her phone was switched off again. Then he thought of his encounter with her at the Candleriggs Sauna, and the prospect of Sunday filled him with an excitement more intense than he'd ever experienced before.

And yet certain fears remained. What if Rose changed her mind about the trip, or postponed it, or decided to leave Sheena behind? What if he couldn't get in touch with Claudia to call it off? How would he handle a confrontation between Claudia and Rose?

By flight, probably. A pity, as it would be a well-matched, heavy-weight encounter.

But Rose had left on time, taking Sheena with her. With some reservations, he could see, about leaving him so much unaccustomed freedom.

'Take good care of the house while we're away,' she had said. 'Though I suppose there's a limit to what even you can do to it in two days.'

What did she think he might get up to? That he might invite a few male friends round for drinks, risking a few wet, circular stains on her antique sideboard? She wouldn't credit him with any more imagination than that. 'Don't worry,' he said. 'The house is safe in my hands.'

'What are you smirking at?'

'Sorry.' He made an effort to appear solemn.

'Remember to set the alarm if you go out. You know how to do that, don't you?'

'I think you care more about this house than you do about me.'

'You don't want me to answer that, Martin. Come on, Sheena.'

She had phoned at two p.m. on Saturday to confirm they'd arrived safely and to check whether he'd gone out. She rang again at ten p.m., at nine thirty the following morning, to see if he was out of bed, and again just before lunch. He'd told her that he'd probably be playing golf on Sunday afternoon, in case she should phone while Claudia was there.

And now Claudia *was* here, with Rose and Sheena safely at the other side of the country.

She was dressed plainly enough, in sweater and jeans, and carried a small holdall. Martin looked anxiously out at the empty driveway as he let her in. 'Where are you . . . ? How did you . . . ?'

'I came in my car,' said Claudia. 'And I'm parked at the end of the road. Don't worry, Martin. This is a discreet service.'

'Of course.' He closed the front door behind her and stood awkwardly beside her in the hall. Claudia, with her usual self-possession, appraised her surroundings.

'This is a really nice place you've got, Martin.'

'Thanks.'

'I couldn't help noticing that it's a bit isolated. At the end of the road, well away from your neighbours.'

'Uh, yes. We like our privacy.'

'That's good. We may need that. Just in case your pleasure gets a bit noisy, I mean. We don't want the neighbours prattling to your wife.'

'I said I didn't want anything too . . .'

Claudia gave her sexy laugh. 'Don't worry, Martin. I've left the whip and the thumbscrews at home. I know just what you need.' She looked at the stairs, which led from the large hall to the floor above. 'So are we going to stay here all day, or are you going to take me to the scene of the action?'

'Of course.' He led her up the thickly carpeted stairs.

'Nice pictures you've got. Is that one an original?'

'I think so.'

They went into the master bedroom. The covers were folded back on the large double bed, the central heating radiator turned on. Claudia walked around the room, stopping at the window, where she looked out at the long back garden and the empty field beyond. She opened the window, inspected the double glazing, then closed it again.

'I thought the main bedroom would've been at the front.'

'No, it's at the back.'

'So I see. Very nice. When did you say your wife was coming back?'

'Tomorrow night. Don't worry. We won't be disturbed.'

'Oh, *I'm* not worried,' said Claudia. 'Right, I'll go and change. You take your clothes off and get comfortable.'

She made for the door. He made to follow her.

'Where the fuck are you goin'?'

'To . . . to the toilet.'

'You never asked permission. I'm in charge, remember?'

'Sorry. Can I go to the toilet, please?'

'OK, but make it quick.'

She waited in the bedroom until he left. When he returned, she was gone. He took off his clothes, lay down on the bed and waited.

And waited. This was Claudia's style, of course, what he had expected, but wasn't she overdoing it a little? He was about to put on his dressing gown and go looking for her when she returned.

She still carried the holdall, though its zip was now open. Her appearance didn't come as a surprise, though he relished it all the same: black PVC underwear, matching stockings and boots, and her white-skinned body was as firm and voluptuous as before.

'Lie on your back.' She put the holdall beside the bed, within easy reach, and crouched over him, her cleavage a few inches from his nose. His interest was growing.

She stroked his right arm, gently prising it outwards from his body. Then, before he had quite taken in what was happening, she had brought a piece of cord from the holdall and was tying his wrist to the bedpost.

'Hey!' he said. 'What's going . . . I didn't . . .'

He tried to get up, but she was sitting on him, pinning him down. 'Sssh!' she said soothingly, stroking his hair. 'It's all right. This is just what you need. Trust me.'

He hesitated, relaxing a little, temporarily overcome by her perfume, the warmth of her body, her overpowering presence. In a moment his reservations had returned, but by then his other wrist was tied. He pulled on each bond, but without success. The cord was soft, but strong, her knots just tight enough to do their job without impeding his circulation. He was comfortable, but he was her prisoner.

His momentary panic subsided. To hell with it. He was going to enjoy this.

She tested the bonds herself, making sure they were secure. Then she got up and stood beside the bed, hands on hips, looking down at him triumphantly. 'Now I've got you where I want you.'

She turned and walked from the room, closing the door behind her.

Martin lay naked in the middle of the wide double bed, his arms pulled apart, like a horizontal crucifixion victim. Then he had a long wait, compared to which the earlier delays seemed like nothing. Where *was* she? From time to time he pulled on the cords, but they held firm, clinging snugly to his wrists. He tried to manoeuvre himself to each side of the bed in turn, attempting to reach the knots that secured him to the bedposts, but the bed was too wide and the rope had insufficient slack. His sexual excitement, which had reached a peak while Claudia straddled him, had now waned. He began to feel the need to urinate, a condition aggravated by his inability to do anything about it.

Outside the room there was silence. What was the bitch up to? Suddenly there came into his mind a half memory, from a few nights ago, of a news programme to which he had only partly been listening. Further speculation about the murders of sauna customers, a theory that the killer might be a woman, a prostitute.

Hadn't one of the victims been tied to a chair and stabbed to death? Jesus Christ! Fuck it, fuck it, fuck it! Why hadn't he paid attention? But the murders had been months ago, the speculation sparked off again by a more recent, seemingly unconnected killing. He hadn't thought that it was anything to do with him. Not then.

But he certainly did now. Christ! What a fucking idiot!

No, it had to be a coincidence. Hadn't it?

He could still hear nothing. Then, after a while – maybe ten minutes after Claudia left, though it seemed like longer – he heard a noise outside the house, behind him, on the other side of the outer wall. He tried to identify the sound. It couldn't be what it appeared to be. It couldn't possibly.

Then, faintly, from downstairs he began to hear further sounds, which he first sought to identify, then to disbelieve. They went on for a long time – at least half an hour, possibly more – sometimes from near at hand, sometimes from more remote parts of the house.

From time to time he struggled again with his bonds. But Claudia had done her work well. All he succeeded in doing was chafing his wrists.

When the bedroom door finally opened, he had entered a lethargic state, lying flat on the bed as Claudia had left him. He jumped at the sound and instinctively brought his knees up, the only defensive posture of which he was capable, a useless attempt to distance himself from the intruder.

A man entered the room. He was tall, just under six feet, and muscular in build. He looked in his mid-thirties, had short-cropped dark hair and wore a grubby shirt and jeans. His shirt sleeves were rolled up, revealing strong forearms covered with blue and red tattoos.

233

He gave Martin a friendly smile. 'Hello there, pal. How you doin'?'

Martin felt unable to reply. Another man appeared, differing from the first only in points of detail. He also smiled at Martin, but said nothing. They both walked past the bed where Martin lay, and took an end each of the Victorian dressing table, one of Rose's most precious family heirlooms. They lifted its solid mahogany frame as if it were balsa and carried it out of the room.

A short while later they returned for the matching wardrobe. This proved to be a little more heavy.

'Better empty it.'

'OK.'

The wardrobe's contents, mostly Rose's clothes, were thrown in a pile on the carpet. They carried the wardrobe to the door, then stopped for a rest.

'Bloody hot work this. I could dae wi' a drink.'

'Don't drink that cola that's in the fridge. It's fuckin' pisswater.'

They resumed work and soon the wardrobe had left the room also. Through the now open door, he could hear their good-humoured comments and curses as they carried it downstairs.

At last Claudia reappeared, dressed in her outdoor clothes again. She smiled at him. 'Hi there, Martin. How's it goin'?'

'How the fuck do you think?'

'Mind yer language.'

'Fuck my language. What the fuck's going on?'

'I thought you might have twigged by now, Martin. How fuckin' stupid are you?'

He was silenced again, as Claudia continued the work of her companions, concentrating on smaller items – chairs, bedside cabinets, bed lights, rugs, clock radio, pictures and mirrors from the walls. The men returned and removed the mahogany chest of drawers. The heap of clothes from the floor and the contents of the fitted wardrobe were bundled by Claudia into large plastic bags. Then she went over to the bed.

'Oops-a-daisy,' she said, yanking the bedclothes from under him and the pillows from beneath his head, leaving him lying on a bare mattress. Another plastic bag was filled and duly removed.

One of the men brought in a stepladder, took down the curtains and pelmet from the window, and unscrewed the curtain rails. While Claudia took these away, he moved the ladder across the floor and removed the bulb and shade from the ceiling light. Then all three of them set about unfitting the fitted carpet. This went smoothly enough until they reached the part under the bed.

'Look, he's pissed himself.'

'Big fuckin' wean.'

Martin was tossed about as they lifted each corner of the bed in turn, to remove the carpet from beneath it. Only the ropes prevented him from falling on to the floor.

Then the carpet was rolled up and gone. Martin was left alone in the room again, lying naked on a bare mattress, on a bed that sat on bare floorboards, in a room stripped of all furniture and fittings. The rest of the house, he now realised, had already been subjected to the same process. He tried to avoid thinking of other items that would be gone: Rose's prized rosewood cabinet, her grandfather's grandfather clock.

Presently, he heard voices out on the landing.

'Is that us done, Agnes?'

'Shut yer mouth, ya daft bastard! I'm Claudia, remember?'

'Sorry, Ag... Claudia.'

A chuckle from Claudia/Agnes. 'I wouldnae worry aboot it. He'll no' be tellin' the polis.'

What the hell did she mean by that? His earlier terror, in abeyance while the gang's apparent intention had been downgraded from murder to larceny, now revived. When Claudia/Agnes re-entered the room, now alone, and walked over to the bed, he resumed his defensive posture, cringing to the maximum extent that his bonds would allow.

'Don't kill me!'

Claudia/Agnes looked puzzled for a moment, then she laughed. 'Kill ye? I'm no' gonnae kill ye. I'll leave that tae yer wife.'

Considered from this point of view, the threat was not very much less.

Claudia/Agnes looked him up and down with an expression of utter contempt. 'What you did tae that lassie,' she said, 'was right out of order. An' from what I hear you've been makin' a habit of it. So you had it comin', ya bastard.'

A moment later she left, banging the door behind her. Soon the large vehicle, which he'd earlier heard being parked at the side of the house, started up again. It was, he now guessed, a large removal van, probably the largest size available. There would have been just enough room for it, provided that the driver wasn't too concerned about the health of Rose's rose bushes or the condition of the grass on the side lawn. Throughout the removal process, the van would have been hidden from the view of neighbours by the trees lining the front drive.

The bonds held well, and Martin was found by his wife and ten-year-old daughter, naked and lying in his own excrement, when they returned late the following afternoon. They had come home early, after Rose's repeated failure to raise Martin on the phone; he hadn't even known about these attempts, as all the phones had been removed.

But his family didn't return quite early enough. By that time, Martin's bank accounts had been emptied, his credit cards used up to their limits and the house's contents distributed among dealers throughout central Scotland.

35

Sex and Violins

Jack wanted to see Annette again, but for some time held back from doing anything about it. On several occasions he was on the point of phoning her at home, but his nerve failed him. A few months earlier he would have lifted the receiver and dialled her number without hesitation. But now there seemed to be an impenetrable barrier between them.

He told himself that he was being stupid. They had not parted on bad terms. There had been a certain awkwardness, but no animosity. She might decline to see him, but she wouldn't snub him. Then there was the message from Candy. Had it been sanctioned by Annette? Maybe not, but Candy probably knew Annette well enough to correctly assess her feelings on the subject. The way was probably clear if he could only make the first move.

On the other hand, there was still the problem of Annette's profession. That was still the biggest obstacle, and his mind hadn't yet worked out a way round it. This consideration and the desire to see Annette again continually pulled him in opposite directions.

The latter impulse finally prevailed late one Saturday afternoon. It was one of his few Saturdays off work, and the pleasure he took in this break was tempered by the fact that he had no idea what to do with it. After a morning spent studying in the local library, he was at a loose end. Saturday was meant to be a time for relaxation, for socialising, and if it was normally spent running around after other people in a bar, it was even more important that it should not be wasted on his Saturdays off. Provided that he had someone to relax and socialise with.

He spent most of the afternoon half-heartedly watching football on television and thinking about phoning Annette. She too would be free on a Saturday, stuck at home with her children. But it would probably be too late for her to arrange a childminder. Would she welcome him visiting her at home after all this time?

By four thirty he could see his evening stretching before him, still stuck at home in front of the TV, perhaps with a few beers to dull the feeling of isolation. He went to the phone and dialled Annette's number.

A young girl's voice answered. It sounded like Linda, Annette's regular childminder.

'Could I speak to Annette, please?'

'She just left for work. Who's that speaking?'

'A friend of hers. Jack Morrison. I didn't know she worked in the evenings.'

'She does sometimes.' Did the girl know what Annette worked at? After the publicity following the third murder it would be difficult for her not to.

'Could you tell her I called?'

'Yes,' said the girl. 'What was the name again?'

Jack told her and they rang off. So the matter was settled, for that night anyway. It would have to be a Chinese takeaway and a few cans of lager. He could always have a pint or two at the Centurion and annoy Les while he was serving. But that meant admitting that he had nothing better to do on his night off. Maybe he could hire a video.

At least Annette would now know that he had got in touch. It would be easier to make a follow-up call. She might even phone him.

Then a new thought occurred to him. Annette had never worked in the evening before, either on Saturday or any other. Maybe she had a new job. Could she have gone back to nursing?

There was one way to check. After some hesitation, he dialled the number. A British Telecom voice told him that it had changed and gave him a new one, which he tried.

'Candleriggs Sauna.'

For a moment Jack was taken aback and said nothing.

'Hello? Candleriggs Sauna.' The woman's voice sounded a little impatient. No doubt they got their share of time-wasting callers. Then Jack remembered. They had changed their name. It had been mentioned in the paper, after that last murder.

'Hello,' he said. 'Could you tell me who's on tonight, please?'

'Certainly. Tonight there's Miranda, Annette and Candy. Do you know them?'

'Yes,' said Jack, 'I do. Thanks very much.'

Yes, he did know them. All of them. Somewhat intimately, in each case. Apart from the name of the place, nothing had changed.

Annette wasn't in Paisley, or working in a hospital ward somewhere. She was in Glasgow, a couple of miles away, waiting for clients. The prospect of an evening at home now seemed even less inviting.

❖

Annette hadn't been particularly happy to get Edna's call. Having to work a second night in a row, at the weekend, sharing a shift with

Miranda and Candy, wasn't her idea of a good deal. She'd be lucky to cover the childminding expenses. Luckily, Linda had been able to come over at short notice.

Edna had asked her to fill in for Claudia, who had disappeared. 'She hasnae showed up for her last two shifts. I cannae get her on the phone.'

'That's funny. Have you any idea what's wrong?'

'Nae idea. The polis have been lookin' for her. They were here on Tuesday.'

'Is that why they were there?' Annette hadn't been working that day, but had heard of the visit. Everybody had. 'I thought it was about the murders.'

'Maybe it was,' said Edna. 'Who knows? They wouldnae tell me what it was about. Now I hear that she's been moonlightin', runnin' her ain visitin' massage service. I can tell you this, she'll no' be workin' for me again.'

For Edna, bringing the police to her premises was the greatest sin anyone could commit. It revived unhappy memories from the bad old days as well as making the customers nervous. And the only offence to run it close was cutting Edna out of her share as middle woman. Annette reckoned that she wouldn't be seeing Claudia again.

So there she was, back on duty, along with the two most popular girls. Miranda and Candy normally tried to avoid being on the same shift as each other, but Edna had talked them into it, in an attempt to revive the visiting massage trade. This had taken a dip after the Trongate Hotel severed their connection; having a guest hacked to death in his bedroom wasn't quite the discreet service they'd been looking for.

The incident had also made an impression upon Miranda.

She had been cleared of suspicion after the police checked her pub alibi; quite a few heads, unsurprisingly, had turned in her direction, and her story had been confirmed. But the feelings which had prompted this unusual diversion on her part seemed to have lingered.

She confided as much to Annette, after Candy had gone off with a customer, leaving Miranda and Annette alone in the lounge together. It was unusual for Miranda to be so forthcoming: evidently she really had been shaken. Annette even warmed to her a little. It made her seem a little more human.

'I don't want to speak ill of the dead,' she told Annette, 'but he was such a horrible man. It made me want to be sick when he touched me. You've no idea what he was like.'

'I have. I saw him on TV.'

'Well, that was it. So did I. If I hadn't recognised him, it wouldn't have been quite so bad. But there he was, bad-mouthing us in public, calling us names, publishing photographs of our customers. Then he turns up as a customer himself.'

'What a damn hypocrite.'

'That's just it,' said Miranda. 'I'm not sure that he was, not entirely. Otherwise I might have handled it better. But I don't think he'd done it before. I think he was a virgin. Can you believe it? He must have been at least forty.'

'Thirty-five, it said in the paper.'

'Really? He seemed older.'

'He must have been really repressed,' said Annette. 'Maybe that's why he was so obsessed with the subject, why he carried on that stupid campaign. He must have been bottling up his feelings for years.'

'And I had to be there when he unbottled them,' said Miranda.

She shuddered. 'It was even worse afterwards. He obviously hated himself, and me, for what had happened. He treated me with total contempt, as if I was something unclean, nothing more than a piece of garbage. He practically flung me out of the room.'

Annette tried not to smile. This was more like the old Miranda. What had touched her most was the affront to her self-esteem. It was her God-given privilege to be worshipped by all men. What right had this one to take a different line? Maybe she had murdered him after all. A quick flurry with the knife, then off to the pub to wind down.

Candy returned and another customer took Miranda away. Annette sighed. She'd had only one customer so far. It looked like being a really slow night.

'I see your boyfriend's here,' said Candy.

'What do you mean? Who?'

'What's his name. Jack, isn't it? I always meant to ask you. What's his beanstalk like?'

'You should know,' said Annette. 'What the hell's he doing here?'

'I wouldnae have thought it was too hard tae work out.'

'But he knows where I live, for God's sake. He's got my phone number.'

'Maybe he fancies a wee change. I'll take him aff your hands if you like.'

'Like fuck you will!'

'There's nae pleasin' some folk.'

❖

Jack had taken the subway to St Enoch Square and walked along Argyle Street towards Glasgow Cross, wondering if he was doing the right thing. Maybe it would have been better to wait until the following day and phone Annette again. But having come this far, there seemed little point in going back, turning a tedious evening into a totally futile one.

Soon he found himself in the familiar landscape of the Merchant City, where up-market wine bars and shops and refurbished blocks of flats mingled with run-down buildings and gap sites. The clocks had been put back the previous week, and there wasn't much daylight left; the gathering gloom seemed to give the neglected parts more prominence, casting a shadow over the areas of bright lights. The neighbourhood seemed to be dragging itself upwards with an enormous handicap, like a man climbing a mountain with a ball and chain fastened to his ankle.

The Candleriggs Sauna was situated in one of the darker side streets; round the corner were the City Hall, several trendy bars and plenty of people on the streets, but here it was much quieter. It was because of this that Jack had noticed the man standing in a shop doorway, almost directly across from the sauna. He gained the impression that the man was watching him. As Jack passed opposite, he turned his head and looked briefly across at the man, quickly looking away again.

He saw a slightly-built man of medium height, well-dressed in a nondescript way. Jack couldn't make out his features clearly, but there was something definitely familiar about him, particularly about the way he was staring at Jack. There was now no doubt about that. Then he remembered where he thought he had seen the man before.

He made up his mind to mention it to Annette. But in the event he was distracted by other things.

His impression that nothing had changed except the name of the place was quickly confirmed. The dark, smelly close and stairs, the pawnbroker's shop, closed for the weekend, the converted top-floor flat, were all familiar. The same woman sat behind the desk, taking his money, noting his name in her book, dispensing the towel and wallet. On his way to the changing room he met Candy coming out of a cabin, then saw Miranda leading a customer from the lounge. Candy greeted him with the usual come-hither smile that she offered all men, both strange and familiar; it was impossible to tell whether she had recognised him or not, though no doubt she had.

With his first sight of the girls he identified one other change in the place. Gone, along with the old name, were the white medical coats and the pretence of legitimacy, a front they presumably could no longer afford after the slump caused by their recent notoriety. Now the girls had switched to the more conventional uniform of low-cut tops, short skirts and sexy stockings.

It was a little disconcerting when he entered the lounge and met Annette in this new context. She was dressed less revealingly than Candy, as befitted their respective personalities, but the change was still noticeable. However, this more punter-friendly image was not evident in her manner towards him.

'Hi,' she said. 'I didn't expect to see you here.'

They were alone in the room, apart from Candy, who had tactfully gone over to play the machine. Jack found himself stuck for words. 'Well, here I am,' he said eventually.

'Here you are,' she said. 'Would you like a drink?'

'No thanks.'

There was an embarrassed pause. Then she said, 'There are three girls on tonight, Miranda, Candy and myself. I think you know us all. Miranda's working just now, but she shouldn't be long.'

'Cut it out,' he said. 'I came to see you.'

'Well, we'd better go through to the cabin then.'

They went to the cabin in silence. He sat on the edge of the massage table and faced her. 'What's the matter?' he asked.

'What the hell do you think? You know my number, you know where I live. I don't hear from you for months, then you show up here.'

'I wanted to see you.'

'You mean you couldn't get me into bed quickly enough, so you thought you would buy your way there?'

'It wasn't like that.'

'Or maybe you thought I wasn't good enough to be your girlfriend, but you could still keep me as your whore. Is that it?'

'No,' said Jack, 'that isn't it. I've been meaning to phone you. I finally did, earlier this evening, thinking you'd be off. I couldn't wait to see you. When I realised you were sitting here, just down the road, it seemed . . . I can see I made a mistake. I'm sorry.'

'You should be.' She had calmed down a little, but he could see that she was still angry.

'I mean, we've met here often enough before. I didn't think that—'

'That was before. I thought we'd moved beyond that stage. Don't you realise how cheap this makes me feel?'

He stood up. 'You're right. I shouldn't have come here. Maybe I should just leave. I'll phone you tomorrow, if you still want to talk to me.'

He moved towards the door, but she was standing in his way.

He stood facing her, feeling awkward. 'It's just that . . . I really missed you,' he said.

Suddenly, she grabbed him and began to kiss him frantically. He was pushed backwards, on to the massage table. She seemed intent upon devouring him alive, as if he were a delicacy she had been too long deprived of. After he had recovered from his surprise, he responded with equal passion. At one point his robe and her clothes were discarded, at another he was fitted with a condom, but neither procedure caused much of an interruption.

Then they were lying side by side, still pressed together in the enforced intimacy of the narrow bed. He had often wondered what the difference would be between their commercial encounters and real lovemaking. Now he knew.

After a while, he got up and lifted his robe from the floor. All at once he felt awkward again. Hesitantly, his hand went towards the wallet in his pocket.

'Don't you dare!'

He lifted both hands in a gesture of surrender, and the robe dropped to the floor again. 'What about Edna's share?' he asked.

'Fuck Edna.'

'No thanks.'

'I'll deal with her cut. You can make it up to me by taking me out to dinner.'

'It's a date,' he said.

After he had showered and got dressed, he went back to the lounge, where Annette was sitting alone. Candy and Miranda, he assumed, were both working. He realised that, before the night was through, Annette too would have other customers, but he was glad he didn't have to see them. Nor would he ever, if he could help it. He wouldn't be coming back here again.

Annette accompanied him to the front door, then initiated a prolonged kissing session before they finally parted. Jack wondered what the woman behind the desk made of it, but found that he didn't much care.

36

Four Jacks

So long a list, so few opportunities to shorten it. Almost as intolerable as the wait between killings is having to select the next subject. So many deserve to die. The satisfaction of administering justice is almost spoiled by simultaneously having to grant so many reprieves.

That's why it's so helpful when a subject virtually stands up and offers himself to me. Like that newspaper owner. With such an insult he was daring me to demand satisfaction.

Now another one has stuck his head above the parapet. Jack Morrison.

After some preliminary investigation earlier in the year, I had put his file aside for the time being, following upon a period of absence. He wasn't forgiven, but recent good behaviour had given him low priority.

Then he comes back and gives me the finger.

His file is now reactivated. The updated chart is conclusive:

Date of Visit	Girls on Shift		
14 Feb	Annette	Sylvia	*Miranda*
20 Feb	Chantelle	Lee	*Miranda*
24 Feb	Melanie	Misty	*Miranda*
4 Nov	Claudia	Candy	*Miranda*

Proved beyond all reasonable doubt. No jury could fail to convict. If it was only recognised as a crime.

My subjects aren't executed without a fair trial.

It's his own fault. Why did he have to come back and provoke me like that, after such a long time? Although maybe the gap wasn't so long after all. During the long wait between the third and fourth murders, I became careless, I didn't cover all of her shifts. It wasn't just negligence, it was frustration at continually having to add to the list without being able to shorten it. That must be the explanation for the gap. While I've been neglecting my duty, he's been slipping through the holes in my net.

Any doubts about my choice – and they were negligible – have now gone.

The practical problems remain. How can I ever again get a perfect location like the show flat or the hotel bedroom? Will I have to settle again for a quick assault, a summary execution, denying us the chance to mull over his fate together?

What do I know about him that might be helpful? He lives and works in the West End, on or near Byres Road. He works as a barman in a busy pub, not the best location in which to isolate a subject.

But he lives alone.

37

Insufficient Evidence

The customer who was in love with Miranda returned the following Friday, early in the afternoon. Annette was on duty along with Miranda and Justine, having done a swap with Cleo in order to get the evening off; she had been landed with the Saturday evening shift again and that was enough for her in the way of weekend work. Miranda was doing a double shift, still being in demand for the visiting market.

Annette recognised the man right away. Although she had never been with him – he had never chosen any girl apart from Miranda – she knew his face well enough. He called himself Johnny, which might or might not have been his real name. He seemed middle-class and reasonably intelligent, but immature. He must have been in his mid-thirties at least, but gave the impression of having become emotionally stuck at an earlier age.

Annette had been given plenty of opportunity to observe him in the past, usually while sitting with him in the lounge while he waited for Miranda to finish with another customer. It was a sojourn which he did not take well. His obsession with Miranda was equalled only by his hatred of her other customers. He never said or did anything about it, or made trouble of any kind – otherwise he wouldn't have been tolerated – but his animosity hung in the air, like an impending thunderstorm, only to be instantly dispelled when his turn came for Miranda's brief attentions.

On this occasion he didn't have to endure his usual frustration; when he entered the lounge, his beloved was sitting beside Annette, waiting for him. Or for someone. She greeted him with the unrestrained delight which she reserved exclusively for every one of her customers.

'Hi there! How are *you*?'

'I'm fine, Miranda,' he said shyly. 'How are you?'

'All the better for seeing you. Would you like a drink?'

'No thanks. I'll just go through when you're ready.'

'Of course. Go into Cabin Two and make yourself comfortable. I'll be with you in a moment.'

Miranda quickly finished her soft drink and got up to follow him from the room, as if it were another routine visit; her next move would be to check in with Moira at the door, a necessary precaution for security reasons, and to provide Edna with a record of the money the girls owed her.

'Hang on,' said Annette. 'Don't you recognise him?'

'Of course I do. He comes to see me quite often. His name's on the tip of my tongue.'

'It's Johnny, to save you looking it up in the book. And he's the one who came here looking for you on the night of the last murder, while you were out on your hotel visit. We're supposed to phone the police the moment he shows his face.'

'No!' said Miranda. 'I didn't realise it was him.' She seemed sincerely appalled at the idea. 'He's a little darling. I think he's quite sweet on me.'

'That's exactly the point for Christ's sake!'

'There's no need to be like that,' said Miranda huffily. 'So what are we supposed to do?'

'You keep him occupied as long as you can. I'm sure you know how. I'll phone the police.' Luckily Justine was with a customer and Annette didn't have to deal with her as well.

'I don't believe it. You want me to go into a cabin with a man you think might be a murderer?'

'I wouldn't worry about it, Miranda. You're the last person in the world he'd want to kill.'

Annette was being sarcastic, but Miranda seemed to take some comfort from her words. 'All right,' she said, with an expression of martyrdom. 'But only because I think you're wrong. It's all been some horrible mistake. He's completely harmless. I can tell.'

'There should be no problem then.'

All the same, Miranda made her way to the cabin with some reluctance. 'How can I look him in the eye, knowing what you're going to do?'

Annette felt confident that Miranda would find some way of holding the customer's attention without having to look him in the eye. She followed Miranda out of the lounge and tried the door of Edna's office. It was locked. At least Edna wasn't around, and there was no need to overcome the biggest obstacle of all.

She approached the front desk, where Moira sat, staring at the closed front door. 'I'll need to use the phone.'

'What for? Edna doesnae . . .'

'I need to phone the police. That man with Miranda, he's the murder suspect.'

'Jesus Christ!' There was no further argument.

She dialled the number Madigan had given her and got through to him straight away. She quickly told him of the suspect's reappearance.

'All right. Keep him there. We'll be right over.'

And they were, almost, though the wait seemed interminable.

Another customer arrived, and went off with Justine, who had just become free, without Annette having to tell her about the crisis. With any luck, the police would have come and gone before Justine and the customer reappeared.

She waited with Moira at the front desk until the police arrived. They both jumped as the doorbell rang, but it proved to be another customer. Moira took his money and sent him on his way to the changing room. He was a regular, who often chose Annette. She hoped he wouldn't be scared away. Maybe the police would manage a quick arrest while he was in the shower.

Madigan, along with a detective constable, arrived about ten minutes after Annette's call. 'Where is he?'

'In Cabin Two, with Miranda.'

But Madigan, showing unexpected tact, didn't seem inclined to burst open the cabin door. Edna would be grateful for that at least. 'Is there a phone in there?'

'Yes.'

'Give her a ring. Tell her to wind up the . . . ah . . . proceedings.'

Annette did as she was told. Miranda said little, but sounded relieved. A few minutes later she hurried out of the room alone. The customer wasn't far behind her, but found his way blocked by the two policemen.

'Police,' said Madigan, showing his warrant card. 'Would you mind getting dressed, please, sir, and coming with us to the station? We'd like to ask you a few questions.'

'What's it about? Where's Miranda?' But his beloved had disappeared, no doubt reluctant to face the consequences of her betrayal.

The constable accompanied Miranda's customer to the changing room. 'When your lovely colleague deigns to show her face,' said

Madigan, 'I'd like the pair of you to come down to the station. I think you both know where it is by now.'

Annette repressed her impulse to make a suitable reply, knowing that it would do no good. It would have been nice, though, to get some thanks for her public-spiritedness.

The constable returned with Miranda's customer, now in his street clothes and looking subdued, and the policemen took him away.

Annette sighed and went to look for Miranda. How long would they have to spend at the police station, enduring insults and not earning? It looked as if Justine would have a good day. At least the other customers seemed to have missed the show and might come back another time.

❖

'It's no good,' said MacDermott. 'We can't hold him. We'll have to let him go.'

'But he's our man,' said Madigan. 'I'm sure of it.'

It was now mid-evening and the suspect had been detained in police custody for more than five hours.

'You may well be right,' said MacDermott. 'But what have we actually got on him? Two witnesses saw him acting suspiciously in the West End of Glasgow. Are we supposed to arrest everyone in Byres Road who looks suspicious? Talk about prison overcrowding!'

'Morag Brown put him at the location of the third murder.'

'And he doesn't deny it. Archer spent the whole evening showing people round his show flat. The suspect admits he was one of them, claims he was looking for a new house in the West End.'

'Come off it,' said Madigan. 'That stinks.'

'But we can't prove it. We don't have any forensic evidence worth a damn. Not at any of the murder scenes. Whoever our man is, he's been very careful.'

'Why was he following Jack Morrison about, taking his photograph?'

'You know what he said. He'd been house-hunting and fancied a pint afterwards. Thought he'd try one or two pubs, see what would be his best local. He didn't take a photo, the girl must have been mistaken.'

'The pubs couldn't have been up to much,' said Madigan. 'Seeing as he still lives in the South Side. For Christ's sake, you can't believe that shite!'

'No, but it's all possible. What have we got that would prove otherwise? Besides, any case against him is based on the supposition that the targets are all customers of Miranda. Jack Morrison says he hasn't been with her for months and I'm inclined to believe him. He seems genuinely attached to Annette Somerville.'

'More fool him. Anyway, we're talking about several months ago. He was a customer then.'

'Briefly. But we can't even prove that the victims *were* all Miranda's customers. We *think* they were, but Madam Edna's books tell us nothing, since half the buggers use pseudonyms. And Miranda doesn't know, she's had so many men.'

Madigan sighed. 'All that shagging. I knew somebody was getting my share.'

'I wondered why you seemed so bitter.'

'Not half as much as I will be if you let him go.'

'I told you, we've got no choice. We've got nothing tangible on him and we don't even have grounds for a search warrant of his house. Anyway, we can put a tail on him. He's not going to rush out and commit another murder – not now that he knows we're on to him. He'd have to be mad.'

'If he's the one,' said Madigan, 'then he is.'

'Mad maybe, but not stupid. Otherwise we'd have got him by now.'

'I suppose so. Anyway, you're the boss. If we find another mutilated corpse tomorrow, it's your responsibility.'

'That's what they pay me for,' said MacDermott.

38

Sufficient Evidence

They thought they had me, but I've been too clever for them. All my careful planning has paid off. I've had to take some calculated risks, but they proved to be justified.

The session at the police station wasn't pleasant, but I managed to keep my head. When they asked me to take part in the identity parade, I was tempted to refuse, but that would have looked suspicious. Besides, what can their witnesses testify to? No one saw me actually do the murders. Apart from the subjects, but they won't be testifying.

One issue has still to be resolved. What do I do next?

The safest course would be to retire. At the moment I'm in the clear because they don't have enough evidence. If I stop the executions, they'll never convict me.

But stopping is out of the question. I couldn't bear the frustration, seeing so many guilty men go unpunished. It would be as if I had never acted in the first place.

The other prudent course would be to lie low for a while, suspend my activities. They won't keep a tail on me for ever, it wouldn't be an economic use of their scarce resources. After one, maybe two months, I'll have more freedom to act.

But I've already had a three-month break. I couldn't stand another one, not so soon. And how can I abandon Jack Morrison when my scheme is so far advanced, when I'm ready to strike? Besides, I won't just be administering justice, I'll be removing a witness.

A compromise. A quick dispatch of Mr Morrison, as planned, followed by a cooling-off period.

First, I'll have to shake off the police tail. It shouldn't be too difficult, as they won't be expecting me to act so soon. What I need to do is lose them without making it look deliberate.

❖

At eight thirty next morning, right on schedule, I ungarage the car and head for the city centre. I've already identified the police car, a grey Ford, parked at the end of the road. This is soon confirmed when I see it in my mirror, following me at what he thinks is a safe distance. I make no effort to elude him, keeping to the main roads all the way.

I join the motorway and cross the river by the Kingston Bridge, then take the Charing Cross exit. After that, even by the easiest route, the one-way traffic system ensures many detours and doubling back; if I lose him in the process, it could look accidental.

As I enter the multi-storey car park, there is no sign of the police car, but I have to assume that it may still have me in view, or that it may not be the only one following me. It has still not appeared, nor has any other car, by the time I have parked and reached the exit that leads to the shopping centre below.

I take the lift down to the shopping centre. It's now nine o'clock and the centre is open, though there are few people about yet. I go into the toilet and sit in a cubicle for ten minutes.

I leave the shopping centre by the front entrance, cross Sauchiehall Street, and walk down Cambridge Street towards Cowcaddens underground station. I have no sense of being followed, but it's difficult to be sure; if my pursuer is still there he'll now be on foot, and I wouldn't be sure of him, even if I dared to look round. During the five-minute walk to the station I feel exposed, but it can't be helped. I'll soon be able to check the position.

I reach the end of the street and go through a pedestrian underpass to the tube station. I buy a ticket at the automatic machine, probably an unnecessary precaution, but it gives the woman at the ticket window the least possible opportunity to remember my face.

I find the platform empty, but while waiting I am joined by half a dozen other people, none of whom looks like a plain-clothes police officer. It's only a quarter past nine, I'm in good time, so I decide to take out one last piece of insurance. My destination is only four stations away, but I decide to take the other line and go the long way round the circle; the underground system is a small one and this will only add about fifteen minutes to my journey. The other train comes first and four people get on it. The remaining two, who board my train, are a man of about sixty and a teenage girl. One of them gets off at St Enoch Square and the other at Shields Road. Unless the police technique is extremely subtle, it looks as though I am definitely free of pursuit.

Where did I lose him? I'll need to get my story right because, even if my plan works perfectly – and it will – they are sure to question me. I must have shaken him off before I entered the toilet, otherwise he could easily have followed me to the tube station. So, shopping in Sauchiehall Street it is. I've already been round the various stores, noting the items I want; on the way home I can pick them up very quickly, obtaining receipts with the right date. Not a perfect alibi, but the burden of proof will be on them. Another example of the careful planning that will continue to keep me out of their grasp. Free, in due course, to dispense further justice.

I get out at Kelvinhall Station, near Partick Cross. Here I am only a few minutes' walk from the home of Jack Morrison, a barman living in a small tenement flat. A nobody. A third-rate person, who thinks he can have his way with my Miranda and walk away unscathed. Now he's about to learn otherwise.

At nine thirty-five I arrive outside his building, part of a long block of identical structures, sandblasted to a mottled, damp-stained yellow. Right above me, on the first floor, is his small cell in this workers' hive. There are a few people on the street, but I'm not dressed in a way that will attract attention to myself.

A modern security door has been grafted to the end of the old close, like a new label on second-hand goods. I press the metal button below his name and wait.

No reply. Have I miscalculated? I was sure he'd be in. I phoned his bar last night, on the way home from the police station, pretending to be a friend. They told me he was due on duty at eleven o'clock this morning. Where would he go before that? He's probably still in bed, after a night out. His last night out. I hope he enjoyed it.

I'm about to ring again when I hear a crackling of static from the little grille. 'Hello?'

'Police. Detective Constable Watson. Can you let me in, sir?' I am standing close to the door, out of sight, I hope, of his window.

A brief pause, then the buzz of the lock being released. I enter and quickly make my way to his flat, already half way up the first flight of stairs when the security door clicks shut behind me. If possible, I want to be at the front door when he opens it, to preserve the advantage of surprise. I arrive there just in time, as the door begins to open, and slam against it with my shoulder, the whole weight of my body behind the assault. As I hoped, he is pushed off balance, falling backwards on to the hall floor. I am ready to straddle him and apply the chloroform, but it proves unnecessary. He has hit his head on the edge of a radiator and is unconscious. Have I killed him? I hope not. I would really miss our chat.

I pull him into the hall, clear of the door, and shut it behind me. Examining him more closely, I see that he is still breathing, though there is blood seeping from a cut on the side of his head. His shirt looks as if it has been put on hurriedly, and his face is damp, his overnight growth of beard half removed. I have interrupted him in the process of shaving, hence his delay in answering the door.

He shows no sign of regaining consciousness and his condition remains the same as I drag him through to the living room and tie him to a chair. He is still out when I return from the kitchen with a cloth soaked in cold water. I gently bathe his forehead, and the still-bleeding wound, being kind in order to be cruel. No response.

If he doesn't wake soon, I'll just have to finish him off as he is. But that would be a pity. I'll give him a little longer. I pass the time by taking a look around. Cheap furniture and carpets, pictures that are merely inexpensive prints. Some paperback books to give a pretence of learning, but I'm not fooled. It's the house of a man with limited means, who misspends his scarce resources going where he shouldn't. My hatred is coming nicely to the boil.

Obligingly, he co-operates by beginning to stir. I bathe his forehead again to help him on his way. He groans and opens his eyes.

A few moments pass before he takes in what is happening. I wait patiently. I know how to do that. The violence of my fury will be all the greater when I finally let it loose.

Better not give him a chance to shout for help. In this warren there will be neighbours above, below and through the walls. I stick my knife to his throat. 'Make a sound and I'll kill you. I'll tape your mouth if I have to, but I'd rather we had a chat.'

'What the fuck do you think you're doing?' he says. How inept. He is probably frightened, still a little groggy, but surely he can do better.

'I thought that would be obvious, Jack. I'm going to kill you.'

At last, fear in his eyes. Also puzzlement. Is he stupid?

'What have you got against me, for God's sake? What have I done to you?'

'What have you done to me? You know damn well. Let me put in one word. Miranda.'

Now it ought to be clear, he should be starting to understand the nature of his offence and the reason for his punishment. Instead, he continues to look confused.

'Miranda? What about her?'

'Do you deny that you've . . . that you've . . . that you and she . . .' I can't put words to the desecration.

'That I've had sex with her?'

I am almost overcome by rage and can hardly speak. 'You admit it?'

'Yes. Once or twice. A long time ago. So what? I was one in a long line. She's a prostitute, for God's sake.'

It takes all my waning self-control not to let go and butcher him right then. But it's not yet time. I make do by slapping his face several times, hard, with the back of my hand. Then I quietly explain to him what Miranda means to me, what we mean to each other. How something so beautiful, so precious has been soiled by him and his like. My face becomes soaked in tears, this time not generated by rage. Can't he see what he's done, what he's put me through? What they've all put me through?

He quietly hears me out. Then he says, 'Look, I'm sorry if you've been hurt. How was I to know? I'd never met you, I'd no idea how you felt. But killing me, killing all those other men, that can't do any good. Quite apart from anything else, the police are on to you now. You can't get away with it.'

How reasonable they all become when they're fighting for their lives! 'Can't I? I've done all right so far.'

'They probably followed you here. Why else would they let you go?'

'They tried to follow me, but I lost them. And they let me go because they don't have any evidence. And now you're going to die, but they still won't be able to prove anything.'

'Look,' he says. 'I think I understand how you feel. But you're not seeing things straight. You're not well. You need help. Why don't you . . . ?'

The patronising bastard! Does he think I want his pity? I slap him again, several times.

Enough of the talk. It's catharsis time. So far he hasn't yelled, but he's likely to start soon, so I cut a section of tape and stick it over his mouth. I pick up the knife again and draw my hand back, ready for the first plunge.

I hear the front door open and close, a woman's voice calling from the hall. 'I'm back. Did you think I'd got lost?' I stand stupidly in front of my bound subject, still holding the knife, not knowing what to do. I did my homework. Painstakingly. He lives alone, so how . . . ? She's still talking as the door opens. 'I had to go to the cash machine. And I thought you said that shop was just round the corner. It's miles . . .'

She breaks off and stands in the open doorway, taking in the scene, a plastic shopping bag in her hand, a look of astonishment on her face. '*Derek*! What the hell?'

I take a couple of steps towards her and stop. What's *she* doing here? What should I do? I'm still holding my knife. But I've got nothing against her. *She's* not on my list. I'm not a random killer.

I hesitate too long, allowing her to recover first. Suddenly she makes a move towards me, swinging the shopping bag, and something hard hits me forcefully on the chin. I stagger back, dazed, letting go of the knife as I try to break my fall. I take only a moment to recover, but it's long enough for her to drop the shopping and pick up my knife.

She makes no attempt to stop me as I scramble past her and run out of the door, out of the house, down the stairs and into the street, with no idea where I'm running to.

❖

Annette made sure that the front door was locked and bolted, then returned to the living room and peeled the tape gently from Jack's mouth; luckily he'd had time to shave his upper lip before the interruption. After that, all she could do was put her arms around him and sob uncontrollably. 'Oh, Jack! My God, Jack!' After a while she settled down. 'That was Derek, Miranda's husband.'

'I know. Don't worry, he won't get far.'

Annette giggled. 'If that's your best line, I'm putting the tape back on.' She giggled again. 'Sorry, I'm a bit hysterical.'

'I don't blame you. Anyway, this bondage stuff is a real turn-on, but . . .'

'What am I thinking about?' She found Derek's knife and cut Jack free. 'Oh God, you're bleeding!' Now spurred back into action, she bathed the wound and found a plaster for it. 'I'd better take you to A&E. You might need stitches.'

'I'm supposed to be at work in half an hour.'

'You'll call in sick. And I'll phone Linda to tell her I'll be late.'

'I think we'd better phone the police as well.'

They did all that, then sat down on the sofa to wait.

'How are you feeling now?'

'My head hurts like hell. Maybe it's just as well. It stops me from thinking about how near I came to being murdered.'

'Oh God, don't remind me. If you hadn't given me your keys...'

'If you hadn't decided to stay the night...'

She kissed him and they were distracted for a while.

Then she said, 'I still don't understand. It wasn't Derek the police picked up. It was one of Miranda's customers.'

'They must have lifted Derek as well. It was him Morag and I picked out in the identity parade. I didn't know who he was then. I didn't realise you and I were talking about different people.'

'But if they had him, why the fuck is he running about loose?'

'They couldn't have had enough evidence. Well, they have now.'

'Useless bastards.'

'He must have been crazy to try again so soon. Anyway, you certainly sorted him out. What the hell did you hit him with?'

'Oh God, I forgot.' She retrieved the bag of groceries from the floor and emptied it, one item at a time. 'The hearty breakfast so nearly missed by the condemned man. Half a dozen rolls. A quarter pound of bacon. A pint of milk. Morning paper. So far, nothing you could call a lethal weapon.' She felt another fit of giggles coming on. 'Just as well I fancied a bit of luxury,' she said, bringing out the jar of marmalade.

39

The Moral of the Story?

'The thing is,' said Jack, 'I understand how Derek felt. He may have taken things to extremes . . .'

'Just a little.'

'. . . but I can see why it pushed him over the edge.'

'I know,' said Annette. 'Even the police managed to work out that much.'

In fact, when it first seemed possible that the murderer might be targeting Miranda's customers, Derek had become a suspect. He had been put in the line-up along with Miranda's possessive customer and had been picked out by both Jack and Morag. 'If jealousy was the motive,' Madigan had said, 'it occurred to us that the husband might just be a possibility. We didn't need to hire a psychologist to work that one out.'

After what had happened, Annette thought Madigan's attitude might have improved a little. Thanks to her, he wasn't having to explain how they'd picked up the killer, then let him go again to commit another murder.

However, Madigan did take the time to tell them about the files found in Derek's house. About how thoroughly they documented the depth of his obsession. How for almost a year he had kept watch outside the sauna during Miranda's shifts. How he had regularly phoned in, posing as a customer, recording the names of the girls who shared each shift with his wife. How he had cross-referenced these with his record of visitors, thereby identifying those who were Miranda's customers. How he had tailed the men on his list, photographed them, made enquiries about them, compiled detailed dossiers on each. How he had even managed to follow Miranda into the Trongate Hotel, in order to identify the bedrooms she was visiting, without his wife ever noticing that he was shadowing her. 'He could have a future as a private eye,' said Madigan, 'if they ever let him out.'

Why had Madigan told them all this? Through embarrassment at how closely disaster had been averted? Or did he think the story contained a moral for Jack and Annette?

'We've got things to work out,' said Jack. 'But I don't want to stop seeing you.'

'Me neither.'

'I've got a university course to finish.'

'And I've got kids to feed.'

'So what do we do?'

'Give it time, see what happens. You owe that much to the woman who saved your life.'

'I can't argue with that,' said Jack.

40

Visiting Time

Miranda's coming to see me today.

Dr Murray says I shouldn't see her, not for a while anyway, not until I'm feeling better. But he says it has to be my decision. I always agree with him that I shouldn't see her, and then I always decide that I will after all.

I think of her all the time. Where is she, what is she doing? Dr Murray says that allowing her to visit only encourages me to perpetuate my obsession, but I know it won't make any difference. I am as besotted with her as on the day when I first cast my eyes on her beautiful face.

She says she's given up the work that drove me out of my mind and brought me to this place. She says she loves me and that she only did it for me. She said the same thing all along, only then she didn't know what it was doing to me. I should have told her, only I couldn't. Instead I pretended that I didn't mind and wreaked my vengeance in secret.

She says that she'll stand by me and that she'll be waiting for me when I get out, whenever that might be.

Can I believe her? I don't know. I don't really know her, even though I lived with her for more than two years. I have no idea what goes on inside her lovely head.

I wonder how Johnny Howard is getting on? He'll never know

it, but my file on him was the thickest of them all, his name always number one on my list. Why did I bypass him? I think that because, unlike the other ver . . . Careful! Unlike the others, I think he genuinely cared for Miranda. While they were taking their unspeakable pleasure, he was suffering almost as much pain as me. Anyway, I'm glad now that I didn't kill him. Feeling that is an important step in my rehabilitation.

I'm also glad that I didn't kill Jack Morrison. He was a minor offender, and he has found his own Jezebel to torment him. I hope he fares better than I did.

I'm told I'll make real progress when I regret killing those other men, but I'm not at that stage yet.

And now here she is, looking as impossible as ever, just as beautiful, dressed just as elegantly and expensively. How can she still afford to . . . ? Caution!

She makes it seem as if seeing me, even in this place, is the most wonderful thing that could happen to her. She gives me her special smile, the one reserved for me alone. '*Hi* there, darling! How *are* you?'

Dr Murray is right. Her visits have to stop or I won't get better. I should tell her right now to go away and never come back. But I won't.

And I never will.

Acknowledgements

I would like to thank the following people for their invaluable contributions to the revival of my literary career over the last few years: Emma Walton and the rest of the staff in the Glasgow area branches of Waterstones, whose championship of my work got me noticed; Dave Hill, whose brilliant covers for my books greatly enhanced this process; and Alison Rae of Polygon, who enthusiastically took notice, the present book being the result.